Kelly McCullough

Spirits, Spells, and Snark

FEIWEL AND FRIENDS

NEW YORK

A Feiwel and Friends Book
An imprint of Macmillan Publishing Group, LLC
175 Fifth Avenue, New York, NY 10010

Our books may be purchased in bulk for promotional, educational, or business use.
Please contact your local bookseller or the Macmillan Corporate and Premium
Sales Department at (800) 221-7945 ext. 5442 or by e-mail at
MacmillanSpecialMarkets@macmillan.com.

Library of Congress Cataloging-in-Publication Data is available.
ISBN 978-1-250-10785-5 (hardcover) / ISBN 978-1-250-10784-8 (ebook)

Book design by Liz Dresner

Feiwel and Friends logo designed by Filomena Tuosto

First edition, 2019

10 9 8 7 6 5 4 3 2 1

mackids.com

This book is for Laura, the love of my life
And in memory of Mike Levy, a scholar and a gentleman

1

When Trouble Knocks

"**ARE YOU SURE** this thing is magical?" Dave slowly turned the Crown of the North under the bright basement lights. The seven diamonds adorning the simple silver circlet barely flickered. "It doesn't look it."

"I'm sure." I touched a finger to the place above my left eye where I carried a mirrored imprint of the Crown's peak—a metallic silver triangle perhaps an inch across with a circle in the middle, like the eye in the pyramid on the back of a dollar bill.

"Have I mentioned how much I dislike that mark, Kalvan?" The rangy fire hare was stretched out on the thick green carpet my erstwhile stepfather had used to mimic the lawns in his model of the Minnesota state capitol. Sparx's fur burned a merry sort of red, though the flames never ignited anything he didn't want them to.

"Only about a million times, familiar mine, but most people

can't even see it." The scar was invisible to most everyone who didn't have magic—Dave being a notable exception.

"That's a good part of why it makes me nervous," grumbled Sparx. "I've never seen a mark like it before, and I'm old enough to find strange magic alarming."

I leaned over and poked his belly, sending the flames dancing through the red fur. "You sound more like a mother hen than a magic bunny."

Sparx gave me his best disappointed-teacher stare—it was a shame he didn't have glasses to peer over. "That's *fire hare*, as you well know, noxious child."

I was thirteen, but I let the *child* thing pass. Sparx is an elemental spirit and old enough that my *mom* probably counts as a child for him. Or my great-grandfather, for that matter. Instead of arguing with Sparx, I ran a finger around the edges of the silver scar again. I'd gotten it when my stepfather, Oscar, threw the Crown at me during our duel at the Winter Carnival a month and a half ago, and I was kind of disappointed so few people could see it. I thought it made me look more adult, not to mention mysterious and even a little heroic, the way a pirate's patch or a mystical tattoo might.

"Do you think it'll do anything special today?" Dave turned the Crown so it framed his dark face—like some antique portrait. "Because it's the equinox and all? Sundown's only moments away."

"I hope not." I shrugged. "What do you think, fuzzball?"

Sparx snorted grumpily. "Given the Crown remains fallow until Summer's reign begins in a month, it seems unlikely, O Accursed Master."

And *that* told me I'd been riding him a little too hard. Technically, Sparx *is* my familiar, but he only calls me Accursed Master when he's teasing or really irritated, and this didn't sound like teasing. "Sorry, Sparx, I'm kind of flipped out about the whole thing. I know Oscar's not the Winter King anymore and we warded the house nine ways from Sunday, but I keep expecting my earth power stepfather to come back up through the floor like something out of a horror film."

Sparx shook his head. "The wards will hold and they run very deep, and I doubt he'd come at you openly even when you are beyond their protection. You beat him at a symbolic level as well as a sorcerous one. That puts a great weight of magic on your side in any future conflict."

I was letting out a little sigh of relief when—

THUMP! THUMP! THUMP!

"Is that someone knocking on your front door?" Dave's voice came out tight and strained. I couldn't blame him—there was six feet of dirt between the roof of the ancient cellar and the much newer house above.

"There's no way we could hear it throu—"

THUMP! THUMP! THUMP!

I felt a fresh touch of winter run icy-footed down my spine. "Sparx!"

The hare vanished in a puff of flame, leaving an arcing trail of smoke that ran from the table where he'd been sitting to the limestone barrel vault above. Several seconds flickered past.

THUMP! THUMP! THUMP!

Sparx returned with a flash, his expression simultaneously serious and bemused. "Sunset has brought you an interesting visitor. You'd better answer that door before your mother thinks to."

I doubted there was much risk of that. Not with my mother . . .

the way she was now. Her mental health issues had gotten considerably worse since the Crown went fallow, but I pushed that thought aside. Something about Sparx's tone made me dash for the spiral stairs leading up to the house proper. Dave dropped the Crown back into the warded circle on the table and ran after me.

I half expected to find a splintered ruin when I got to the front door, but the wood looked fine. The knock came again, only . . .

rap rap rap

The taps sounded so gently this time I could barely hear them.

What the . . . I yanked the door open and found myself facing a tall, slender, professionally dressed woman with sooty-black hair in a pixie cut and the amber eyes I'd only ever seen on my mother and in the mirror.

"Hello?"

"You must be Kalvan." Her voice was rich and full, yet somehow colder than it had any right to be. "I've *so* been looking forward to finally getting the chance to meet you. I can see a lot of Genevieve in your face."

Okay, that's a little weird—Genevieve is my mother's name. "Got it in one. But I'm afraid I don't recognize you . . ."

She extended her hand and I shook it bemusedly. Her fingers were icy—literally, like a steel handrail in the winter cold.

She smiled, and the expression set a weird combination of concern and anticipation dancing along my nerves. "Don't you, then? I'm your aunt Noelle."

Memories of old conversations and older pictures shocked through me and I suddenly had trouble breathing. Now she'd said it, there was no doubt this was my mother's older sister. Noelle looked exactly as she had in the picture on my mother's dresser. A picture that had been taken three years before I was born and a few weeks before Noelle died.

"Don't look so surprised, nephew. I can see from your heart and your familiar you've learned how magic runs in our family." She nodded at Sparx, who had taken up a perch on the railing of the stairs to the upper level. "I've known Genevieve needed me for some time, but the bonds of the grave are horribly strong, and I hadn't the power to burn them away. Not till tonight's turn of the fallow months severed the last vestiges of Winter's hold on both power and my sister. Now, how are we going to break it to her?"

My dead aunt stepped past me, and I started to turn to follow her. "I, uh . . . huh, oooooof." But then—as my back touched the wall—I found myself gently sliding to the floor when my knees turned to butter.

"Are you all right?" Noelle stopped midstride.

"I . . . maybe?" I felt awfully light-headed.

Dave pushed past her and squatted in front of me. "You don't look so hot."

Sparx nodded. "Try putting your head between your knees."

Something about the hare's voice made me suspicious. "You knew!"

Sparx blinked innocently and his eyes seemed to grow to three times their normal size—like a cartoon rabbit's. "Knew what, O Accursed Master?"

"That it was my aunt at the door!"

Sparx shrugged. "There's a strong family resemblance in the hair and eyes, even if your coloring is more like your father's." I was much darker than either my mother or my aunt. "What's your point?"

"I . . . but she's, uh . . ." I trailed off as I caught an amused twinkle in my aunt's eyes.

"Dead?" she asked gently.

"Yeah, that."

Now she laughed. "He's a fire hare; he couldn't possibly have missed it."

Dave abruptly sat down beside me. "Wait, you mean that thing she said about the *bonds of the grave* . . ."

Noelle nodded. "A major difficulty, but not impossible given the proper circumstances and sufficient motivation." She canted her head to one side. "Right; I'm guessing neither of you is a tea drinker, so it had best be hot chocolate." Without another word, she turned and headed deeper into the house with Sparx trailing along behind.

Dave reached over and pinched me viciously.

"Ouch! What's that for?"

"I wanted to make sure you weren't dreaming."

I blinked. "Aren't you supposed to ask someone else to pinch *you*?"

He shook his head. "When *I* dream about zombies they look like zombies, not like some lady who could be a partner at the law firm where my mom works. If it's a dream, it's all you, buddy. Mine are nothing like this crazy."

I glanced at the red spot on my forearm. "I don't think it's a dream."

"Then we'd better go after her."

We found Noelle in the kitchen with the teakettle held between her hands like a basketball. Even as we entered, steam began to pour from the spout. "Now, where are the mugs?"

"Left of the fink, fecond felf up." Sparx dropped onto the table and let a pair of hot-chocolate envelopes fall out of his mouth.

Within a few moments, Noelle had offered us each a neatly stirred mug, though she didn't take any herself. "My sister is above." It wasn't a question, and she turned toward the back stairs as she spoke—the house was a duplex my stepfather had converted to single-family living. "Come on, you can drink on the way."

I looked at Sparx, hoping for some clue. I mean, the script for pretty much every vampire or zombie movie ever said I should be trying to put her back in the grave. Like, yesterday. But movies about the undead didn't normally start anything like the way the last ten minutes had unfolded. Add in that Sparx didn't seem alarmed . . . In fact, he just smiled and jerked his chin toward the stairs my aunt had already started climbing.

So, taking a huge slug of hot chocolate, I followed her. "Aunt Noelle?"

"Yes, dear?"

"Mom's not really herself." *Understatement of the year!* She's never been all that tightly moored to reality's shore, and now that I'd driven my stepfather away, she seemed to be drifting slowly but steadily farther and farther out to sea. "In fact, she's pretty fragile."

"I know. It's not the first time. I'll see what I can do."

Riiiiiight. The dead lady was going to bring my mom back to reality. This was *so* not going to end well.

My mother was sitting cross-legged on the floor of what had been the upstairs dining room, with all the lights out. Her back was to us and she didn't turn. Her long black hair hung in thick tangles, and the red velvet dress she wore had broad tears along the hem.

She'd arranged the full skirt around her in a loose circle and the rips showed dark in the moonlight.

I turned on the kitchen lights and a bright rectangle reached across the floor, stopping just short of the edge of her skirt. "Mom?"

"What is it, Kalvan?" She still didn't turn around. "I'm trying to find the place where flint meets steel."

"Uh . . ."

"It's important because steel and flint are earth, but together they beget spark, and spark becomes fire."

As with so many things my mother said these days, I didn't know how to answer. "We've got a visitor."

Noelle walked around in front of my mother. "Genevieve?" Her voice came out as gentle as if she were trying to soothe a fussy baby.

"There you are." My mother sounded relieved. "How was the drive-in? I'll never understand what you see in those awful spy movies."

Noelle blinked once, then smiled. "It was all right. Not my favorite by a long shot, but not bad. The popcorn was terrible."

My mother laughed. "It always is."

Dave poked me in the ribs and mouthed, *What the heck?*

I shook my head. One of my mother's more bizarre habits is restarting a conversation in the middle, days or even weeks after you thought it was over. I couldn't tell whether this was that or something else related to her current condition.

My mother leaned back and put her hands on the floor behind her. "Have you changed your mind about Nix? You know how much I hate to fight with you about anything important."

I twitched. *Nix* was my long-absent father's name, and it almost never passed my mother's lips. Or mine, for that matter. I knew so little about my father, but asking Mom to tell me more was pretty much the same thing as asking for a fight or a flip-out, so I'd learned to avoid the subject.

But Noelle made a noncommittal gesture with her hands, and went on as if it was nothing important. "I'm still not sure I think Nix is the best idea you've ever had, but I'm no longer convinced he's the worst."

"I said he'd grow on you."

I held my breath as I waited to hear more, but Noelle caught my eye, lifted her chin, and flicked her gaze beyond me, suggesting without saying a word that I find something else to do. I didn't want to go, but her expression told me I'd better. I nodded and caught Dave by the wrist before heading back down the stairs. Sparx seemed to think it would be all right, and I didn't know what else to do.

I dropped into a chair at the kitchen table and glared at my familiar. "I want some answers, bunny boy."

He responded rapid-fire style. "Yes. No. I don't know. Maybe. It wouldn't surprise me. And, I think she's going to do more good than harm for your mother."

"Huh?" This came from Dave, behind me.

Sparx rolled his eyes. "*Yes*, she really is dead. *No*, it's not the first time I've seen something like this. *I don't know* how it works, but sometimes the door to death swings the other way. *Maybe* it has something to do with Oscar's scheme to keep the Crown going back and forth between him and your mother. It certainly *wouldn't surprise me* if that was the case. As I mentioned when we first found out about Oscar, the Crown is supposed to pass to a new head with each turn of the seasons. Interfering with that was bound to have some very unpredictable and nasty effects."

"You are the most frustrating creature I have ever met." I glowered at Sparx.

"Hey, I live to serve."

"Sure you do." I sighed. "Do you really believe she'll do more good than harm?" I'd cheerfully invite a dozen zombies into the house if they could help my mom.

Sparx flicked his ears back and forth in the rabbit version of a shrug. "Your mother's reaction gives me hope. Sometimes the ties of the past can shift things magic dare not touch."

I winced. While my mother's problems were mostly brain chemistry, the fire in her nature only made them worse. When her condition first started deteriorating I'd asked if we could use magic to help, but Sparx felt it would do little more than add fuel to the flames already consuming her.

Sparx put a paw on my wrist. "Why don't I stay home and keep an eye on things while you're at school tomorrow."

I nodded. "That'd make me feel better."

Dave punched my shoulder. "Come on, let's watch a movie and pretend we're normal teenagers with normal problems."

Dave yanked the covers off my bed. "Get up, slughead, you need to shower so we can catch the school bus."

I wanted to strangle him, but he was already off to the bathroom by the time I finally worked up the energy to move. Normally, I hate morning people, but Dave is a rare exception. Sort of. Anyway, I owe him. Since the end of Oscar's run as the Winter King had pushed my mom across the line into deeper instability, he'd been staying over pretty often to help keep *me* sane.

Shivering in the early chill, I stepped over Dave's sleeping bag and grabbed the first pair of jeans and tee I could find. By the time I caught up to him in the bathroom, he was already showered and dressed. Twenty minutes later we were at the stop and waiting for a bus to take us to the hippie experiment where we both go to school, better known as the Free School of Saint Paul. Or, more simply, Free.

I missed Sparx, but knowing he had my back with my mom was a huge relief. Also, as much as I hated to admit it, not bringing him meant I would be less distracted. He was invisible to most people unless he made an effort to show himself, but that only made it worse when he played silly tricks no one but Dave and I could see.

When the school bus arrived, we headed for the back. We were first aboard for the long ride and had our pick of seats. As usual, Dave pulled out a book while I just leaned my forehead against the window and stared blankly into the predawn streets of Saint Paul. We'd had another snowfall a few days previously so the yards were all white, but it wasn't very deep and temps were running above normal.

Somewhere along the line I drifted over the edge from mostly awake to mostly asleep, which was fine till the bus hit a pothole big enough to house a hippopotamus and bounced my head off the window so hard that sparks danced across my vision. I was still trying to shake off the impact when a glance down a passing alley made my blood run cold as meltwater.

For one brief instant I saw—or maybe only thought I saw—a

man, tall and gaunt, clothed all in rags, with skin like granite and eyes colder than the hardest ice. He was crowned with silver and leaning against a wall, his arms crossed as though he were waiting for something or someone. He smiled as our eyes met—a terrible, predatory smile, and I shivered. His features reminded me of Oscar as he had looked in the moments before our duel, but he was bald above the Crown and far too thin. Between that and the whack I'd taken, I couldn't be sure if it was my stepfather or not.

"Did you see that?" I demanded of Dave.

"See what?"

"The man in the alley. He had a crown. I think it might have been Oscar."

"What?" Dave leaned forward to look out the window, though we were long past the alley. "Are you sure?"

"No. Not at all. To start with, I was half asleep, and then, when we hit that pothole, I banged my head so hard I still have stars in my eyes. That's why I'm asking you."

"I'm sorry, Kalvan. I was reading. I didn't see anything. You say he had a crown? Was it the Corona Borealis? Because . . ."

"I don't know. It kind of looked like the Crown of the North, but I only got one quick glimpse and I think the stones were wrong— dark rather than clear or white. But what if it was?" I fought back a moment of panic. If Oscar had gotten into my house again, he would have had to get past Sparx, and my mom was there, and, and, and . . .

Dave squeezed my shoulder. "It's all right, Kalvan. I'll call. Switch places with me so I can do it without the driver noticing."

I nodded, but didn't say anything. Even if everything was fine, there was no guarantee anyone would pick up. Sparx doesn't do phones. My mom is . . . well, not entirely there at the moment. And my aunt? Who knows how the dead might act? But we swapped spots anyway and Dave bent down below the level of the seat, dialing his phone inside the mouth of his backpack.

He had the volume turned really low so as not to draw attention, and when someone answered he spoke so quietly I could barely hear his side of things. "Noelle? This is Kalvan's friend Dave. Can you go to the basement and check . . . Oh, you're in the basement? Great. Can you see the table with a Crown on it? You can? And the Crown's fine? Thanks!" He hung up. "Kalvan, it's—"

"Yeah, I heard. Thank you."

I should have felt better, knowing the Crown was safe, and that the guy in the alley couldn't have had it. But somehow that only made me worry more. If it *was* Oscar, where had he found a new crown? What kind of powers did *it* have, and what was he up to now? If it wasn't him, who was it and why had he looked at me that way? But then, what if I hadn't really seen what I thought I saw? It was all so confusing.

Before I could figure out any of it, we rolled up to the school. All the Older Learning Center teachers were out front corralling their advisees as they came off the buses. BTW, for those tuning in late, OLC is what we call grades 7–12 at my experimental school.

I blinked and turned to Dave. "What's that about?"

Dave rolled his eyes. "Field trip. You remember that, right? Como Park Zoo and Conservatory ring any bells?"

"Oh yeah, no. I completely forgot." Which meant I was going to get mighty hungry come lunchtime, as I'd neither remembered to pack something or to hit my mom up for cash to buy food. "One more way for today to go wrong, I guess." I winced. "I don't suppose you brought an extra granola bar?"

Dave laughed. "I didn't, but don't look so glum. Mom gave me money for lunch and I think we can stretch it enough for two if we're quick and we aren't too picky about what we eat. Come on."

As we piled out onto the sidewalk, Dave caught my backpack and pulled me between our bus and the one in front of it. I saw Evelyn—the drama teacher who was our advisor—throw us a disapproving look, and I shrugged helplessly at her.

"Come on!" Dave said again. "We can just hit Doughboy if we run."

I was still worried about the man with the crown, but we could deal with that after the immediate crisis, so I pounded after Dave. "Great idea!"

"Of course it is. It's mine." Dave flashed that big infectious grin of his and started to really book it.

The bakery outlet store was two blocks from the school. Unfortunately, we weren't the only ones who'd decided bakery surplus was the best bet for lunch, and there was a line. My Free School student mentor, Aleta, was there with her girlfriend, Jenn, and they both smiled our way. Josh Reiner, my sometimes-enemy sometimes-ally in the weird secret world of magic, was there as well, and the look he gave me suggested today was a watch-my-back kind of day.

Since we'd arrived relatively late, all the good muffins and snack cakes were gone from the past-best-by bins. So we just grabbed a baker's dozen of whatever was left at the bottom of the heap without really looking and dashed to the back of the line.

"Hey, Dave." It wasn't until she'd spoken that I recognized the girl in front of us, Morgan Shears, who was in Rob's advisory group; morning embarrassing me again.

Morgan was nearly three years older than me and a good couple of inches taller even without the high-heeled boots she was wearing now, which *might* be why she mostly looked over me. Morgan did a lot of dance, which put her in a group that kind of overlapped with theater nerds like me. She had wavy brown hair, dark eyes, a snub nose, and a scattering of freckles.

She also had dimples that showed when she smiled, as she did now. "Hey, Kalvan. Grabbing lunch?"

"Hey, Morgan, yeah," I kind of mumbled in a morning-ate-my-brain sort of way.

Dave grinned. "And breakfast. Gonna be a long day and we'll need a serious sugar fix to get through it."

Morgan laughed, and the dimples reappeared. "Too true."

Then she was checking out and too busy to talk to us anymore. As we hurried out the door after our turn, I felt a sudden impact in my face and the whole world went white and cold for a second. My first thought was an attack by the Winter King and I started to pull fire from my heart. But then I heard a harsh laugh and Dave yelling at Josh and realized it was only a snowball.

A second later, Dave hissed at me, "Cool it!"

"What?"

"Your glove is on fire."

I glanced down and saw red and gold dancing along the blown-out fingertips. "Oh, oops." I quickly shook the flames out, hoping no one else had seen them, and curled the burned tips into my palm.

Josh laughed even harder, and I had to throttle back the urge to cook him on the spot. Mostly because he was a bitter water sorcerer himself and he'd probably have kicked my butt. Instead, we all dashed back to school where Evelyn scolded us for being late, shepherded us onto the last bus, and got everyone settled. By the time I next remembered the man in the alley, the bus was so packed it was too late to talk to Dave with any privacy. I decided to let it go for now since there was nothing I could really do about it till I got home to Sparx.

The buses rolled to a stop beside the Como Conservatory—an enormous greenhouse with multiple wings. It's big and warm and the air is so soggy you can practically swim in it. Once Evelyn finished a quick lecture about being responsible, not embarrassing the school, and meeting the group for a lunchtime check-in, we all piled off and scattered. Eighty-five percent of the group headed toward the zoo, while Dave and I opted for the conservatory in hopes of avoiding the crowds.

Aleta and Jenn went the same way we did. So did Josh and a couple of the other rougher older boys. Morgan, too, along with another dancer, Lisa Alvarez. She was in Rob's advisory group, like most of the dance crowd, and much closer to our age than Morgan's— though they were good friends. Actually, most of the kids who'd been at the bakery were there. Birds of an unprepared feather, maybe. Or creative minds running in the same gutters. Or something like that. Twenty-five or so of us, anyway. Once we got inside the big central dome most of the crew went right or down the center path, but Dave and I went left like we usually do since it's the best way to avoid crowds.

Only Morgan and Lisa came our way as we headed into the sunken-garden wing. It was my favorite of all the greenhouses, with a long narrow koi pond running down the middle. We walked along one side of the pool while the girls walked on the other, but the vast room was so quiet, there was no privacy and none of us spoke much.

As we got closer to the far end, my right foot started itching like crazy and I had to suppress an embarrassing urge to tear my shoe off and scratch. Eventually, we came together as the greenhouse opened out into a circle where a lot of weddings were held.

I couldn't help but notice how pretty Morgan looked there on the edge of the pond, and I found myself wanting to say something clever to make her dimples come out. *Not* that I thought I was in her league or anything—I was way too short and young for that— but I liked her smile, and I wanted to see it again.

Screaming "Get out of the way. Delver!" and shoving her and Lisa into the muddy pond was *not* part of the plan. But then, neither was the giant badgerlike creature who had risen out of the earth in the flower beds off to our right with a thick stubby crossbow cradled in both hands. He came up right on the edge of my vision and I might not have seen him in time to push the girls out of the way if my itchy foot hadn't kept pulling my attention to that side.

As it was, I had barely an instant to react before—

TWANG!

2

Badger, Badger, Badger

FOR ONE FRACTION of a second that felt like it lasted about three hundred years, the stone bolt from the crossbow looked and sounded like the world's largest bumblebee as it headed straight for my right eye. But, at the last instant, it seemed to turn, and I felt a burning kiss on my cheekbone followed by the crash of breaking glass.

Before the badgerlike delver could redraw his bow, I aimed my palms at him and opened the place in my heart where fire lived. Torrents of red-and-yellow flame shot toward him. Driven by fear and anger, the fires came out *much* more forcefully than I intended. Instead of a tight burst, I launched a gigantic wave of flame.

The delver grunted something short and hard in the language of stone, raising a shield of earth from the garden bed, and the roaring sheet of fire washed over and around it. The fire struck the glass wall behind and dozens of panes shattered in the sudden heat, but I kept right on pouring my heart into the flames.

"What was that about!?!" Lisa demanded.

Dave yelled, "Kalvan, shut it down! The delver's gone, and there are going to be official-type people all over the place in about one minute."

I closed my fists and snuffed the flames, though several plants continued to burn fitfully while fire danced along my fingertips for a couple of seconds longer. "We're going to need a *really* good story . . ."

Morgan pulled herself out of the pool. "Maniac with a Molotov? That'd explain the burns, and there's plenty of broken glass. Ran out through that giant hole you made?"

Dave nodded. "Uh, yeah, that might work."

"You're fire," snapped Morgan. "Can you do silvertongue?"

How did she know about that? "I don't like to—"

The older girl cut me off. "But you *can* do it. Good; that'll make them believe it no matter how daft it sounds. Lisa, you and I play dumb and cute. That usually goes over well with authority. Dave spotted the nutball and tackled us into the water—we didn't see anything after that. That'll let Kalvan do most of the talking."

"Why Dave?" I felt a little hurt he was going to get the credit for my quick thinking.

Morgan rolled her eyes. "He's black and, unless I'm wrong, he doesn't have powers. There are going to be cops all over the place, and it would be a *lot* safer for him if he's clearly the hero." Then she grimaced. "Don't worry about it, Kalvan, I'm not going to forget who *actually* ruined my dress."

I winced at the way she'd phrased it, but she was right. I'm pretty much a white boy, even if I've got some of my dad's complexion, since that's how I was raised, and official-type people generally treat me as such. Add in that silvertongue, which means I can talk my way out of a hole better than just about anyone, and Morgan hadn't said anything I shouldn't have thought of myself. While I dithered, Dave jumped into the pool and started splashing muddy water on his face and arms.

"You and Lisa can do magic?" I asked. "What element?"

"I'm air, *obviously*," said Morgan. "You don't think that bolt turned away from your face all on its own, did you? Lisa's—"

The other girl's voice cut across Morgan's. "It's complicated, and now's not the time. Let me see that cut." She leaned in so close her nose grazed my cheekbone. "There's some dark influence of earth on that wound. Let me . . ." She mumbled something low and growly, then licked her index finger before running the tip of it along my cut, which tingled at the contact. "That should take care of it."

"I . . . uh, thanks." *That wasn't weird at all.*

Before I could say more, she held up a hand, and for the first time ever I noticed her eyes were more gold than brown. "Sirens. A long way off, but lots of them. Means we won't be alone much longer."

I was going to say *I* couldn't hear anything, but then—in the same moment Dave climbed out of the water—doors at the far end of the greenhouse burst open and an older woman came through accompanied by a security guard.

"Bomber had on a parka with the hood up, so we never saw his face," added Dave.

Morgan nodded. "Good, no description. Gloves, too." She turned to me. "You're on."

I took a deep breath as the guard came running up to us, and then I began to speak quickly and breathlessly with the power of fire dancing on my tongue and filling my throat. "Oh, thank goodness you're here!"

I followed the script we'd concocted and almost believed it myself as I poured my magic into the words. Sparx says fire is the most dangerous element—tricky to work with and prone to unexpected blowback. Silvertongue is especially treacherous, since it plays with the mind of the listener and no one listens more closely to what you're saying than you do yourself. Use it too much and you can lose all sense of the truth or even reality—which makes it especially scary to me given my mother's problems. By the time I was done, *I* could barely remember what really happened, and I wondered if any of my companions would without me reminding them with fire on my lips.

The cops arrived shortly after, and the fire department with them. Blankets and towels were found for the others, and they bandaged the long, shallow cut on my cheek. I had a brief, panicky moment when they inspected the pane broken by the crossbow, but they never found the bolt, and I heard someone saying fire did weird things.

We repeated our story over and over for the next two hours, until, eventually, they handed us back over to the authority of our teachers, where we got to tell the story again to Rob and Evelyn. They made a much more skeptical audience—it was no surprise to me that Morgan had been able to put together a good story on the fly. The Free School isn't always perfect where it comes to teaching academic lessons, but we sure learn how to work the system and the refs, and our teachers know it. Still, silvertongue is *very* convincing and I'd worn the story smooth with frequent use.

Finally, lunchtime came and everyone stopped grilling us. Morgan ducked off to the bathroom while the rest of us settled on a couple of benches. That's when Dave and I discovered pretty much everything we'd grabbed out of the bin had . . .

"Raisins!" Dave held up the package of cinnamon rolls in disgust. "Who puts raisins in cinnamon rolls?"

Lisa nabbed one of the buns. "I like raisins. Here, you can have some of my jerky as a trade." She held out a couple strips of dried meat.

Dave grinned and took one. "Does this make us all friends?"

Lisa smiled and broke the roll in half. "Cinnamon rolls and jerky isn't quite the same as sharing bread and salt, but I think it's close enough to count for a declaration of alliance."

Morgan returned just then, wrinkling her nose distastefully. "Temporary at best, Lisa." She shifted her attention to Dave and me. "But we'll definitely need to talk about this whole thing at some length later. Of course, for the next week or two we'll have to snub you boys hard if we don't want stupid rumors flying around."

I must have looked wistful, because she singled me out with an amused look. "No offense, Kalvan. You're cute enough for your age, but that's about four years too young for me. Oh, and I still need to make you pay for destroying this." She tugged at the hem of her badly stained dress—formerly cream, now duckweed green with black streaks from the muck on the bottom of the pool. "I am soooo taking this out of your hide."

I wanted to laugh, but something about the look in the depths of her eyes made me wonder where the joke ended and the strips out of my back began. Before I could think of a good response, I saw our science teacher, Tanya, heading our way with a stern look on her face and a purposeful stride.

"Kalvan, could I have a word with you?"

Her expression didn't allow for a no, so I nodded. "Of course, Tanya." Again, for those tuning in late, part of being a Free Schooler is calling all your teachers by their first names.

As Tanya turned to lead me away, Morgan caught my eye. Pointing at the science teacher with one finger, then herself and Lisa simultaneously with two, she made a very slight shake of her head and a lip-zipping motion. I bobbed a nod to let her know I'd understood. Tanya—an experienced windwalker who had recently begun tutoring me in magic—didn't know about the girls' powers. That, or Morgan wanted me to pretend she didn't, or that *I* didn't. In any case: Don't tell Tanya anything about her and Lisa. Seeing as she'd just saved my life with that gust of wind, I felt I ought to play along.

Once we'd put a little distance between us and the others, Tanya leaned against a wall and gave me a very hard look over her glasses. "Is there anything you want to tell me?"

"Not really, no," I said with complete honesty. I didn't use silvertongue; and not only because I had no idea if it would work with Tanya being a magical adept. I'd pushed way past any reasonable margin of safety and I was having flashes of false memory trying to blot out what really happened.

"Kalvan Middlename Monroe."

"Sorry. Jerk reflex. I, uh, the story I told the police isn't quite true."

"That's a good start."

"How did you know?" I had to ask.

She snorted. "So you can figure out how to avoid my catching on in the future?"

"That had crossed my mind, yes." There was no point in lying *after* you got caught.

"Let's just say silvertongue leaves traces for those who know what to look for. Especially when you layer it on as thick as you did today."

"I'm sorry. I couldn't afford to tell the truth."

She simply raised an eyebrow, so I continued. "We . . . I was attacked by a delver. I had to defend myself with fire and then I needed to cover my tracks."

Tanya winced, then sighed. "That does change things. I still don't like it, but better a white lie than getting tossed in the psych ward for telling the police you were attacked by an earth elemental. Was it that delver who worked with the Winter King? I ask because they don't normally come out in the open, so I have to believe this one had a grudge or was directed to attack you." I'd told her the whole story of my conflict with my stepfather soon after she started teaching me magic. "What was his name?"

"Cetius." I shrugged. I had vivid memories of my stepfather's henchbadger, and it wouldn't surprise me if Oscar had sent him after me again, but . . . : "I don't know. One delver looks pretty much like another to me."

There were probably all sorts of ways someone with more practice could tell delvers apart, but I hadn't spent enough time with them to get there, and I hoped I never would. I considered telling her about the crowned man I thought I'd seen in the alley this morning, but I was starting to doubt myself on that one. I'd been more than half asleep at the time, and I'd spent much of the night worrying about Oscar and the Crown, and my zombie aunt. I wanted more evidence about what I thought I had seen before I started telling anyone as official as a teacher.

"What about Sparx?" Tanya asked. "He'd be able to tell if it was Cetius."

"He's home keeping an eye on my mom." I might have to explain my dead aunt at some point, but I decided now was not a good time.

Tanya's demeanor went from stern to worried in an instant. "Is she all right? I know she hasn't been at her best since . . . the Winter Carnival."

It was a brief pause, but I noticed and it hurt. My duel with my stepfather again. I'd won the fight, but my mother's already dubious mental health was a casualty of the battle. A huge part of why I'd had to take Oscar down was that he'd been using her to enhance his evil magic. The horrible flip side was that his earth powers had been the main thing keeping her stable, since he needed her coherent for his schemes. When I broke his power, I also broke her strongest anchor to the real world. Mostly I managed to avoid blaming myself by not thinking about it, but Tanya's hesitation and her obvious concern hit me like a brick in the face.

"She's not noticeably worse," I lied around what felt like a pound of broken glass in my throat. "But she isn't working today and I thought she'd feel better for the company." My mom's a freelance accountant, which makes for weird hours.

"All right, but if she gets too bad, you'll let us know, won't you?"

"Of course." *No chance.*

Neither Tanya nor Evelyn had ever said anything about having to report my situation to the state if things got out of hand, but they didn't have to. The fear was always in the back of my mind when I told any of my teachers anything about my life at home. If Child Protective Services ever got involved, they might take me away from my mother, and the thought terrified me. Though I honestly didn't know whether that was more on my behalf or hers.

"She'll be all right. Her next job starts Thursday," I lied again. "She always does better when she's working." True but irrelevant.

Tanya sighed and looked skeptical. "All right. Now, tell me more about this delver."

So I did. Mostly. I skipped over the part where Morgan saved me from the delver's bolt, of course. And I took credit for coming up with the fake story, implying I needed silvertongue as much to make Morgan and Lisa forget things as to keep the cops and everyone else from thinking I was crazy. I was pretty sure Tanya didn't buy *everything* I told her, but if not, she kept her suspicions to herself.

Most important, she didn't ask about Morgan and Lisa and magic. But, again, whether that was because she didn't know anything about their powers or for some other reason, I couldn't say. There was simply too much about magic I didn't know, having only discovered it and my powers a few months previously.

At the end she nodded. "I'll go take a look at the Conservatory now. Not that I think it'll do much good. Earth and air are opposites and much of what the delvers do and leave behind is alien to me."

"Will you let me know if you find anything important?"

"I might. Oh, and, Kalvan, on the not getting caught front . . ."

"Yes?"

"If you want to use fire magic and not have anyone figure it out later, you might try to avoid scorch marks on your shirt cuffs. *You may be immune to fire, but your clothes aren't.*"

I'd been too distracted until then to notice, but Tanya was right. The cuffs of my turtleneck—fashioned from some kind of bright blue sports fabric—had blackened and melted away from the heart-fire that poured through my hands.

Sparx took one look at me as I came in the back door and tsked, "I let you out of my sight for one day, and you come home covered in filth and white gauze. What did you do to yourself?"

"This?" I touched the bandage on my cheekbone. "It wasn't me. It was a delver crossbow. If Morgan hadn't been there . . ."

It was only in that moment I truly realized how close I'd come to dying and what that would mean for my mother. For the second time in as many days I found myself suddenly weak-kneed and sliding to the floor. With a flash and a puff of smoke, Sparx crossed the distance between us in an instant, landing in my lap.

"Breathe." His face was inches from my own as he pressed his chest against mine. "In. Out. In. Out. Again."

"I—"

"Not yet. For now, I just want you to breathe. At least until you stop crying."

"I'm crying?" I touched a finger to my cheek and discovered he was right.

"Yes. Now, in, out. Breathe with me." The big hare stayed in my lap for the next several minutes. Finally, he nodded. "Better. Let's try again. You look like you've had a rough day. What happened?"

When I got to how my cheek got sliced, he whistled. "A daylight attack in a human space is very unlike the delvers, even if it was Cetius pressing a vendetta for your stepfather's sake or on his orders. I don't like that part of this thing at all. Neither that nor the crowned man you may or may not have seen. I'm also curious about your itchy foot. That reeks of coincidence, and seeming coincidence in the magical world rarely is. Go on."

I felt some of my earlier sense of panic returning as I recounted what happened next and I had to work hard to keep my breathing calm and even. I was sweaty and shaky by the time I finished.

"Let me have a look at that cheek." He leaned in closer and sniffed at the gauze. "Hmmm, not sure what the girl did, but if there was any malign influence there, it's gone now. Finish the story."

When I was done, Sparx canted his ears toward me, looking thoughtful. "So, this Morgan you promised to cover up for with Tanya? Pretty girl, pale and tragic, a few years older than you?"

Sparx had seen all of my classmates, even if Dave and Josh were the only ones who'd seen him. "I don't think I'd call her tragic look—"

"Never mind. You say she's a power of air?"

I nodded. "I didn't *exactly* promise to cover up for her." Even if she *had* thanked me for it after Tanya left.

"No, but you did cover up for her, and that's much the same thing. It's interesting that I didn't see the power in her before this, and I wonder about the why of it. What about the other girl? The one who doctored that slice. I'm not sure I know who she is."

"You haven't seen her very often." He'd been hiding in my bag for most of the classes I shared with Lisa. "She's in Rob's group, like Morgan, and closer to me in age." I paused, trying to picture Lisa. "Long black hair like my mom's, but she usually wears it in a braid.

Brown skin about like mine . . . sharp chin . . . high cheekbones. Eyes almost golden. You know, she's nearly as pretty as Morgan."

"You say that like you're surprised."

"Well, I usually see them together, and I've never paid all that much attention to her until today."

"Sounds like someone has a crush on this Morgan girl."

My face went hot and red. "I do not!" Well, maybe a little; but if so, it was a stupid crush that was never going anywhere.

"Of course you don't. Sorry I mentioned it."

"You're smirking," I growled.

"I am not. Rabbits can't smirk. Our faces aren't built for it. That's a known fact."

"*A*, as you've so frequently pointed out, you're not a rabbit, you're a fire hare. *B*, tell it to Bugs Bunny."

"Okay, maybe I'm smirking a little." He held his paws up a few inches apart. "But you really ought to see your face." The hare opened his eyes wider than they had any right to go and stared off into space with a big dopey grin. "Oh, Morgan, thank you for rescuing me, I've always hoped—"

At that point I dumped him off my lap before stomping through the kitchen and dining room to my bedroom, where I tossed my bag onto my bed and tore off my scorched and bloody shirt. My jeans were in better shape, though they had duckweed and filth from the bottom of the pond spattered here and there.

I'd just stripped them off when I heard a throat-clearing noise from my doorway and spun around angrily. "Sparx! If you don't st— Oh, hi, Aunt Noelle, I was just—" That's when I realized I was down to briefs and socks and yanked the blanket off my bed to cover myself, tumbling my backpack to the floor with a crash.

Noelle laughed, a simultaneously engaging and chilling sound with weird harmonic undertones. "It's all right, Kalvan, I can wait a bit to talk to you, but in the meantime, please don't open the shades. Daylight . . . is a problem for me. Even this weak winter light. Your mother and I are in the basement. Come down once you're clean and dressed." She walked away as silently as she'd arrived.

"Interesting." Sparx spoke from his favorite perch atop my shelves.

Since I hadn't noticed him slipping in, either, I about jumped out of my skin for a second time. "Don't do that! And what's interesting?"

"When you cross that section of floor it creaks and groans like a mouse orchestra tuning up for the big night. For her, nothing." His nose crinkled in thought.

"Maybe she's more ghost than zombie?" I offered as I wrapped a towel around my waist.

Sparx shook his head. "She's neither, and plenty solid."

"You're plenty solid, but I've seen you walk through walls."

"That's different and expected. I'm an elemental spirit, both flesh and flame."

"Neither of which can pass through this." I slapped the wall beside the bookcase.

Sparx snorted. "Ordinary flesh and flame, no. But in my case both are as much made from the stuff of magic as anything. No, I follow the old rules perfectly. Your aunt, on the other paw . . . Your aunt is something I've never seen before."

"Is that good or bad?"

"For my curiosity? Excellent. For your mother? So far, so good.

For everything else?" He raised both paws pads up. "As with most things, only time can properly answer."

"Have I ever mentioned that you're very reassuring?"

"Not even once."

"There's a reason for that." Though I had to admit his teasing had pretty deftly taken my mind off my earlier worries by irritating me—one of his favorite tricks. "Now I need to go clean up so I can have a nice chat with my crazy mom and her dead sister."

3

Sell by ... Too Late

"STALE BREAD, old canned goods, really any food past its expiration date. The older, the better." Noelle held up the jar of red currant jelly she'd been eating with a spoon so I could see the best-by date—April 18, 1987. "This is *perfect*. Genny found it in a box of our mother's stuff in the attic when she went looking for childhood toys. It should sustain me for some days. More recently expired food is less effective, but can be made to serve."

I couldn't help myself. "Gross!"

Sparx leaned forward and peered into the jar—though I wondered how well he could see anything given Noelle had unscrewed most of the lights. "Fascinating."

Noelle shrugged. "Necessary. And, rather surprisingly, quite delicious."

My mother looked up from where she was sitting on the floor, an ancient Black Canary action figure held in one hand and Batgirl in the other. She shrugged. "Noelle's always been a little odd."

Said the expert, I managed not to say.

Then, as if she was reading my fearful mind, "It's all right, Kalvan. I'm not that far out there at the moment. I know Noelle's dead and the current situation is temporary. She explained it while you were at school."

Because that's super *reassuring!* "I . . . uh, that's good, Mom. It's just . . ."

"You're worried." She sighed. "You probably should be. I'm not . . . I can't hold it all in my head right now. Sometimes I can tell exactly what's real and true, but too often I can't. Oscar used to anchor me, and before him, your father, Nix. But now I'm adrift. Noelle is helping as best she can. She got me to check the bills today. I was late on the power and the trash, and they were about to cut off the Internet."

"What?!?" It hadn't even occurred to me to think about that stuff. Realizing we'd come so close to being cut off made me feel like I'd eaten live worms for lunch.

"Don't worry; I got it all sorted."

Noelle nodded. "Automatic bill pay is a marvelous thing."

"For how long?" I asked, feeling sicker by the minute. I had no idea how much money we had, or if my mother would be able to work regularly, or anything about our finances at all, really. I'd never needed to know.

"Quite a while. I shifted nearly all of the money out of the joint savings account and put it into my own checking. That way if Oscar comes back he can't . . ." Her eyes widened suddenly as if she was seeing something over my shoulder. Then she turned away, back to Batgirl and Black Canary, singing softly. "Ash and char, sun and star, wind and smoke, ash and oak . . ."

Before I could say anything, Noelle caught my wrist and headed for the stairs. "Don't. We need to talk." Her grip was soft and cool, but unbreakable, like a steel tool with a rubber grip.

With Sparx trailing behind, Noelle led me up to the back hallway—a windowless space that was probably the second darkest spot in the house after the basement. "She's been like that off and on all day. It's not the worst I've seen her, but . . ."

"But what?" I demanded.

Noelle took a breath and sighed. It was only then I realized she'd had to consciously choose to breathe. She did it again now, before she began to speak. "Genny's always had issues, Kalvan. Since we were little girls. But it got especially bad when she first tried to go away to college."

"Tried?" I didn't like the sound of that.

"Yes. She ended up in a mental institution for a few months. Genny sees and hears things that aren't there sometimes, and most of her problem isn't about magic even if that's where it started. It's brain chemistry. Depression, delusions, hallucinations, paranoia sometimes. Her medications cover some of that, but she also needs anchors to help her sort the real from the imagined when things get bad. People she can trust to be real. Back in her college days, that was me and your grandmother—Grandpa Howard was already dead when she had her first episode—but neither of us had the right sort of powers to do anything for her magically. Fire only feeds the flames of her madness. Later, Nix did much of the work. Then, apparently, Oscar."

"What—Nix? You say that like my dad had magic, too."

"Of course." Noelle nodded. "He was a powerful sorcerer and a good one, and he used his skills to help your mother. I assumed you knew that."

"I . . . really?" I was so confused. "I don't know *anything* about my dad. Mom never talks about him. I thought from that first conversation you didn't like him."

"I didn't. At least not at first, but he grew on me. Much of it was simple prejudice on my part. Earth powers have always made me nervous. Dirt smothers fire, and all that."

"Hold on, my dad had the same kind of magic as Oscar?" The idea made me feel like I'd swallowed a grumpy rat to follow the worms. "That's terrible! Oscar was the worst thing that ever happened to me, and my dad was an earth power, too?"

"*Is* an earth power, Kalvan. Is. He's still alive . . . ish. Honestly, I wish he hadn't passed beyond any reaching."

Wait, what now?! Before I could ask anything more about my dad, Noelle continued.

"As much as we had our differences, he was always good for Genny, and she's in a bad place. If there was any way at all to reach him . . ." She shook her head. "Unfortunately, that's completely impossible. Death has given me a connection with earth that's letting me help more than I used to, but I won't be able to stay very long. Here in the North, life is weak and easier to fight while the snow flies, but spring will come. At some point after that I will lose the battle. Too soon it will all be on you and—"

"Me!?!" That drove every question about my dad out of my head. "But we both know fire can't help her, and I don't know what to do, and I'm only thirteen, and—"

"And it's not fair. Not even a little bit." Noelle put her hands on my shoulders and looked me straight in the eyes. "I know all that, but lots of things aren't fair. Like having to master the Darkness, or dueling with Oscar, or being attacked by delvers. But you handled all of that, and I'm sure you'll manage this, too."

Which makes exactly one of us, I thought.

"How?" I whispered.

"I don't know, Kalvan, I don't know. But I know you'll find what you need if you search inside yourself." For one brief moment, she looked as if she wanted to say more. Then she shook her head and turned away.

Sparx tapped the side of the big steel mixing bowl, making rainbows ripple on the inch of gasoline in the bottom. "I think we're ready."

I knelt beside him in snow gone slushy with the spring melt, and glanced anxiously around. "I hate this idea. Someone is going to call the cops about thirty seconds after we light the gas."

"Which is why we're doing this on the railroad tracks a few blocks from home and not in your backyard."

I nodded warily. "Does it really have to be at midnight?"

"Yes, and a full moon would help, but this can't wait. We don't know how long your aunt can hold herself free of the grave, and your mom's not going to get better on her own. We need to figure out what you can do to help her, and the fire bowl is the best tool I know when you're looking for hidden answers."

"I—eep!" I pointed at a pair of yellow eyes that had suddenly appeared on the slope above us. "What's that?"

Sparx looked up. "Coyote, I think. Big one."

"In the city? And why are its eyes glowing?"

"They're not glowing, they're reflecting. There's a streetlight on the slope behind us. And, sure. With the parks and the lakes and the cemeteries there's a lot of cover and decent hunting between all the fat squirrels and half-tame rabbits."

"Like you?" I jokingly poked him in the ribs, though the glowing eyes gave me the creepy-crawlies.

"No, not like me. Animals actually see what's there even when you humans do not, O Accursed Master. No coyote wants a mouthful of fire."

"So, why is it staring at us?" The yellow eyes held my own.

"How should I know?" He sighed. "Look, if it really matters, why don't you ask it?"

"For starters, funny bunny, I never learned to speak coyote."

"It's not all that different from fox. Listen." He let out several sharp yips and something between a howl and a long bark.

The eyes blinked. Then the coyote, if that's what it was, let out a low whine and a couple of yips of its own.

Sparx yipped back twice and the eyes lowered as though their owner were settling down to wait. Sparx turned back to me. "See? Nothing to worry about. Now can we get back to doing what we came to do?"

"What did it say?"

"*She* said this valley is her territory, and wanted to know if we were planning to stay long. I don't think she likes people very much, which is quite sensible for an urban coyote. I told her we'd be gone soon enough, but she might want to move off for a while anyway."

"That seems like an awful lot to say in a couple of yips." I eyed him skeptically.

"It's a very concise language and as much conveyed by subtle movements of the ears and nose as by words. With that settled, would you please light the bowl? It's cold out here."

The eyes still made me nervous, but Sparx was right and the slush had long since soaked through the knees of my jeans. Breathing in and then slowly out again, I framed the words I would need and began to speak in the language of fire. "Ash and char, sun and star, wind and smoke, ash and oak."

As each word left my mouth it formed itself into a glowing ideogram, hovering briefly in the air before dropping down to land on the edge of the bowl. *Ash* went first and landed beneath Polaris, the star of the north. *Char* took station on the south side of the bowl. The others followed, filling in the eight points of a fiery compass rose. I'd never used the next few lines in a real spell; only practiced them as part of my lessons.

"Words of fire, light a pyre. Words of art, open hearts."

The ideograms slid down into the bowl, igniting the gasoline, which bloomed into a flower of cobalt fire. Now I had to imagine what I wanted to see and know, and hold that in my heart while I spoke the final piece of the spell.

Show me what I need to help my mother. I still had trouble with a lot of fire magic, but this part felt easy. There was nothing in the world more important to me.

"Flame of earth darkness brightens. Flame of truth the blind enlightens."

The heart of the fire flower brightened and clarified until it looked like a sphere of aquamarine embedded in the center of an enormous candle's perfect flame, or one of those onion domes you might see capping an orthodox church.

Please. I need to see.

For several long seconds nothing happened. Then, slowly, like a face taking shape out of the random arrangement of tiles in a floor, an image began to form. It took me several beats to recognize it as the back of a person's head, dark haired and leaning forward. Even as I realized what I was seeing, it turned, exposing a too-familiar face.

Oscar! Oscar, as I had only seen him a few times; with all the planes of his face gone hard and flat, his features as cold and inhuman as if he were a stone playing at being a man. A power of earth and rock. The Corona Borealis winked into being on his brow, dark and tarnished—Winter's Crown.

"No." I leaned backward, away from the flames. "I won't let us fall into his power ever again." If Oscar was the only thing that could help my mother, there was no hope.

"Wait," said Sparx. "The vision is not yet finished."

The Crown shimmered and Oscar's features began to change and flow. Moving with the slow, inexorable pace of lava devouring a village, it became another face. My real father's—the one I saw in my dreams sometimes with a clarity my memories didn't possess—but still carved from stone. The Crown had vanished. *But this doesn't make any sense. My dad can't help; Noelle said he was beyond any reaching* . . . Before I could finish my thought, the fires flickered again, restoring the Crown while Nix's features blurred into . . .

"NO!" This time I shouted and leaped back, kicking the bowl over in my hurry to get away from the vision and spraying liquid fire across the slushy ground.

"No." More quietly, but just as emphatic, because the last face I had seen in the fire was mine. My face as hard and granite-cold as the others; my face in stone and crowned with the Corona Borealis in all its summer glory.

"I don't understand." I glared at Sparx across the broad puddle of burning gasoline. "I don't understand any of it. What's going on? Why did it show my father? Then me as a creature of earth? And as the Summer King?"

"I don't know." Sparx shook his head. "And I don't like it. The Crown is fallow, but when the season turns, someone must become the Summer King. At first I thought it might be your father, given his face in the vision, but then it ended with you."

"You don't think it's going to be me, do you?"

"I very much hope not." The hare looked more worried than he had at any time since we fought my stepfather. "The Crown should never go to one so young. It's a magic for the mature, both of body and spirit. I doubt you have strength to bear it."

"But?" I glared at him. "You didn't say it, but I know there's a *but*."

"*But*, barring death or other special circumstances, the reigning monarch may choose their own successor. When Oscar threw the Crown at you it left a mark where it shouldn't have . . ."

"Oh." I touched the silver pyramid I had thought so dashing when I first noticed it, and swallowed hard.

"That's not good."

"No." He hunkered down in the slush and started pulling the flames from the burning gasoline into himself. "It's not."

"What about the other part, my face in stone? Is there something there you don't want to tell me, too?"

Before he could answer, the coyote suddenly threw her head back and let out a long, mournful howl that seemed to go on forever, rising and falling until it became . . .

"Sirens!" Sparx's ears popped straight up. "That's probably about the fire. We'd best make ourselves scarce."

I couldn't hear them yet, but I nodded and followed him away from the tracks. It wasn't until I bent to duck through some brush that I thought to wonder about the coyote and her timely howl. But when I glanced at where I'd last seen her eyes, I found only darkness.

I half wanted to question Noelle more about my dad when I got home, but the vision of him looking so much like Oscar haunted me. Earth power scared me, and I didn't think I could bear it if he turned out to be pretty much the same sort of man as my stepfather. Besides, if he couldn't be reached anyway, maybe it was better not to know. In the end, I couldn't bring myself to ask.

After a nearly sleepless night, I zombied my way through the first two hours of my classes with Sparx hiding out in my bag. I'd tried to convince him to stay home and keep an eye on my mom, but after the delver attack, he flat refused to let me out of his sight.

Third hour was Modern American History with Rob. As with most academic-type classes at Free, the room was set up with long tables forming a sort of squared-off U shape around the outer edge of the classroom with the teacher's desk in the opening. All the chairs were on the outside of the tables, facing toward the center. The effect was to create a big circle with the teacher's place only slightly more important than the students'. There was some lecturing, but part of the Free School deal was that you were supposed to read up on the topic so classes could happen as a give-and-take discussion of the material.

Most of the time I liked it that way, even when it meant I had to work harder than I would have in a regular school—there was no faking it if you didn't do the homework or know the material some other way. But today was a big exception. I was totally zonked and having a brutally hard time keeping my eyes open.

When Rob started talking about the debates in the House of Representatives leading up to the Iraq War, Dave actually had to elbow me a couple of times to keep me from nodding off, and I caught some very disappointed looks from Rob. I tipped my chair back onto two legs, leaning my shoulders against the wall and balancing there in an effort to force myself to pay attention or fall on my ass.

It was soooo hard to stay awazzzzzzzzzzzzzzzzzzzz . . .

BANG!

"Augh!" The back of my head bounced off the wall hard enough to make the room flash bright white for an instant. "What?!? George Bush! Oil! Desert Storm!"

I blinked madly, trying to bludgeon my brain into working. Around me, the whole room broke out laughing. I looked up into the eyes of the teacher staring at me from the other side of the table.

"Did we have a nice nap, Kalvan?" Rob's voice dripped sarcasm. "Are we refreshed and ready to take on an exciting assignment in the world of history? A five-hundred-word paper perhaps? Delivered aloud to the class in one week? On the subject of today's discussion. We are? Excellent." He picked up the yardstick he'd used to smack the table and went back to his desk.

Dave leaned in close and it was only then I noticed he and Ellen were hanging on to my chair so it wouldn't tip backward and dump me on the floor—probably at Rob's direction. "Sorry, man, but you started cutting Zs with a noise that would have done the old band saw in the shop proud. I couldn't cover it. Rob called your name twice before he came over."

I shook my head slightly, not wanting to draw any more attention than I already had. "S'okay, s'not your fault. I should have just skipped class and caught a nap. Think I'll do that 'stead of lunch."

Dave nodded. "Good plan."

I managed to keep my eyes open through the fifteen minutes until the bell rang. Then, while most of the kids headed for the cafeteria, I made my way to the back door of the main stage. I knocked—twice slow, three times fast, twice slow again. It opened a few minutes later and a senior named Clayton waved me inside before heading back onto the stage where he started running lines from a play with some girl whose name I couldn't remember.

There were ten or twelve students scattered around the ridiculously oversized theater—a remnant of the much-better-funded mechanical arts high school that had originally occupied the building. Free had inherited the building third or fourthhand, probably because it was cheaper to house us in the worn-out old school than tear it down. I was too tired to even pretend to say hi to anybody, so I headed around to the front of the stage where a panel that was supposed to be locked let me slip into the darkness beneath.

The distance between the boards above and the black-painted concrete below was about two feet at the front of the stage, but the floor sloped down as you moved toward the back, where there was nearly four feet of clearance. Decaying props and bits of scenery filled most of the space, with a few narrow aisles that allowed actors access to the trapdoors in the stage above. I could hear kissing noises in the darkness down one of the side paths. Normally that would have been enough to send me back the way I'd come.

Instead, I went on until I got to a little three-quarter-sized recliner against the back wall. I'd spent a week sleeping there in the lead-up to my duel with Oscar, so it was a bit like coming home . . . in a weird sort of way; and I was out in seconds.

. . . and *for* seconds. Or at least that's how it felt when I woke up as my chair went over backward and landed with a thump and a big puff of dust while I flailed around wildly.

". . . the heck?" I blinked muzzily at the face above me. They were bending forward so their features were upside down in relation to me and difficult to sort out. But not for long. "Josh!"

"Mornin', pumpkin." He wore a grimly satisfied sort of smile that made me want to punch him in the nose, as I'd done once before.

Before I could respond in any way, there was a bright flare and Sparx appeared on my chest, interposing himself between me and Josh. "Back off, bitter water boy!"

Josh chuckled. "Aren't we a feisty little bunny this afternoon?"

I put a calming hand on Sparx's back where the flames rippled and churned angrily. "What do you want, Josh?" I didn't like him, but for reasons that had nothing to do with friendship, he'd helped me against Oscar and I owed him.

"Mostly to see you land on your face instead of your back, but I don't always get what I want. Herself wanted me to tell the stone man's son that a fancy crown won't keep his head on his shoulders and that delvers dig deep and think shallow." *Herself* was an elemental spirit and the embodiment of the Mississippi.

"How wonderfully vague." I gently shoved Sparx off my chest

and sat cross-legged on the back of the overturned chair. "At least it's not something half as specific as a riddle this time. I *loved* the last pair."

Sparx put a paw on my thigh. "Kalvan . . ."

"What?!"

"When one of the great elementals decides to warn you about something, it's best to respond politely and gratefully. She didn't have to give you clues for the fight against your stepfather, or spit you out when you went under the ice after the duel."

Josh smirked at that. "Listen to the bunny; you'll live longer."

I rolled my eyes. "Well, then, I'll be sure to send her a thank-you card as soon as I figure out what she's talking about. In the meantime, I've got classes."

What I really wanted was more sleep, but that wasn't going to happen. I sure didn't want to sit around chatting with Josh, but I couldn't make him go away since he's twice my size and has magic to boot. So I snatched my backpack and pushed past him to the nearest trapdoor leading onto the stage. Shoving it open with a crash, I climbed up between Clayton and his scene partner, who both glared at me. I ignored them and kept going.

"Kalvan!" Josh followed me out into the hall. "I'm not done with you—" He stopped speaking abruptly and turned back toward the theater when a small knot of girls came around the corner—which was a huge relief.

Right up until the girls started giggling and one said, "Hey, Morgan, isn't that your new boyfriend?"

I saw Morgan and Lisa then and blushed hard.

Morgan's face darkened as well. "Stow it, Angie."

"Look at those red faces," said Angie. "I think I'm on to

something. What *were* you and Lisa doing all alone with Kalvan and his little friend at the wedding garden? It sounds awfully romanti—"

The girl's voice cut off abruptly as Morgan dropped and pivoted, kicking the legs out from under her in a move straight out of an action film.

"Oh yes, I'm head over heels in love with a boy who barely comes up to my chin." Morgan rolled her eyes as she came back upright, then stepped in close to me. "It's *so* much fun when I have to bend over to kiss him. See." The boots she wore gave her seven inches on me and she made a show of leaning way down to bestow an air kiss a few inches from my unbandaged cheek.

Then she shoved me away hard enough that I stumbled and landed on my butt before she turned back to the other girls. "Is that what you wanted to see, Angie? I hope so, since it's a one-time event, because barf."

And wasn't *that* just great for my ego. I mean the idea of me and Morgan going out—if I were even really interested in going out with someone—was about as likely as a gopher dating a racehorse. Morgan started to walk away. I didn't move—mostly because I didn't want to draw her attention.

The sharp voice of our principal, Aaron Washington, cracked out. "Morgan, Angie, Kalvan, my office. Now." His eyes scanned the group. "Lisa, you too. Let's go."

Great.

4

Wind in the Illows

THE PRINCIPAL STARED at the four of us across his desk, a disappointed frown on his face. I resisted the urge to confess to crimes I hadn't committed and waited for someone else to crack. I'd ended up in Aaron's office any number of times over the years, but this was the first time I was *actually* innocent. It was a refreshingly novel experience.

The silence stretched out and Aaron rubbed his right temple where the tight black curls were beginning to silver. "Well?" More silence. "Fine. Morgan, why did you blow a kiss at Kalvan and then knock him down?" So, he'd seen at least that much. "Is this about what happened at the conservatory?"

"It is." Morgan's voice came out tight and clipped. "Someone said he was my boyfriend, and I wanted to make it very clear he wasn't."

"Because blowing him kisses and knocking him over conveys that so much better than the obvious age difference . . ." Aaron sighed and visibly suppressed the urge to roll his eyes. "Well, that's a start. Would anyone care to explain why Angie was also on the floor when I came around the corner?"

Angie coughed. "I, um, I'm the one that teased Morgan about Kalvan. When she got in my face, I, um, I tripped."

Tripped? I thought, in the same moment that Aaron raised an eyebrow and said, "Tripped?"

Angie nodded vigorously and I wondered why she wasn't ratting Morgan out. It was the perfect opportunity for a little revenge, and she'd already admitted to the teasing, which was the only thing *she'd* done wrong.

Aaron's eyes shifted. "Lisa, is there anything you'd care to add? You *were* present for both this incident and the one at the conservatory."

"That all sounds like what I saw, Aaron."

"Kalvan?"

I shrugged. "I wasn't really paying attention until Morgan knocked me on my butt."

"Right. Lisa, Kalvan, you're not in trouble. Angie, that wasn't nice. Consider your next free period a detention, which you will serve in the library." He quickly scrawled a note and handed it to me. "Drop this off at the library for me, please, Kalvan, since it's on your way." *Why did he know my schedule that well?* "Morgan, you stay. Everyone else can go."

When we got out to the hall I turned left toward the library, and Lisa fell in beside me. Angie went the other way, *fast*.

"She looks scared," I said.

Lisa nodded. "She should be. Pissing off Morgan was stupid."

I didn't argue. If you'd asked me about Morgan a month ago, I'd probably have said she was pretty, that she had a sweet smile and dimples, that she was a dancer, and that she seemed nice enough. That would have been it. She hadn't made much of an impression on me because we didn't run in the same circles and she was a couple years older. But that was before seeing that kick, and before the conservatory. I owed Morgan my life. Almost involuntarily, I reached up and touched the edge of my bandage, reminded again of how close the bolt had come to hitting me in the eye. When I did so, Lisa suddenly looked down at her left wrist, rubbing it as though it ached.

"That was a heck of a takedown," I finally said.

"Morgan's a black belt. For her, that was gentle."

"I didn't know that."

She finally met my eyes again. "There's lots you don't know about Morgan." We turned into the stairwell and were briefly out of sight of anyone. Lisa caught my arm and turned me to look at her. Once again, I was struck by the golden color of her eyes, which was almost as weird as my own amber. "Be careful, Kalvan. Morgan's a good person to have on your side, but she can be . . . dangerous."

"All right. But why are *you* warning me? I thought Morgan was your best friend."

Lisa smiled, though there was something sad about the expression. "That she is."

"And?" I looked at her expectantly.

"And you could have acted to protect yourself first when that delver popped up with his crossbow. But you chose to try to save us instead. I owe you for that, and I always pay my debts." Lisa put one foot back behind the other and bent her knees briefly in something very like the curtsy I'd seen some actresses use instead of a bow. "See you later, Kalvan." She turned away, heading down the stairs, while the path to the library took me up.

After I dropped off the note, I continued on to Tanya's home-room, arriving right with the fourth-period bell. There was a short line in the hallway ahead of me since this was the period when Tanya dealt with her independent-study students. They were mostly doing stuff in the sciences, which was her main teaching area. But I was pretty sure at least a couple of kids were there for purposes similar to my own. If so, it was impossible to tell which ones were which from where I waited with the others—Tanya's desk was at the back of the room, and for reasons I suspected were magical, conversation didn't carry from there to the doorway.

I was last in line. As I stepped into the room, Tanya waved a hand, and a sudden breeze blew the door shut behind me. I startled at the slam. "Did I do something wrong?"

Tanya shook her head. "No, I just want to make doubly sure of our privacy. Sit down, Kalvan. Is Sparx home with your mom again?"

There was a flash like someone had flicked the world's largest lighter, and my familiar flared into being on the desk. "No, I was abandoned in the—Oh, burn and blight it!" He had arrived on a pile of tests, igniting the top one, which he now had to stomp out. "Sorry about that, Tanya."

"It's all right; he was going to fail anyway." She waved it off. "Abandoned?"

"Never mind." Sparx flicked his ears. "Kalvan was simply being a typical adolescent. Nothing to worry about."

Tanya snorted. "If you can say that being a typical adolescent is nothing to worry about with a straight face, you've clearly never taught at a public school."

"Fair enough."

I sat down and crossed my arms. "If you two are done pretending I'm not here, what's up?"

"Ooh," said Tanya, "he's turning into a teenager." She shifted her eyes to Sparx. "Always a *great* time with a power of fire. Good luck. You're going to need it."

"Don't I know it!"

I rolled my eyes but kept silent because I was outnumbered.

Tanya shifted back in her chair so she could more easily speak to both of us. "I took a good look around the conservatory, but I didn't learn anything about the delver. I'm a windwalker and earth is my opposite. I can't read it well under the best of circumstances, and these were most definitely not that. Which is why what I *did* find worries me." Tanya frowned. "The air in the wedding garden had been very badly disturbed."

"I'm not sure I understand . . . ," I said.

"When someone passes through a room, they leave a record in the currents of the air—drag lines, patches of fresh turbulence, heat signatures. Wanting to learn more about how air moves is what drew me into science originally." She smiled. "My powers allow me to see the way your breathing affects the space around you right now. Depending on the strength of the interactions and what follows by way of interference, I can also read things that have happened in a space for some amount of time afterward."

"So, you can see if someone walked through a room after they've left?" That was pretty cool—she'd make a great detective. Which, if you looked at it the right way, was kind of what a scientist was.

"Exactly." Tanya nodded. "Though some traces only last a few minutes, strong scents might leave patterns that last for days, and powerful enough magic can change things for weeks or even years, depending on what kind and how it's used."

"Oh." *Now how am I going to get out of telling her about Morgan and Lisa?* I glanced at Sparx, willing him to honor the fact I didn't want to give the girls away. "You saw some sort of magic in the conservatory? Beyond mine, I mean, and that delver's?"

Tanya nodded. "A windweaver was there, though I couldn't say exactly when. They smeared over all traces of their passage in a way that made it impossible for me to tell anything beyond the fact they'd been there between the time you were attacked and my arrival."

"So, they were there *after* I was?" Maybe I wouldn't have to rat on Morgan after all.

"Yes," said Tanya. "Possibly during or before the attack as well, but I have no way of knowing since they blurred everything so badly. I could barely even see any evidence of what *you'd* done, and a firestorm of the kind you described should have left traces that would be obvious for several days at least. This windweaver pretty much nuked the evidence."

"That's the second time you've used the term *windweaver*, but you call yourself a *windwalker*. Is there a difference?"

I caught Sparx rolling his eyes and giving me his best you-never-do-your-homework look.

Tanya sighed and her expression mirrored Sparx's. "I'm pretty sure it was in the book you're supposed to be reading. Windweavers are both much rarer and vastly more powerful than windwalkers. I *thought* I knew all the windweavers within a hundred miles, but apparently I've missed one. I called all four of the others and if any of them know about the one from the conservatory, they weren't willing to tell me. That a new windweaver has revealed themself now, in the wake of the fall of the Winter King, is very worrying."

"You think this has something to do with the Corona Borealis?" I didn't like that at all, especially knowing who the windweaver probably was—I doubted a third master of air was in the conservatory between Morgan and Tanya.

"Power attracts power, Kalvan," replied Tanya. "That scar your stepfather gave you marks you as a major player, and that will draw foes and friends both. Doubly so in the magical chaos created by dethroning a monarch. Even if Oscar weren't still alive and likely to want revenge, simply possessing the Crown would make you a target."

"Why didn't you tell me that weeks ago?" I spoke as much to Sparx as Tanya.

My human teacher spoke first. "I didn't want to alarm you. I was hoping it wouldn't start so soon."

"What about you, bunny boy?"

"My reasons were similar, and it wasn't until last night's fire bowl that I began to worry the Crown might actually have fallen to you when Oscar struck you."

"And after?" I demanded.

"You were exhausted and completely flipped out last night, and it didn't seem a good time to add to your burdens. Then it was morning, and we both know that telling you anything in the morning is as effective as trying to light fire to a bucket of water."

I couldn't argue with that. "All right, now what?"

Sparx turned to face me, putting his back to Tanya. When I asked my question, he flicked his gaze toward her and back to me in a pretty clear don't-you-think-you-should-tell-her-about-it manner. I pretended not to understand. Morgan saved my life and I owed her silence if that's what she wanted.

"Could you two back up a moment?" Tanya sounded more concerned than ever. "Tell me about scrying the fire bowl. You saw a vision that makes you think Kalvan might be the coming Summer King? That would be much more dangerous than simply holding the Crown through the fallow months. He's far too young!"

Sparx nodded. "Assuming nothing happens to stop it, yes. I think when Oscar threw the Crown at him, he symbolically chose Kalvan as his successor."

"Tell me about the vision." So we did. At the end Tanya shook her head. "That's not good. Between the scar and the fact he's the child of both the most recent Summer Queen and the last Winter King . . ."

"Oscar's not my dad!" I said very firmly.

"Yes, of course," Tanya apologized. "That was an insensitive way to put it, even if that's how it plays out magically and symbolically. I'm sorry." She frowned and then took a deep breath. "I think we may have to change your course of study."

That surprised me. "What? How?"

Sparx looked thoughtful, but didn't say anything. Though he was technically my familiar, he was also my main teacher when it came to magic, what with being at least four or five hundred years older than me.

When Tanya saw he didn't have anything to add, she continued, "Up till now Sparx and I have been focused on getting you to master the basics of fire magic. Everything else you're going to do rests on that foundation, and it can be quite dangerous to try the more advanced sorts of spells without it—you've been incredibly lucky so far. Having you perform the full familiar summoning without all the proper groundwork was a very risky move on Sparx's part."

The fire hare shrugged. "I was pretty much cooked without it."

"I know, but considering all the things that could have gone wrong . . ." She shuddered.

"Could we get back to the *course change* thing?" I asked.

"Right." Tanya set her shoulders. "I think we need to start teaching you some of the more advanced sorts of defensive magic. Starting today."

Sparx agreed. "He needs to learn how to address the other elements."

I looked from human teacher to hare mentor and back. "Didn't you just say that could be really dangerous?" They nodded in perfect unison. "This is because of the Crown?" Again the nods. "That bad?" A third nod. "Oh."

Yikes.

"I hate this, and I'm never going to figure it out," I grumbled, dropping the polished ball of granite into the big silver basin at my feet and splashing water all over.

Several drops spattered Sparx, flashing into steam with a hiss. "No, you won't." He sighed. "Not if you don't improve your attitude."

He flicked his ears grumpily and hopped onto the lab bench, bringing him closer to my eye level. Embarrassed, I turned and walked away. Well, as far as the confines of the small space would let me. Once upon a time, the glorified closet off the science room had been a darkroom—I'd had to look that up—and it still had the big air lock–type door designed to keep light from getting in and destroying the film. The tanks of chemicals and developing tubs were long gone, but the workbenches remained and a fume hood stood in one corner now. It was a perfect place to conduct small experiments—both scientific and magical—that were safer done in isolation.

"Kalvan, you're acting like a five-year-old! Well, or a fifteen-year-old . . . same behavior, different motivation."

It was my turn to sigh, but I went back to the bench. "I'm sorry, but first there was the vision in the fire, and now I have to learn words from the language of earth. It feels like the universe wants to turn me into Oscar."

Sparx snorted his frustration, and jets of flame shot from his nostrils. "Hardly. Whatever else you think about Oscar—may the fires of blame claim him for eternal torment—he is a highly disciplined sorcerer, and a master of both his element and the higher magics. *You* can't even master yourself. Besides, Oscar isn't the only power of earth out there. Your real father—"

"I DON'T WANT TO TALK ABOUT THAT!" I clapped a hand over my mouth, shocked at my own vehemence. "I . . . I'm sorry. I just . . . I'm kind of a mess right now. I can't get the thought of that crossbow bolt out of my head—the sound of it, the slice on my cheek, the certainty that . . ." I shuddered and shook my head. "Now all this. The Crown stuff. Learning *earth* words when I'm a fire power. Visions of Oscar, and discovering my dad is like him . . . it's all gone weird and scary, you know?" The more I thought about my dad and Oscar, the more I wished Noelle had left me in the dark.

Sparx sighed, and some of the tension left him. "You have already been forced to face much no one your age should have to deal with, and now I'm asking you to do more than you're really prepared for. You have done so well that sometimes I forget how very young you are. I wish I didn't have to push you, but Luck or Fate has singled you out, and you must either rise to the occasion or fail and fall into darkness. You have no other options."

I took a deep breath and consciously suppressed the urge to argue. "You sure know how to cheer a guy up there, Mister Doom and Gloom." It wasn't much of joke, but it helped ease my frustration. "I'm really glad we had this pep talk. You've got me revved up and ready to take on . . . well, something small and not very fierce. Maybe a geriatric mouse with a trick knee and one paw tied behind its back? Yeah, I think I could almost manage that. You should totally become a life coach!"

Sparx snorted again, this time sans flames. "Better. A little late, but better. Let's try this one more time, shall we?"

I pulled the stone from the water, holding it in front of my right eye and giving it a good glare. The spell was something called the Dragon's Wings. For me, it was ninety percent fire magic, but for reasons I had kind of tuned out, it wouldn't work properly if I didn't do an invocation of all four primary elements—which statement sort of implied the existence of secondary elements, but Sparx had refused to get into that.

So, time to try again. "Issilthss!" The name of the wind in its own tongue . . . sort of. I couldn't really pronounce it, much less spell it, what with all the weird susurrations and hissing sounds. The human throat was as ill suited to the task as any human alphabet, or, at least, that's what Sparx had told me about elemental tongues, and I quote: "you big, bald thumb-monkeys." Whatever the case, when I spoke the word, the still air of the darkroom suddenly stirred and came alive around me.

"Kkst*ta!" Fire. My own element and one I *could* actually

pronounce properly by letting the fire of my heart speak through my throat, crackling and popping like a log on the hearth.

"Bglbgleb!" *Yeah, right. Gargle, gargle, glub, glub, and I'm going down for the third time.* Water was never going to be my friend, and my mangling of its name barely produced a ripple in the basin . . . if that. I was pretty sure I'd flubbed it, but that didn't mean I was off the hook.

I still had to try, "Drooododor!" The globe of rock grew suddenly heavy in my hand and I felt a connection run from it straight to my heart, which went cold and hard, slowing in my chest and—

"NO!" I shouted in fear, and pushed back against that sense of being *invaded* by stone with all the fires of my soul. Earth was my enemy. Oscar had proven that.

Searing pain filled my hand and the suddenly red-hot stone fell into the basin. It hit with a hiss and cloud of steam, and the water began to bubble and roil. I focused on that instead of the black bundle of agony at the end of my arm.

My knees started to go weak and spongy, but before I could collapse, Sparx—seeming to have grown to three times his usual size—was pressing his forehead tight to my injured palm, fur blazing bright. Somehow, in complete opposition to everything my logical brain knew about fire and burns, he felt like ice where he touched my skin, and the pain began to ease.

With the blood roaring in my ears, I put my back against the wall and slowly slid to the floor. Sparx held contact all the way down and beyond as the world went red and then white before finally fading completely away.

∽

As soon as the school bus got out of sight, I yanked my glove off and squatted to soak my hand in a deep puddle of melt water. That eased the pain of the blisters, but only a little, and I swore quietly as I waited for the ice-water to numb things further.

Dave whistled. "That burn looks *really* nasty, Kalvan. Are you sure you should be dipping it in such filthy water? Maybe you should see someone about it?"

I shook my head. "Sparx says it *ought* to be gone by tomorrow because the injury is mostly of my element." When I couldn't stand the cold any longer I pulled my hand out of the puddle and looked at the thick white blisters that carpeted my palm and the insides of my fingers. "I think they're starting to go down a bit already." *Maybe. I don't know.*

"They are." Sparx spoke over my shoulder from his perch in my backpack. "I know it doesn't feel like it, but you'll barely be able to see them in the morning. Besides, the burned hand teaches best and—"

"Sparx," I growled as I lifted the backpack off my shoulder with my good hand so I could look him in the face. "Would you please shut up?"

Dave shook his head. "Chillax, dude."

Sparx simply raised one eyebrow and crossed his forelegs on his chest.

I took a deep breath. "I'm sorry if I sound whiny. It just hurts a *lot*, and you and Tanya have me really spooked about the Crown. Oh, and there was that guy I saw in the alley, and nearly getting shot in the eye yesterday." I was *never* going to forget the angry bee sound the bolt made as it kissed my cheek.

"I thought everything was *supposed* to get better after I defeated Oscar. I mean that's how it works in the books—you beat the bad guy and then it's happily ever after. But, my bad guy is still out there." Not to mention that the idea of becoming somehow like him as I had in that vision was almost as scary as what was happening with my mom. "And . . ." I trailed off when I realized I didn't know where I was going. This was sooooo not my day.

Dave punched me in the shoulder. "Come on, you're looking a bit crispy around the edges and not just the hand. Let's get you home. It's a good thing for you I'm sleeping over."

"Why?"

"Because you could clearly use a real meal and no one else is going to fix it for you."

He might have a point. My mom didn't do her best cooking when she was phoning it in from the moons of Mars, and my aunt . . . well, I really preferred my meals to come with expiration dates that fell at some point in the future.

"Hey," I grumbled, "I can microwave a gas-station burrito with the best of them!"

"Exactly. You've been eating way too much garbage."

Dave poked me in the ribs and I blinked my eyes open. It seemed like I'd drifted off only minutes ago.

"Whazzup? It's not morning yet, is it?"

He shook his head. "Nope, it's just shy of the witching hour."

"Did I miss a meeting?"

"You wake up worse than anyone I've ever heard of. You know that, right?" Dave sighed. "You have homework, remember?"

"I . . . oh, yeah." Some of the things Tanya and Sparx wanted me to learn had to be accomplished or prepared at specific times or places. "You don't suppose it could wait till tomorrow night?"

All the sympathy went out of Dave's expression and his tone took on something like disgust. "Dude, you are a piece of work."

That woke me up. "Huh?"

"I know things have been hard for you, what with your stepdad turning out to be an evil sorcerer and all, but I cannot believe how much of an absolute lazy jerk you can be about this magic stuff."

"I'm . . . sorry?"

"Yeah, you are. I'd give my right hand to be able to do the stuff you can do now, and—"

"Stop!" Sparx's fur flared suddenly bright from his perch atop my bookshelves. "Never say things like that."

"Like what?" asked Dave. "That I'd give my right hand to have my own magic?"

"Yes, that. Exactly! Do not say such things."

Dave looked baffled and maybe a little hurt. "Why not? People say things like that all the time. Besides, it's true."

Sparx hopped down to land on the bed. "Ordinary people may be able to get away with it. But *you* have become part of the world of magic and are no longer anything like ordinary, and the truth of the thing makes for all the more reason not to speak of it. You never know who or what might be listening."

"Wait, I thought you had to be born to it, like Kalvan," said Dave.

"Not at all." The hare shook his head. "It might be easier for someone with Kalvan's family history, but there are as many ways to acquire magic as there are stars in the sky."

"So, you're saying a trade *is* possible?" Dave's voice came out somewhere between scared and wistful.

"Quite possible and very, very dangerous. Especially the way you framed it, with no specifics about what sort of magic you want. There are many varieties of enchantment, and not all of them are things you would wish on anyone you cared for. Curses are as real as blessings. If the wrong power heard you, it might take your hand in exchange for making you into a monster your own mother wouldn't recognize."

"Oh." Dave swallowed hard. "I was imagining elemental powers like Kalvan has, or Morgan, or even Josh. I didn't know there were other options."

"More than you can possibly imagine," said Sparx.

"Okay, then. If anyone is listening, I think I'll keep the hand, thanks."

"Better," said Sparx. "Now, we need to get going or we'll lose our window of opportunity."

As we were heading out the back door, my mother came stomping down from upstairs. She was barefoot in a blue taffeta ball gown and her long black hair was a wild and filthy cloud around her face. "Kalvan, the plants are eavesdropping again. I'm sure of it. Would you be a dear and pour bleach on all of them?"

I felt sick, but I nodded. "Sure, Mom." Then I turned back toward the door.

"Where are you going?" She sounded intensely suspicious, which meant she probably hadn't been sleeping, possibly for days.

It wasn't the first time she'd gone paranoid on me, and I'd learned some decent coping strategies. "I don't think we have enough bleach in the house, Mom. I'll need to run to the store."

"Oh." She turned, took two steps up the stairs, and then stopped.

"Hang on." She reached into the bodice of her dress and pulled out a couple of twenties. "Here. Get some milk while you're at it."

After we got outside, Dave squeezed my shoulder. "My dad can get like that when he's in a manic phase. Does she really think the plants are out to get her?"

"I don't know. The first time it happened I thought she might be talking about bugs in the plants—the electronic kind—but that was before I really got involved in the magic world. Now, I live with a talking rabbit, so who knows?"

"I'm so sorry, man."

I shrugged his hand off. "I'm dealing with it." Sometimes, if you pretend not to care, you can almost even convince yourself.

"Ouch!" I jerked my hand back and the shard of obsidian I'd been balancing on my burned palm dropped to the ground between the pottery cup filled with clear water and the nearby railroad tracks.

"What happened?" Dave asked from beyond the edge of the magical circle.

"The rock bit me!"

Sparx poked at the black stone. It came from Oscar's magical supplies and had been partially shaped into a spear head. "I don't sense anything that would cause such an effect. Describe the sensation."

"It. Bit. Me," I growled. "I still don't see why I should have to work with stone at all. I'm a child of fire. Rocks hate me."

"Rocks do *not* hate you." Sparx took a deep breath. "And your wants are neither here nor there for the purposes of this exercise. The highest formal magics touch on all the elements even when they draw most heavily on one. If you're going to protect yourself properly, you will have to learn how to address and invoke the other powers."

"It's hardly fair."

Sparx's fur flamed suddenly bright. "Fairness is not an element in magic. Neither is it one that life pays much attention to. Which is something else you will need to learn. Now, tell me *exactly* what happened when you spoke the word of stone. And 'it bit me' is not an acceptable answer. Your hand is neither bleeding nor more swollen than it was before. If anything, the blisters have gone down. So, it did not *bite* you. What did it do?"

I took my own deep breath. Sparx was right, and I knew it. "I . . . it's hard to explain. Maybe it's because it was Oscar's element, but when I speak words in the tongue of earth, I feel . . . weird inside. Cold and hard and hollow all at once." *See also: Rocks hate me.* But I didn't say that bit out loud.

"Better." Sparx nodded. "Tell me more."

"When I said the word for stone in its own language, it felt like a barb of ice came out of the shard and ran through my veins until it pierced my heart. It . . . hurt. But not like a cut or a burn . . . more like when I think about my mom's problems."

"That's—" Sparx's words were cut off by a sudden high howl.

I turned and saw a pair of glowing golden eyes coming up fast. It was the coyote again and she was running straight toward . . . "Dave!"

The coyote leaped and I got my first clear view of her. She looked huge, like Great Dane huge. Or, at least, that was my brief impression before she hit Dave, driving him backward over the line of the magical circle and into me.

We hit the ground in a tangle of limbs and fur, and that was the moment when the earthquake started.

5

Over Under Sideways Down

TAKE ONE LARGE COYOTE, two medium-sized thirteen-year-old boys, one enormous hare—who, by the way, happens to be on FIRE. Add a grab-bag of magical oddments, some of which have sharp edges. Place all ingredients in a large clear glass bowl with a couple of gallons of slush and mud. Shake till thoroughly mixed.

That's what the next few seconds felt like from the inside. I can only imagine how it looked from the outside. The circle of protection had been cast to contain me, Sparx, and not a whole lot else. Which would have been fine if it had not also been forced to accommodate Dave and the giant coyote in the middle of an earthquake. Because as soon as they entered the circle, the spell hardened up, creating a transparent magical dome of force stronger than steel. This prevented us from leaving and anything else from entering.

Why that happened, and why it hadn't *before* the pair fell on me, was beyond me in the moment. The most important thing was that it probably saved all of our lives, as scant seconds later at least a dozen stone crossbow bolts shattered when they struck the invisible dome surrounding us—another delver attack! Or, at least, that's how I pieced it together later.

At the time it was pretty much: OW! HEY! STOP! GRRRRRR! WHAT?!? OWWW! DON'T! YIPYIPYIP! *SIZZLE!* ARGH! GRRRRR! *TWANG! CRACK!* OWWWWWWWW! And so on.

Eventually, we settled into something resembling a rest state. I say *resembling rest* because half the blisters on my palm had been torn open, I had a fuzzy coyote paw with very long nails lodged firmly in my ear, and Sparx was pinned between my left knee and Dave's now badly singed parka sleeve.

To top it all off, I was about sixty percent upside down, with only my shoulders and the back of my head in contact with the ground. There may even have been some swearing of the sort I can't report anywhere my mother might see it someday. What had brought the whirling, tumbling slap-fight of death to a halt was Sparx's repeated shouts that the coyote wasn't attacking us, and "STOP MOVING ALREADY!"

Within instants of ceasing to struggle, I heard a sharp crack and saw a puff of dust and shards of rock bursting outward as something hit the invisible dome about two inches from the place my nose was pressed against it. It took me back to the attack at the conservatory in an instant and panic burned through me.

I tried to leap backward. It went about as well as could be expected. OW! HEY! STOP! GRRRRRR! etc. This second time the big BLEND button on our collective mixing bowl got pressed was mercifully much briefer than the first, and ended in Dave asking the obvious question.

"What the heck is going on?"

"Delvers," Sparx answered in a tone that held more resignation than panic.

"Is Oscar out there?!?" I demanded.

"Not that I can tell. Not aboveground anyway. Though Lisa might have a better sense of things."

CRACK!—another bolt shattered angrily on the dome and I flinched involuntarily.

"Lisa?!?" The question burst from my mouth without any conscious intervention from my brain.

"Yrrrrs." There was a distinct growling undertone to the word and the sense that the throat making the sound was not intended to do so. "Been krrrping eye on yrrrr."

"You're a werecoyote!" said Dave. "That's awesome!"

"Grrrrrr . . ."

TWANG—CRACK! I tried desperately not to think of the bolt that had nearly struck me in the eye only a day before.

"No, she's not," Sparx translated unnecessarily—the tone of the coyote's growl was pretty clear. "It's much more complicated, and this is not the time to go into it."

"I don't know," I said, trying to distract myself from the thought of delvers with crossbows. Now that I knew Oscar wasn't out there I was starting to cope again. "I don't have anything else pressing on me at the moment . . . well, except for the paw in my ear."

Sparx snorted grumpily. "You've gone awfully sarcastic. I think I may be a bad influence on you, my boy."

"Show of hands?" asked Dave.

CRACK!

"I'm trying to raise both of mine," I answered.

"Forrrrr which I orrrt to slap you," growled Lisa.

"Could we all please get back to the point?" demanded Sparx.

I attempted a shrug. "I doubt it." There was something about the situation, even with the crossbow bolts, that invited snark. Or, possibly, it was hysteria.

"Because if we don't," continued Sparx, as though I hadn't spoken, "in about five minutes, when the circle of protection goes down, we are going to end up as the world's biggest and strangest pincushion."

"Five minutes?" That shook me.

"Maybe a little more, but not much. This ring was designed for light duty, and forcing it into the higher energy state needed to keep us all safe from the delvers' bolts is burning it out *very* quickly."

So *that* was why it went all solid and stuff.

"Which means," said Sparx, "we need a plan for when I shut it down."

"You're going to shut it down?" Dave sounded more than a little scared, and I was right there with him. This *was* frightening.

"It's that or let it fail on its own, which could go incredibly wrong. Like thunderbolts and lightning wrong."

Very, very frightening. I forced the thought aside. "Right. Suggestions?"

"Lisa and I can move a lot faster than you two-footed types. Especially from the places we're all starting. Which means the initial counterattack is on us."

"What about me and Dave?"

"You remember the protective spell that blew up in your face this afternoon?"

"The Dragon's Wings?" I winced as I thought back to the moment the attempt had backlashed through my hand. "What about it?" Though, of course, I knew.

"This time you're going to get it right."

"What if I blow it again?"

"Don't. It'll be the only thing between you and the delvers' bows. Here."

I felt the stone shard that had bitten me earlier press against my burned hand. Air was available in abundance, of course. Though we'd broken the mug I'd been using earlier, the slush soaking through the shoulders of my jacket would provide water enough. That plus the fire in my heart was all I really needed.

But I couldn't do it. Not . . . "Here? Like this? Now?"

"Yes, yes, and the final step will need to wait until I release the dome, but also, yes. And remember: If it blows up in your face, you won't be the only one getting hurt."

"You've got this," Dave said far more confidently than any sane person.

Riiiiiight. I squeezed the stone so hard a few more blisters burst. Not that it mattered. I was going to get one chance and I was going to fail. And then I was going to die. Still, I had to try.

"Issilthss!" *Or something like that.* The language of air did *not* trip naturally off my tongue. It was meant to sound a bit like wind in the grass, but when I said it, it always came out like something a really honked-off garter snake might hiss at a cat. Even so, I felt the air in my lungs go suddenly cold and crisp.

"Kkst*ta!" *Better.* I'd mostly mastered the crackling sounds of the fire tongue even if they could never be properly written with human letters, and I felt the words ignite an answering burn in my heart.

Insert gargling sounds here. Loosely: "Bglbgleb!" So I did that.

Despite my poor efforts, the slush soaking my jacket began to bubble and fizz like soda water.

I squeezed the stone even tighter and spoke slowly and sonorously. "Drooododor!" Nothing! *Don't panic.* "Drooododor!" Again, nothing. *Okay, maybe panic a little.* If I failed on a third recitation, the spell's budding structure would collapse with results that could fall anywhere between a small bubble popping and the stone in my hand returning to the lava that gave it birth.

I opened my mouth to try again, then shut it with a snap. I might not like the way the stone bit me earlier, but the effect came from a true connection between my heart of fire and words of stone. Maybe I could reverse that and speak the word for earth *from* that place of pain in my heart. I reached inward, recalling the cold, hollow, hurting feeling, focusing on it. There! Sorrow/anguish/loss washed through me.

So cold. So hard. So . . . "Drooododor!" Only not that at all. The real word came out of my mouth in the deep tongue, stone spoken by stone.

The pain I felt in my heart jumped to my ribs and then ran upward through the bones of my shoulder into my arm and onward to my hand. For one brief cold/hard/hollow moment I *was* the obsidian shard. Then it was gone. The sensation and the stone both. Vanished, like some thinnest leaf of ice melting into the palm of my hand and taking my pain with it.

The heck . . . But I didn't have time to think as Sparx spoke then.

"Good! Now, hang on to what you have built, and take the next step."

I took a deep breath, envisioning what I wanted to happen. "Ash and char, sun and star, wind and smoke, ash and oak."

The words in the language of fire rolled easily up my throat and along my tongue, sliding through my lips and forming themselves into ideogrammatic glyphs, like and yet unlike the ones I had summoned to aid me in my divination with the fire bowl. These were born of fire but tempered and transformed by my invocation of the other elements. Water bound them. Earth hardened them. Air fed them.

Before this moment, I had heard Sparx and Tanya explain the theory. Now, I felt the difference on my tongue and lips and the skin of my face. I had no bowl or other vessel to catch the ideograms this time. Instead, they slipped along the surface of my cheeks and neck, rising to perch themselves in my hair like a fiery halo. I could feel them burning there, bright and hot and dangerous. It should have made me nervous at the very least. It did not. It filled me with the sort of wild confidence I sometimes felt on the stage in front of a good audience.

"Are you ready?" Sparx asked.

Much to my own surprise, I heard myself answer, "I am," in a voice that sounded deeper and harder than my own.

"Yrrrs."

"Not even a little bit, but let's do this thing." Dave sounded scared.

"You've got this," said Sparx. "When I release the circle, Dave, I'll need you to hit the dirt. Lisa and I will each move to deal with the delvers in our own way and—"

"I'll cover Dave and invoke the Dragon's Wings," I added for him.

"Finish the incantation," said Sparx. "I'll release the dome as you speak the final word."

"Word of fire, dragon's ire. Word of air, wings a-flare. Word of water, shield from slaughter. Word of stone, harden bone." In response, I felt the ideograms grow hotter and somehow heavier, weighing on my brow like a crown of iron.

"Words of power, a voice that sings. Open wide the dragon's wings!" The ideograms flared very bright and slid down from my hair to form a pair of flaming lines on my shoulder blades. "Drooododor! Bglbgleb! Issilthss! Kkst*ta!"

The dome fell, and in the very same instant I rolled over, covering Dave with my own body as I envisioned great flaming wings sprouting from my back. I felt each ideogram like a hot brand on my skin as threads of fire slid down and inward, anchoring themselves painfully in the bones of my back and shoulders. Pseudo nerves, formed from nothing more than words and will, spun up and out along with phantom bone. A thick skin born of fire and smoke and the stuff of fairy tales filled in the gaps between the long batlike phalanges growing from the ideograms burning in the flesh of my back.

In the next few seconds I felt a dozen sharp flares as the heavy stone bolts of the delvers struck the great wings I had bent to cover Dave and me like a shield. But my spell held and the bolts shattered and fell around me in a shower of red-hot shards.

Fear faded slowly, becoming a terrible, deep anger. If only I *really* was a dragon I could turn against my attackers and make them pay for trying to kill my friends and me. In that moment, I felt the spell shift as I connected to it on a deeper level, below art and thought and even magic. The flames that made the skin of my wings flowed together with the fires in my heart to become one at the same time I felt their bones merging irrevocably with my own.

My rage burned suddenly brighter. I wanted to turn and rend my enemies, to sink yards-long talons into delver flesh and rip them apart before catching them in my jaws and throwing back my head to gulp them down—fuel poured down a fiery gullet, a dragon's . . .

Wait, what now?

I blinked and pulled myself out of dragon fantasies, realizing as I became fully myself again that for a few brief moments I had been more than half a dragon in my heart. *Weird!* Nothing Sparx or Tanya had talked about when they were teaching me the spell had prepared me for that. It seemed like an awfully big oversight if that was supposed to happen, and a very different sort of mistake if it wasn't. But I didn't have time to worry about a spell gone funny right now. Not with the delvers about.

Or, wait, maybe worrying about it was *exactly* what I needed to do . . . A mad idea occurred to me. Though the bolts had stopped striking my wings, I had little doubt the delvers were still out there. Sparx was tough and I had no clue what all Lisa could do, but there were at least a couple dozen of the badgerlike creatures to deal with, and only the two of them. Which meant they needed my help, and I thought I knew just what to do.

I looked down at the face of my best friend and saw the fire of my wings burning bright in his eyes. "Dave, will you be okay if I go help the others? Can you get clear? I can promise you one heck of a distraction."

He nodded, his expression rueful. "Yeah. I doubt they have much interest in me as my boring old magic-less self. I'm only a target because of the rest of you."

He was probably right, but I didn't like the bitterness I could hear in his voice. Unfortunately, I had no idea what I could do or say to make him feel any better, and I didn't have time to figure it out. "I'm going to move up and left in a few seconds, and I want you to roll right and run for cover when I do."

"Your right or mine?" asked Dave.

"Mine."

"Consider it done." He slapped my shoulder. "Go!"

So I did. I sank the tips of my wings deep into the muddy ground. Water boiled in an instant, exploding outward into a huge cloud of steam. Then I flicked my wings up and back, flinging hot mud and rocks in every direction as I rolled to the side. When Dave bounced to his feet and bolted for the brush along the edge of the tracks, I snapped my wings out and down, throwing myself twenty feet into the air. At the same time, I reached into the structure of the spell with my will, touching that greater connection I had found with the magic. Then I took a deep breath and . . . *twisted*. Either this was the worst idea I'd ever had, or it was going to be AWESOME!

The ribbons of fire that tied my wings to the bones of my back and shoulders punched outward, reaching through flesh to anchor themselves in my ribs before sliding down to my pelvis and up along my jaw and deep into my skull. Like a giant flower blossoming from a slender bud, a massive bloom of magic and flame opened out from my skin, shaping me into a dragon to match the wings. I roared my anger and poured a stream of fire down upon a delver who was drawing a bead on Lisa's back with his crossbow.

His fur flashed red and gold as it burst into flame, and he screamed in anger and pain as his shot went wide. But he didn't die. Instead, he dove deep into the earth, quenching the fires in darkness. I turned my attention toward another delver, but she was already sinking out of sight. A dragon's rage burned in my heart and I sent a flaming blast that ignited the hair on her heels before she, too, vanished. I started to look for a third, but they had all fled. And a good thing, too, as the drain of the expanded spell exceeded the fuel of my soul in that very instant.

Between one blink of the eye and the next, my fires went out. The dragon vanished from my heart and the world in the same breath. And then . . .

I fell.

My everything hurt. That was my first impression. I felt as though someone had turned me inside out, thrown me on the grill for an hour, and then turned me backside right before rubbing me down with a mix of gravel and thumbtacks. Well, except for the part where I wasn't dead. At least, I hoped I wasn't . . .

I opened my eyes . . . or, rather, not. Not at first anyway. When I tried, I discovered even my eyelids hurt.

"I think he's waking up." Lisa's voice, sounding more than a little surprised.

"I told you he was tough." Dave.

"Lucky." Sparx.

This time when I told my eyes to open, they did. Light stabbed through them and skewered my brain. "Ow." Turns out I had a headache, too.

Sparx leaned down to stare into my face, blocking about three quarters of the light. "That was really, really stupid."

"If I agree, will you keep your head between me and all that bright?"

"No." The hare moved away and light kicked me in the back of the eyeballs again.

I recognized the ceiling—our basement. "Could someone turn off the spots?" There were only a few still screwed in, but that was a few too many.

Dave nodded. "Sure." He didn't move.

It was going to be that kind of conversation. "Fine. *Will* someone please turn the lights down." Dave grinned and vanished from my line of sight. "Thank you." I closed my eyes while I waited for the bright to go away. "By the way, what happened?"

Lisa laughed. "Why, six impossible things before breakfast, of course."

"Huh?" I blinked up at her, realizing only in that moment that her eyes in human form were the exact same shade of gold as her coyote shape's. "I don't understand."

"When I use a word," said Lisa, grinning, "it means just what I choose it to mean—neither more nor less. Also, thanks for saving me again."

Dave returned just then. "I think that she's suggesting we're on the other side of the looking glass here."

"Did somebody hit me in the head?" I asked.

"Yes," said Sparx. "You did, with the earth and a forty-foot windup."

"Huh?" I didn't . . . but then I did. "Oh, you mean that I fell and smacked my head." I pulled myself up into a sitting position against the wall—it hurt.

Sparx nodded. "That, too. It's a wonder you didn't break every bone in your body. What were you thinking?"

I opened my mouth to answer, then paused. "Actually, I'm not at all sure it *was* me. Thinking, that is. I believe it was the dragon. Speaking of which, I have a bone to pick. You didn't tell me the spell could turn me into an *actual* dragon. If I'd known that, I'd have practiced harder."

"I didn't tell you that because it can't."

"Are you saying I wasn't a dragon?"

Sparx tilted a paw back and forth. "Only sort of, and the spell had nothing to do with it."

I gave him a hard look. "I'm pretty sure it did, actually. About ten seconds after I cast the spell I was wishing I *really* was a dragon, and that led me deeper into the magic. Pretty soon I was thinking like a dragon. It was a short step from there to becoming one."

Sparx opened his mouth to say something, but Lisa shushed him. "Let him tell us about it."

So, I did. When I finished there was a long silence before Sparx spoke. "None of that should have happened. Well, none of it but the wings."

I looked at Lisa. "You know something about this stuff. What do you think?"

She shrugged. "It's not precisely my kind of magic, but it's worth remembering that bodies shape minds."

"Is that what being a werecoyote is like?" Dave asked—rather wistfully, I thought.

She shook her head and growled. "I. Am. Not. A werecoyote."

"Then, what—"

She cut him off. "Force of nature. Leave it at that. You wouldn't understand the rest. Not from the outside."

Sparx hopped between them. "What did you mean about bodies and minds?"

Lisa shrugged again. "Again, not my kind of magic. But it sounds to me like the spell was supposed to imitate a dragon's wings, fire in this case because it's Kalvan. What if he managed to go a step further and turn imitation into the real thing?"

"A real live dragon?" Sparx shook his head. "There's no way the spell could have done that. I'm not even sure how it managed to make him look like one."

Lisa raised an eyebrow. "I didn't say the spell was responsible, and I wouldn't be so sure about it only being a seeming."

"I don't . . . oh." Sparx's ears went straight up and he turned and looked at me. "Hang on a tick, I need to check something." The hare jumped into my lap and . . .

"Hey!" If I could have leaped away, I would have, but I was fresh out of the kind of muscle control involved in sudden movement.

I'd seen Sparx poke his head into walls and other solid objects on any number of occasions, but this was the first time he'd poked his head into me. It felt . . . weird. Like the tickle of a cough in the back of your throat . . . only fuzzy and gentle, and not entirely unpleasant. I could feel his presence running along my ribs and spine. A moment later, he withdrew his head and front paws from my chest.

Dave's eyes were wide. "That's not right."

I kind of agreed with him, but I let it go. "What did you find?"

"That we're going to have to be super cautious about what spells we teach you."

I raised an eyebrow and he continued. "Lisa was right, you actually were a dragon there for a bit and it left a mark."

"It did? That doesn't sound good."

Sparx shook his head. "It's not. Although it's not terrible, either. The ideograms imprinted themselves in your bones, like permanent anchor points for a set of dragon's wings. That part's bad, and I don't know any way to fix it, but there are some plusses, too."

"Bad how?" I asked.

"That spell will come easily to you in the future. So will the dragon. Too easy. And you'd be better off avoiding both."

"Why?" I asked. "Being a dragon worked great for getting rid of delvers."

Sparx flicked his ears grumpily. "Except for the part where it used up all your available magic and left you drained and unconscious in midair. Do that too often and you might burn out your magic completely, or worse."

"Worse?" My voice broke as I said the word. "Because that sounds pretty awful. Tell me about worse."

Lisa spoke then. "Wear the path to a shape that is not yours too deeply and you might never fully return to yourself. You might become a dragon in truth."

"I . . . that would be bad?"

"Very," said Lisa and there was sadness deep in the well of her eyes.

"Good to know. Good to know." I found myself getting lightheaded. "Why don't we focus on the positive. You mentioned some plusses?"

Sparx nodded. "Yes. The dragon within strengthened your bones, though whether the effect will last we can't know. That's the reason you didn't break anything in your fall."

"Oh. That's great."

"What's going on down here?" It was my aunt's voice.

Before I could say anything the room started to swim around me. "I think I'm going to faint now."

And I did.

6

Stones Better Left Unturned

I **WOKE FEELING** like a plate of baked death with a steaming pile of the mornings as a side dish. Dave killed the alarm and aimed me at the bathroom while he gathered up my backpack and other things. A shower helped, but I was stiff and sore all the way to the bus stop and right on through the day's classes.

For a mercy, it was a low-drama day, with no one and nothing trying to kill me, or enlist me to a cause, or anything at all out of the ordinary for a thirteen-year-old kid at an experimental school. When I saw Morgan and Lisa, the former snubbed me and the latter flashed me a smile when no one else was looking. Josh gave me his usual murderous glare whenever we passed.

The only thing really out of the ordinary was Dave, who seemed awfully quiet and down. I figured it was because of the whole magic thing, but I didn't have any idea what I could do to help. After my third comment about the previous day was met with a giant bowl of MEH, we both more or less stopped talking and pretended everything was normal until we said good-bye at the end of school.

When I got off the bus at my stop, Sparx poked his head out through the top of my bag and put his front paws on my shoulder so we could chat.

"You know, when you do that, I feel like I've got the world's biggest and funniest-looking pirate parrot riding with me."

He snorted. "Very funny, and—oh, hey, Kalvan, don't . . ."

SPLASH!

When I stepped off the curb I put my foot down on what I thought was a bit of crunchy ice. It turned out to be slush floating on top of a puddle that must have been ten inches deep. The water instantly filled my boot and I started swearing.

". . . step there," he finished quietly. "I think the storm drain is blocked."

"Clearly," I grumped as I looked around for a stick or something to poke the drain with—if someone didn't clear it, I'd probably do the same thing tomorrow. "Man, the melt is running strong this year. There's practically no snow left."

"You've no one to blame but yourself."

"Huh?"

"Because the Winter King didn't finish out his reign."

"Oh." That made me look around for delvers or other bad magic, but my quiet day remained so. No giant badgers, no Oscar, no angry river spirit, nothing. That was good. I could use more quiet in my life. "I hadn't thought about it. Oh, and I wouldn't use the word *blame*. After this last year I'm ready for an early spring and a loooong summer."

"Be careful what you wish for, O Accursed Master."

"Why?"

"Messing with the seasons is like any kind of meddling in magic—it can have *major* unforeseen results."

"Isn't that the story of my life now? I did kind of *change into a dragon last night.*" Which was sort of awesome, even if it was weird and frightening at the time.

"That you did."

On an impulse, I turned left, heading for the railroad tracks instead of home.

"What's up?" asked Sparx.

"I want to check out the place where last night happened. I . . ." I paused for a second, trying to figure out how to explain what I was doing. "I guess I need to prove to myself that it, well . . . *is*. I don't know if that will make any sense to someone who didn't grow up in a house with a person who isn't fully connected to reality, but sometimes I just need to see physical proof that the stuff I remember is legit real. Especially when it's weird stuff."

"Actually, that makes a *lot* of sense. Let's go."

Considering the scale of the battle, there wasn't much to see. Even knowing what to look for, the patches of disturbed earth where the delvers had come and gone were hard to spot. Faint char marks showed where my wing tips had pressed into the mud as I launched my dragon self into the air. But again, they weren't something that would attract the attention of someone who didn't know to look for them. Besides, they didn't really *prove* anything.

So far there was nothing really dramatic to . . . *Wait—there!* Right in the center of the circle of smoothed ground where we'd built our ring of protection—a huge clawed footprint, like a dinosaur might have left. The broken remnants of a pottery mug lay nearby, which reminded me . . .

"Sparx, what happened to the stone I used for the Dragon's Wings?"

The hare blinked. "I have no idea. You didn't have it when Lisa and Dave dragged you back to the house after you passed out. I guess if I thought about it at all, I presumed you dropped it during your transformation." He looked around. "Maybe it got dragged under by one of the delvers."

But none of the disturbed patches were anything like close enough to the ring for that to make sense. A truly horrible thing occurred to me then and I glanced at the hand that had held the spearhead. I remembered the sensation of stone melting into my flesh as I spoke the word invoking earth all too clearly.

"I didn't drop it."

"All right . . . then, where is it?"

I held out my hand and whispered, "I don't know. I think it became a part of me when I summoned the Dragon's Wings." I quickly described the stone sinking into my palm and taking the pain in my heart with it. "What does that mean?"

Sparx smiled sadly and nodded, like I'd confirmed a theory.

"There's something you're not telling me, Sparx. You *know* something!"

"I know many things," replied Sparx. "Others I only suspect or guess at."

"So, what *exactly* is it you suspect or guess about that stone?"

The hare shook his head. "It's not about the stone." Then he crossed his forelegs on his chest—waiting. Clearly, he felt I had all the clues I needed.

"Sometimes, I hate you so much," I grumbled. But then, "It's about me. What does it mean about me?"

"Good. You're almost there."

"I . . . wait. Back when I first tried the Dragon's Wings in Tanya's work room, I felt the stone tugging at my heart. You can't mean . . ."

Sparx nodded. "Stone answers to stone, just as fire answers to fire."

"But I'm a child of flame!"

"On your mother's side, yes. But if your father really is what Noelle said he is, you are also a child of earth."

I felt like he'd kicked me in the chest with those enormous feet of his. I *couldn't* be a power of earth. That was my stepfather's element. The thought made me want to throw up.

"How can I belong to two elements? I didn't know that was possible!"

Sparx shrugged. "It's quite rare for humans, but not unheard of. It would do much to explain why you became a dragon if your connection to the original spell was doubled by coming at it from two elements. Well, and when the delver attacked you at the conservatory you spotted him because of an itchy foot. That could well have been the earth warning you."

Another memory came back to me—one that made me feel even more hollow and empty. "When we were trapped in that delver cell after Oscar took me prisoner, and then I dug my way out, you were surprised at how well that magic shovel thing I made worked on the stone—almost concerned . . ."

"I had forgotten that, but yes. You shouldn't have been able to tunnel your way out nearly so easily. At the time, my main worry was that you were under the influence of some enchantment of your stepfather's, a spell of stone that was interacting with your own magic and might betray us. Now . . . well, that may have been the first sign of another element waking in your soul. Or, the second, really. The first was probably your resistance to Oscar's spells of control. Stone resisting stone."

I remembered Oscar bending over me and touching a knife to my chest and saying there was something deep in my heart that resisted the weight of stone as no flame should. He wanted to cut me open to see what it was, but finally decided he needed me alive more than he needed answers. The thought that my core of resistance was because deep down I was like Oscar, that my heart and his were the same somehow . . . No! I wouldn't believe it. I *refused* for it to be true. Without another word, I turned away from the tracks and started walking home.

When I got there, I threw my backpack into my room and stomped off to play video games and melt my brains. Sparx let me brood, but it didn't help. There's something about shooting zombies that loses its appeal when you've got one for an aunt. Which reminded me I'd been avoiding her since our last conversation, the one that ended with me hearing another bunch of stuff I didn't know how to cope with.

I still didn't *want* to think about any of it, but I was starting to wonder if maybe I needed to grow up a little and deal. I waffled around for a bit, but Noelle was the only person I had access to besides my mother who had known my father. And, unlike Mom, Noelle seemed willing to talk about him. Eventually, I tossed my controller aside and went looking for her because I needed to know more.

The basement brought back more memories of my stepfather.

Even though I had briefly claimed it for my own, I tended to think of the deep stone barrel vault as Oscar's territory. It still contained his big models of downtown and various highway projects. It also held the cabinets with his tools, both mundane and magical.

"Noelle?" I called into the dimness.

"Back here." I found her sitting in an overstuffed chair with her legs drawn up underneath her at the far end of the basement. She set aside her book as I approached. "You look like someone turned your best friend into a newt."

"What?"

"Never mind. Rough day?"

I nodded. "Rough day, rough week, rough month, rough everything . . ." With a sigh, I sat on the edge of a model of an overpass. That put us at the same eye level. "I'm a little fuzzy on last night, but I'm guessing somebody let you know I was a dragon for a while."

"Yeah, your friend Dave told me what happened. He thought I should know, though he seemed almost as down about the whole thing as you do today. Frankly, I'm a little surprised. When I was your age I would have loved the idea of turning into a dragon."

I grinned. "It is pretty cool. Well, except for the part where Sparx says I might get stuck that way if it doesn't burn out my magic completely." *That* was a lot less cool. "But that's not why I'm feeling down. What can you tell me about my dad?"

"Oh." She pressed her fingers together and looked serious. "Nothing that will make you very happy, I suspect."

"Last time we talked you said he was an earth power . . ." I took a deep breath. "Like Oscar."

"Earth power, yes. Like Oscar? I don't think so. Not from what

I've been able to get Genny to tell me about your stepfather. Though I didn't see it at first, Nix was a good man. Or, is a . . . well, it's complicated. You look a lot like him, actually."

"Do I?" The face I'd seen in the fire bowl didn't look much like mine. At least, not to me. "I'd wondered . . ."

My mom almost never mentioned my dad, and the few times I'd tried to start a conversation about him hadn't gone at all well. In fact, they'd gone so badly I'd mostly trained myself not to think about him—all part of growing up in a house with a fragile mother. Still, there were times when I looked in the mirror and couldn't help wondering about that side of my heritage.

I was much darker than my mom, who was icy pale despite her soot-black hair. If you went purely by coloring, you might have guessed I was maybe part Native American or Mexican, but when I'd asked Mom about that, she'd given me a gentle but definite no. But every time I'd pushed her about where, *exactly*, my dad's people came from she went ballistic on me or vanished into the ozone— occasionally both.

Looking in the mirror didn't tell me much. Beyond being dark- ish, I didn't have a face that looked strongly like anyone else I'd ever seen. It was super frustrating, which was another reason I'd trained myself not to think about it. I didn't even know my dad's last name, since my mother used the Monroe she'd inherited from her parents. For all I knew, he was just an especially dark white guy.

Now, after all these years, here was my chance to find out more. "Where was he from?"

Noelle took a deep breath and I more than half expected her to put me off like Mom always did. "He was . . . not from this world."

Or, you know, she could spout something crazy, like my mother would have. I sighed. "It's okay, Noelle, I don't really—"

But she held up a hand. "No, really. He was a lord of earth, much stronger than any I'd ever met before, though I understand Oscar is almost as strong and was stronger still before you broke his hold on the Crown. Nix had a power to him like bedrock, hard and cold, with hidden roots. He said it was because the country where he was born was buried within the heart of stone."

I didn't want to interrupt when she'd already said more about my dad in two minutes than any three conversations I'd had with my mother, but I couldn't help myself. "That doesn't make a lot of sense."

"I didn't think so at first, either. But I know he took your mother there . . . to his home, I mean. She said they traveled by ways that ran deep beneath the earth and beyond. That they led to a place like one of those weird old novels about a hollow Earth. Green and beautiful with the sun always shining at the center of the sky."

"And you *believed* her?" I asked. "My mom?" I didn't add *the crazy lady* but she knew what I meant.

"Not at first, no. For obvious reasons. We fought about it. Later, I learned more about Nix and his people and how they had gone there from our Earth thousands of years ago. Ultimately, I did come to believe her, but it was too late. I . . . died before we had a chance to reconcile our differences. It's one of my biggest regrets, and she's in no shape to sort it out now. Speaking of which, have you figured out how you're going to stabilize Genny once I have to go back to the grave?"

The question hit me extra hard given what I'd learned at the railroad tracks. I shook my head mutely. I wasn't ready to deal with any of that.

"Kalvan, I know this is difficult, but you don't have a lot of time. You *need* to be thinking about this."

There was nothing in the world I wanted to think about less, especially now. "I don't even know where to start!"

My aunt's eyes flashed suddenly angry. "Start with what Nix and Oscar did for her."

I threw my arms wide. "That was all earth magic. I'm a fire power!"

She lifted one eyebrow and her gaze sharpened, as if to say, "Oh, really?"

Another punch in the gut—she knew! "Sparx told you!"

She rolled her eyes. "Don't be foolish. Your familiar had nothing to do with it. I have known what you are from the moment *your* power called me out of my grave. I've only been waiting for you to admit it to yourself. I figured after what happened at the tracks last night, you might be ready."

"I . . . uh . . . What now?"

Noelle pinched the skin of her arm. "This? Is the stuff of earth. My will is born of the fire of our family—rekindled from the ashes of death by the awakening flames of your soul. But my dead flesh remained inert, frozen like the cold, hard ground surrounding it, until the stone in your heart likewise awoke with the turning of the fallow Crown."

"I don't understand."

She touched the silvery pyramid on my forehead. "This is the mark of the Corona Borealis. Your fate was tied to it in the moment you received that scar. When the fallow turned, it freed the earth to sing together with the fire. That music is what brought me from the grave."

"I didn't realize . . ."

She smiled again, sadly now, and there was a deep love and compassion in her eyes I had only seen directed at my mother until then. "I know. It was obvious you couldn't hear the quiet stone voice of your heart from the moment I arrived—that you had blocked it out. How could you not, when you have only known earth as the tool of your deadliest enemy?"

She leaned forward and touched her hand to my chest. "Oscar wounded you more deeply than you can yet understand. I wish there were some way I could spare you the trials to come, but my time is brief. Summer will arrive all too soon, and then I must depart—a failing spell falling back into dust. If you aren't ready to help Genny by then . . ."

"But I'm *not* ready. Mom needs you. *I* need you. Isn't there some way to keep you here?"

Noelle shook her head. "Not that I can see."

One of the fundamental problems of being thirteen is that no matter what else is going on in your life, you still have to go to school. A fact I was rather forcefully reminded of when I bombed my third-hour math test. The one I forgot to study for because my life was a mess. I don't really like math. Not because I can't do it. I'm actually probably better at it than most of the kids in my class, but—and, it's a *big* but—I have to keep up on my homework, and I'm terrible at homework.

It's a side effect of being smart, actually. It's easy for me to coast in a lot of classes. All I have to do is pay attention while the class is going on and say the occasional smart thing in discussion and teachers count it as a win. I mean, sure, I have to do some reading for things like my American government class, but I read a page a minute or better, and half the time I can catch up in the first few minutes of class if I didn't do it ahead of time. I might get some side eye, if I'm too obvious, but teachers like to see the book open in front of you. If you can make it look like you're just trying to find the right bit to quote, you're golden.

That doesn't work with math. Well, not with algebra anyway. When I was doing simpler math, I could sometimes just read a problem and figure out the answer in my head and write that down. But in pre-algebra my teacher wants us to solve problems using specific steps and rules, and when I don't keep up with the homework, I don't know the way I'm *supposed* to solve things. So, while I was pretty sure the sheet I handed in at the end of the hour had a lot of right answers, I was probably out of luck because I definitely hadn't shown the right way to get there.

"How'd you do?" I asked Dave as we headed for lunch together.

"All right. You?"

"I face-planted." I smacked the palms of my hands together. "Splat."

"Huh." He shrugged.

"You all right?"

Another shrug as we reached the stairwell.

"I hear it's casserole with mystery meat in the caf today. You want to sneak off to Doughboy and then eat in the theater?"

"Nah." Dave shook his head but left it at that.

"Are you sure?" I really wanted to talk to someone who wouldn't expect me to suck it up and simply be okay that I shared an element with Oscar. "I'll buy."

Dave stopped walking and looked at me shrewdly. "What happened?"

I swallowed and then stalled. "I'm not sure this is the best place to talk about it."

"Kalvan, you're my best friend, but I'm having a rough week, too. I don't have a lot of patience for games at the moment."

"All right. So, you know Noelle told me my dad was an earth power, too, like Oscar."

"Uh-huh." Dave's answer came out flat, almost cold. "You were pretty flipped out."

"Well, it turns out I inherited his element, too, and—"

Dave held both hands up. "Stop."

"What?" I blinked.

"I'm pretty sure the next thing to come out of your mouth is going to be a bunch of woe-is-me, and I can't do that right now. I can't listen to you complain about inheriting a second set of superpowers, when I don't even have a first set. I'm sorry, but no." Then, while my mouth was still hanging open, he turned and walked down the stairs.

I decided to skip lunch then because my stomach felt like it was full of lead. Instead, I went up the half flight to a little landing with a couple of windows that looked out over the hill behind the school and a door that led onward to the roof. It was locked, of course, but the doorknob provided the second of three steps that went from radiator, to doorknob, to the top of the window frame, and then up into the drop ceiling.

One of the main ducts ran from left to right above the window, providing a wide, bench-like spot where a guy could lie down with his head propped on his pack—which I proceeded to do. I wasn't the first, of course—candy wrappers and other, less savory garbage bore witness to previous visitors. I'd discovered the spot at the end of the previous school year after I noticed a senior going up the steps and then vanishing. It wasn't big enough for more than one person and you had to lie down if you wanted to be comfortable, which is why I hadn't made it one of my regular hidey-holes. But I was sure Dave wouldn't think to look for me there, and *that* was the important thing. As I settled in, Sparx climbed out of my bag.

"I deserved that," I said.

Sparx didn't say anything, but he didn't need to. We both knew I was right.

"I'd give him my earth powers in a heartbeat if I knew how. Happily." I took a deep breath. "Is that a thing?"

The hare shook his head. "That's not how this stuff works. Also, giving up a thing you don't want isn't much of a sacrifice."

"Ouch, but you're right. I just . . . I don't know what I'm going to do, Sparx. Even if I had the first idea of what I was doing, the thought of using earth powers makes me want to barf. But I can't not help my mom. And now there's this thing with Dave. I didn't ask for any of it and I feel like I'm getting worse at dealing with everything instead of better."

"I'm sorry, Kalvan. If I could take some of this load off your shoulders, I would, but Fate or Luck has made it your burden to bear."

I suppressed the desire to scream, speaking bitterly instead. "That's just great. Perfect, really. Any thoughts on how I might go about doing that?"

"Despite the sarcasm, yes, a few."

"Like?"

"Why don't we dig around in all the stuff Oscar left behind and try to figure out how, *exactly*, he kept your mother stabilized."

"Aside from the fact I hate everything about it *and* the idea of doing any earth magic, that's not a bad suggestion. Oh well. At least it will have to wait till after school."

When the bell rang, Sparx tucked himself back into my bag and I quickly climbed down to the landing. I really didn't want to go to my next class—Acting—not when I was on the outs with Dave, and I paused to stare out the window. At first what I was seeing didn't really register. But then, like one of those optical illusions where a scene suddenly becomes visible within a chaos of dots, I realized I was looking at a man.

He was leaning against a ridge of rock exposed by the fire I'd accidentally caused in the fall, and his ragged clothes blended into the stone like some sort of camouflage, which was why I hadn't seen him at first. But this wasn't just any man, this was the same bald and ragged beggar I'd seen on the morning of the conservatory trip. As our eyes met across the distance, he raised his hand and touched the forepeak of the crown in a kind of salute.

Then, before I could respond or call Sparx out to look at him, he wavered and vanished so completely it was like he'd never been. When I told Sparx about it, the fire hare went and inspected the hill but couldn't find any evidence someone had been there. Not so much as a footprint in the mud or the least bit of magical turbulence. He didn't say it, but I got the distinct feeling he thought I'd imagined the whole thing.

Acting class was just as miserable as I expected, and Dave didn't really talk to me for the rest of the day. Not even at our brief afternoon advisory where he rather pointedly sat across the room from me. On Fridays, the half-hour meeting usually gets abbreviated to a ten-minute check-in and announcements because everyone is anxious to get outside. Especially if it's a nice day, which it was, with temps hitting the high forties and green showing here and there.

"I know you all want to get out into the sun, so I'll keep this brief," said Evelyn. "If the weather holds, we'll do spring cleanup on Monday. Make sure you wear something durable and easy to wash. That's all I've got. What about you? Trina?"

The one senior in our class grinned. "I had a good week. Aced my civics test and got a bunch of work done on my graduation packet, including getting the writing half of my coherent communication certificate." At Free, you graduate by proving you're ready to go out into the world. Most of that involves getting teachers or other experts to sign certificates of competency in various areas.

Evelyn looked around. "Saladin?" A sophomore.

He shrugged. "All right, I guess. Classes are going decently, anyway."

"Dave?" she asked.

"I'm fine. Did okay on the math test. Meeting my dad for dinner tonight."

Evelyn nodded, though I saw a hint of concern pass across her face. She knew about Dave's troubled relationship with his dad. Not to mention that his tone sounded anything but fine.

"Kalvan?" She turned to me next.

I decided not to pretend I was happy, but also not to give up the real reasons. "Could be better. Bombed the math test. Need to do a lot of homework this weekend." I put on a big obviously fake grin. "Really looking forward to that!"

She raised an eyebrow and glanced from me to Dave as if to ask why weren't we sitting together, but I pretended not to notice.

Several hours later, Sparx and I were back in my basement

poking around in the space under Oscar's old granite-surfaced desk. We'd thrown aside the plastic chair mat to expose the stone beneath. The cement that floored the rest of the open space gave way to a huge square slab of icy gray granite about eight feet on a side there. The stone was identical to that in the desk, except for a rougher finish that blended surprisingly well with the aging cement. I don't know that I'd ever have noticed it if I hadn't been actively searching the basement two months before.

Even then, I hadn't found it, so much as it had found me. Or, us, really. A spell trap of my stepfather's grabbed both Sparx and me, pulling us down into the stone. The memory of slowly sinking into the freezing cold granite came back to me now, like dozens of slithering icy fingers sliding along my skin. I had to fight the impulse to bolt.

"Do you really think this will help us find what we're looking for?" I poked the granite nervously with one booted toe.

"No, I find crawling around under desks in the lair of an evil sorcerer to be relaxing. I don't know why anyone goes to Hawaii when they could be doing this instead."

"Probably just avoiding sunburn." I gave him the hairy eyeball. "You know what I meant."

"Well yes, and the answer is that it mostly depends on you."

"Huh?" I was confused. "You're the expert."

"And you're the one with earth powers and a link to the Corona Borealis. If this leads anywhere, that's how we're going to find out. It's not normal stone, or I could pass through it." He thumped the rock with one fiery foot.

"Oh. Did I mention how much I hate everything about this idea?"

Sparx snorted. "Only about seventeen times, but you still agreed to try."

"I did, didn't I? All right, so what do I *actually* do?"

"Start by touching the stone with your hands. See if that tells you anything."

With a sigh, I squatted down and cautiously placed the palms of my hands against the granite. "Nope, there's noth—oh, wait . . . drat, I'm getting something."

Again, I felt that cold, hollow pain developing in my chest like I was missing some important organ or I'd lost a friend. The stone under my fingers began to warm and pulse faintly. It should have been creepy; instead, it reminded me of a cat's purr. This time, there was no immediate sense of connection between the feelings in my heart and hands. It needed something more. But what? I closed my eyes and tried to blot everything else out—most especially my discomfort with the whole idea of earth magic.

Then I had it. You know that hot, tight feeling you get in your forehead when you have a fever and a headache? When the lights are too bright so you have to lie in the dark and just hold still? But then your mom comes in with a wet washcloth and puts it across your eyes? There's this sudden intense moment where your world narrows to that strip of cool relief. This was like that, only more localized. I felt the triangular scar the Corona Borealis had left me like an ice cube pressed into a fresh burn.

"I'm going to need the Crown," I whispered.

"I'll get it." I heard a thump and then a faint rutching sound from the place where we had confined the Crown inside a ring of protection. "Here." Cold metal touched the back of my left hand.

Without opening my eyes or lifting my other hand, I raised the

Crown and set it in place. Cool relief spread outward from my scar to circle my whole head. The purring of the stone grew louder and the ache in my heart deepened. Almost there . . . Guided by impulse, I placed my left palm beside my right and very gently pushed down on the granite. For one long second nothing happened. Then, my hands sank into the rock like it was a liquid and I lost my balance, tumbling forward and plunging deep into stone.

7

Rock-Solid?

IT WAS LIKE sliding through a gigantic brick of half-set Jell-O—squishy and soft and slick as black ice. And it went on a lot longer than I'd have liked. It ended abruptly when I rolled headfirst into a dark space filled with echoes. The impact when I landed on my back left me gasping, while my bruises reminded me it was only the day before yesterday I'd fallen out of the sky.

I was still trying to figure out where I was, when I felt a distinctly fuzzy sensation in my guts and red light blossomed as Sparx poked his fiery head out of my rib cage. His front paws followed, becoming solid as he braced them against my chest and pulled himself out into the open. Imagine that horrible scene from *Alien* where the thing claws its way out of the guy's chest, only disturbingly cute and without all the blood, and you'll have a pretty good idea what it looked like.

Sparx caught the look in my eye and shrugged. "Sorry, couldn't pass through that rock on my own, and I didn't know if simply grabbing on would be enough."

"'S all right. I'll be fine." *Once I forget how that looked, and this queasiness passes anyway.* "Where are we?"

I lay on my back with the top of my head inches from the nearest wall. Closest to me, a band of smooth granite perhaps eight feet wide ran from the floor to the slightly domed ceiling. The rest of the stone was gray-green and rough, shale or limestone—more like the walls of a cave than anything shaped by man. The room, or cave really, was a rough triangle maybe thirty feet on a side with rounded ends. The granite band stood in the middle of one wall with a dark door-like opening in the point opposite. The other two points were closed. Other than Sparx and me the room was empty.

"Somewhere under the house." The hare hopped off my chest and started toward the door, taking the light of his fur with him.

I didn't like the darkness and didn't feel up to making my own fire just yet, so I quickly followed. The opening led into a small, circular room with three more doorways, left, right, and forward.

I glanced right first into another triangular cavern. "Is that . . . ?"

"The room where Oscar threatened us before?" Sparx nodded.

A lurid red granite altar crouched in front of a throne of some glossy black stone. Overhead, a mirror of the altar stone hung from the ceiling like a great crimson bat. The last time I was here I'd been laid out on the altar with Sparx, while Oscar held an obsidian dagger to my chest as he decided whether or not to cut my heart out.

I had no desire to revisit the place, but I made a quick circuit of the room to see if there was anything not immediately visible from the door. Nothing. Not even the tunnel Cetius had used to carry me away only a month ago—gone without a trace. *Creepy.*

"Do you think Oscar's been back?" I asked.

Sparx shook his head. "No. The wards we laid to protect the house and surrounds should extend well below this level. If he'd even tried to challenge them, I'd have known about it."

"Good." Those wards had been a crap-ton of work and I'd needed Sparx's guidance at every step of the process. It was nice to know it was worth it.

The next cave—yet another triangle—was as empty as the first. Our final stop proved more interesting. A huge and elaborate diagram had been carved into the stone floor, which had been smoothed and polished to a mirror finish.

"What is all that?" I asked as we stood in the doorway.

The hare shook his head, looking troubled. "I see some things I recognize, but others are wholly foreign. Take the overall structure. That circle within a circle with the signs of the elements between is something you might see in any greatspell. But the triangle surrounding it? And the diagrams within the points there? No idea."

I stepped past Sparx when I spotted something weird in the farthest corner of the big-spell structure.

"Wait!" Sparx yelped. "Don't cross that . . . line." But he was too late. "Or . . . well, I guess it's okay then. But that's not how I'd have chosen to find out."

"Huh?" I stopped and turned back. "What are you rattling on about . . ." But my voice ran down as I watched the expression on his face go from relieved to alarmed in perfect synch with a sudden change in the illumination as the outer structures of the greatspell lit with a flickering silver glow. Only the circle in the center remained dark and cold.

"Kalvan?" Sparx sounded artificially calm, like someone who

doesn't want the fact that they're about to tell you that you're standing two inches from a poisonous snake to cause you to make any sudden movements.

"Yes." I tried to emulate his tone. Maybe if I *sounded* calm I would stay calm?

"I want you to hold perfectly still and not panic."

"Are you sure? Because *I* was thinking this might be the perfect moment for panicking. I was also thinking of coming back to you. Quickly."

"I don't think that would be a good idea yet. I don't know if you've noticed, but the Crown is flickering in time with the diagram."

"It is?" I tried to look up through my eyebrows at the Crown on my head, but I couldn't see it directly. "Is that good or bad?"

"Yes. Almost certainly."

"Which?"

"I don't know, but I would prefer to find out as gently as possible. Can you touch the Crown for me?"

"Sure." I reached up and placed my fingers on the metal where it rode above my temples. I couldn't feel any difference from normal. "How's this?"

"One-handed would have been better, but I suppose that works. Now, very, very carefully, lift the Crown away from your head about three inches."

So, I did that.

"Interesting," Sparx said in that same artificially calm tone.

"What?"

"Well, you know how there aren't any patterns on the Crown? How it's all smooth silver except for the stones?"

"Yes." I had no idea where he was going with this.

"Well take a look at it now."

I moved the Crown down to where I could see it. "Wow!" Fine lines of light danced through the metal like lace or the veins of a leaf, while the rest of the surface remained cool and dark. "Why couldn't we see them before?"

"Now, this is a bit of a guess, but I'm going to go with it: No one was stupid enough to run into a giant alien spell while wearing the Crown before this."

"You know, that's so crazy you might even be right. But don't let it go to your head; I'm sure it was an accident."

"How a kid your age got so sarcastic I will never understand."

"I blame my familiar. Now, moving on to my original question . . ."

"I honestly don't know why they've been invisible till now. Maybe it's because they're inside the metal rather than on the surface. But that's not actually the detail you should be focusing on."

"Oh. Why not?"

"Because a much more important point is that the patterns in the Crown are very like those in the diagram you're standing on."

I looked from Crown to floor and back. "All right. What does that mean?"

"No idea, but it's certainly not a coincidence. Now, before we do anything else, I have one more thing to tell you, and I want you to be calm about it."

I didn't like the way he said that even a little bit. "All right. Hit me."

"The mark on your forehead is glowing along with the rest

of this stuff and it has the same patterns running through it. Only, with the scar, the lines are dark and the voids between are bright."

"Really? My scar is glowing?" I could hear my voice rising sharply.

"Uh-huh."

"That's great. I love that. Best thing ever. You're *sure* I can't panic?"

Sparx shrugged. "I'm sure it would be a bad idea."

"All righty then." I swallowed hard and kept it together somehow. "Any suggestions for what I ought to do next?"

"Why did you cross the line into the diagram in the first place?"

"I noticed something over in the far corner."

"What . . . oh. I see. I think you'd better go have a look, but please, please don't touch it."

"Aw, man, you're no fun at all." I forced my voice not to shake or squeak. "I suppose *next* you'll be telling me I shouldn't feed the trolls, swim with selkies, or ride the unicorns. On a possibly related note, what should I do with the Crown?"

"Put it back on. The greatspell seems to recognize it, and it hasn't zapped you yet, so maybe the Crown is protecting you. Oh, and don't cross into the circle of protection on the way. We don't know what it's for in relation to the rest of the spell, and I'd prefer not to activate it."

"Would entering it do that?" I asked.

"No idea, but let's not find out."

Moving very carefully, I set the Crown back on my head and edged between the circle and the outer lines of the triangle to get to the far corner. The patterns were of a type with the ones on the Crown and my forehead, only much bigger, with a large oval void that matched the place the center stone of the Crown was set.

A porcelain doll about as long as my hand lay in the oval on the floor. It was a near perfect image of my mother, with ice-white skin, sooty-black hair, amber eyes, and a red velvet dress. The one major deviation was the forehead of the doll, which had three wide cracks in it, as if its skull were trying to split apart from the inside. Each of the cracks had been filled with a sliver of stone—one green, one black, one brown. It was the creepiest thing I'd ever seen and I wanted nothing to do with it.

"What is it?" Sparx called from his place by the door.

"A doll." I described it.

"Hmm." Then he spoke like he was reciting from an ancient memory: "*Life comes from the earth, death returns to the earth, the earth is the beginning and end of the circle.*"

"What's that from?"

"I don't remember—something I learned long ago and far away, to be sure. The colors brought it to mind."

"Can I come back now?" I *really* wanted to get away from that doll and the part of the spell built around it.

"I want you to do one more thing first. Get as close to the inner circle as you can without crossing the line and tell me what you see. We really should have brought your magic journal along. You could have sketched it all out."

"Yeah, that would have been great." I tried to sound like I agreed with him while secretly being just as happy not to have *another* homework assignment. The blank leather-bound journal Tanya had given me as a home for my magical notes and diagrams was perhaps my least favorite thing about being a sorcerer-in-training. "Maybe next time."

"You can do a rough version from memory when we get back upstairs."

Goody. With a sigh I turned to the circle. "There's a big seven-pointed star thingie in the center. It's asymmetrical and looks like the points are full of more of those filigree designs from the Crown." There were several less-recognizable structures that I described to the best of my ability—each obviously an important part of whatever this spell was supposed to do.

When I finished I glanced up and found Sparx shaking his head. "There's a lot there that's beyond me, though whether that's because it's earth magic, or because it's tied to the Crown, or simply because it comes from some tradition I've never studied, I can't say."

"That's not even a little bit reassuring, bunny boy. What do you think it does?"

"I don't know, though I suspect a good bit of it is aimed at helping your mother keep herself grounded in the real world. Well, that and some of it is probably for keeping her under Oscar's thumb."

That second bit caught me like a knife in the gut. It made me want to destroy the whole thing, but I couldn't help remembering my aunt saying it was up to me to ground my mother now. "Which parts are which?"

"I don't know, and we don't dare blindly experiment with something that complex and potentially dangerous. We're going to need to find someone who knows more about this sort of magic before we can do anything important with it. Come on out of there, but do it slowly and gently. I'm standing at the exact place you crossed into the spell. It's probably best if you exit the same way."

"All right." I started to make my way back to Sparx, wishing the whole time we'd never found the thing. Or better yet, that it didn't exist at all. "Are you sure this is safe?"

"Not at all. I'm quite sure it isn't, but you have to come out of there sometime."

"You are the world's least reassuring magic rabbit. You know that, right?"

"Yeah, it's actually on my résumé, right after 'doesn't get pulled out of hats.' Now, are you going to cross that line on your own or should I write you an instruction book?"

I nodded and stepped over the line. Nothing happened, and I breathed a little sigh of relief. "I don't suppose we can pretend this thing doesn't exist from here on out?"

"You tell me." Sparx pointed behind me.

Even though I was no longer inside the diagram, the triangular structures in the corners continued to glow faintly. *Not good.* I lifted the Crown from my head so I could look at it, but its lights had gone out and I could no longer see any evidence of the lines within.

"Oh. What about my scar?" I tapped my forehead.

"It's gone dark as well, which is good but not sufficient."

"Not sufficient for what?"

"To ease my mind. It's looking more and more like the Crown will fall to you in a month, and that terrifies me."

"Why?"

"Why which?" He jerked his chin at the spell structure. "The way that has reacted to you and what it revealed about your scar are what makes me think you are the coming Summer King. As to why it terrifies me . . ." He paused so long I thought he might not answer, but then, with a sigh, he spoke again. "The Summer Monarch should be an adult fully grown and in complete control of their powers. You are neither, and I fear that taking the Throne with all that it entails could destroy you or drive you mad."

I swallowed hard. "I . . . Are you sure?"

"Not in the least. I don't know enough about the Crown and its magic to be sure of anything, but I know that others who have come to one of the great thrones unprepared have faced similar fates."

"Oh." Another horrible thing struck me as I remembered the way he had come to be my familiar. "The soul trap Oscar made for you . . ."

Sparx nodded. "Yes, if you die before we solve that riddle, so do I."

"So, who do we ask about this?" I glanced back at the pale glow of the greatspell and shuddered. *Not good at all.* "Tanya?"

"For starters," agreed Sparx. "But I won't hold my breath. She's a power of air, and whatever else that thing is, it doesn't look like any air magic I've ever seen. Besides, air is earth's opposite. Now, let's go see if you can get us back out of this cavern."

Up felt basically like a reverse of *down.* Touching the stone and willing my way back to the basement started a process that is probably best likened to being a bit of banana caught in the straw of a really determined giant's banana malt. First I was sucked into stone that had been rendered temporarily gelatinous. Then I was drawn upward through the mess. Finally, I shot out the top fast enough that I actually dropped back onto the floor with a bit of a thump.

"Now what?" I asked.

"You do your homework. I need to see if I can find some answers.

I may be gone a while. Don't worry and don't do anything stupid." With a puff of smoke and burst of flame, he vanished.

I headed upstairs, but both motivation and my magic journal eluded me, so I ended up reading a book after poking around in my room for half an hour. Sparx didn't return before bedtime. The next day was Saturday and I slept till the crack of noon. It was much needed, and I picked up my book and munched on a granola bar rather than go looking for breakfast. Sparx came in through the wall beside my pillow an hour or so later.

"Any luck?" I asked.

He shook his head. "No, and I've spread a wide net. I even talked to the selkies."

"The muskrat girls who were teasing me last fall? I thought you didn't like them."

"They're actually not bad when I'm not worried about a very drownable boy who's under my protection. A bit scattered perhaps, and quite dangerous in a negligent who-knew-humans-couldn't-breathe-water sort of way, but they understand a thing or two about water magic."

"I thought you said the spell was earth magic."

"No. I said it *could* be, but that's not the same. I wanted to cover all the points of the star."

"What about Tanya?"

"I think that's your job, don't you? She's your teacher and she'll want to see your sketches of that spell both to know what you're talking about and as a gauge of your progress."

"Oh. Yeah. Good thought."

Sparx sighed. "You didn't do your homework, did you?"

"I figured it would be better to do it on the spot instead of from memory. I was also thinking of using one of the big sketch pads from Oscar's design supplies, so I can get more detail. My journal's pretty tiny." Plus, temporarily mislaid, though I didn't mention that. Sparx gave me a very hard look, but my stomach growled then and supplied me with a perfect excuse to get out of bed.

Aunt Noelle had lunch waiting when I finally got there, along with a report on how my mom was doing. The first was good if a bit stale. The second was not great—she'd been yelling at plants again, which made me want to hide under my bed or change my name and move to another state. So I tried to pretend everything was fine, and it wasn't until I was three quarters of the way through a giant bowl of recently expired macaroni and cheese I even remembered my aunt was dead.

Which all goes to show there's nothing so strange you can't get used to it. Except . . . that's when I kind of fell apart. Because, well . . . everything, ultimately. But, the trigger? She. Was. Dead. The woman who made me lunch. The woman who was taking care of my mom when I couldn't handle it anymore. My aunt. Sixteen years dead.

I dropped my spoon with a clatter as the thought sank in. One of the big reasons I worry about going like my mom is that I know how much I take after her. If I let it, my brain will cheerfully spin itself into a real mess. I could feel it trying to do that now, which meant I needed some time by myself to get my thinking straight again.

Normally, if I want to be alone, I turn inward, crawling into the back of a closet or some other tight space. I'm something of a claustrophile. But right then I wanted to get as far away from the earth and the darkness of the grave as possible. So, when I left the table, I went up.

Out of the kitchen. Up the back stairs. Along the tiny hallway to the attic stairs, and up again.

The attic was long and narrow, with steeply slanted ceilings, and we mostly used it for storage. The previous owner had started converting it into a third apartment, but he'd never gotten around to doing things like putting a door on the bathroom or trim around the big skylights I'd come seeking. But even standing in the direct sunlight pouring through the nearest window didn't seem like enough. I wanted . . . no, *needed* more.

The pivots on the rarely opened window above the attic's kitchen sink squealed. Even with the melt, the air that poured in was cool and sharp across my face. It was also fresh and free. It was only the work of a moment to climb onto the counter and slip out through the narrow opening. The roof beyond was dangerously steep, but thanks to the slope and the sun, neither wet nor icy. I used the skylight as a sort of ladder to get to the peak of the roof, and from there I scrambled a few yards to the place where the broad brick chimney pierced the shingles just off the centerline of the house.

The bricks were warm in the afternoon sun, and I gratefully put my back against the rough surface as I settled into the little dip between chimney and roof peak. My calves and feet were on one side of the ridgeline and the rest of me on the other as I set out to empty my head of all the things I didn't want to think about. After a few moments, I realized I was shivering, though I wasn't cold, and there were tears blurring my eyes.

"Kalvan?" Several minutes later, Sparx's voice came down from above, gentle and quiet.

I flicked my eyes upward and saw him perched on the chimney—he'd probably ridden the smoke up—but otherwise I didn't respond. More minutes passed in silence and shivers.

"Kalvan . . ." Still quiet, but more insistent now.

I sighed. "Yes."

"Are you all right?"

"Not even a little bit, but thanks for asking."

"Is there anything I can do?"

I shook my head. "No."

I could have said more. I could have talked about how much less insane my life was before the day he'd walked into it. How I used to be just a regular kid. Admittedly a smart kid at a weird school with a weirder mom, but still someone who could at least *pretend* to be normal on days when being strange was too hard. I could have yelled at him about ruining my life, and I sort of wanted to.

But that wouldn't have been honest or kind, because *none* of it was his fault. My life really wasn't even a little bit normal before Sparx showed up. I just didn't *know* how screwed up it was. Without Sparx, my stepfather would still have been the dark wizard who had courted my mother and put her under a series of enchantments because he wanted to use the fire of her soul for his own evil purposes. I would probably have stumbled into my own powers without Sparx's interference, but I almost certainly wouldn't have handled it as well. In virtually every way possible he had made my transition into this new life better and easier.

But I still had to fight the urge to yell and rage at him. Had to fight it so hard my hands hurt from squeezing them into fists. That my teeth wanted to explode from clenching my jaw. That it felt like I was swallowing acid as I forced the words to stay inside. Not because any of it was his fault, but simply because he was there and weird and sometimes he said all the wrong things. And *that* made it both harder for me to bite my tongue and easier. Because it was a battle I'd fought a million times before. Because I knew how deep my words could cut. Because sometimes people are fragile, and you have to be gentle with them no matter how much it costs.

Because my mother.

Simply allowing myself to think that thought had as big an impact as any spell. I stopped shaking and I stopped crying and I started breathing again. It wasn't really Sparx I was mad at. Nor my dead aunt. Or even Oscar, who had left his giant doom spell in the secret subbasement. It was my mom. Underneath all the other things, I was sooooo very mad at her for not being the type of mom I saw on TV, kind and nurturing and *there*. The type that made you a normal breakfast, and bandaged your cuts, and, most of all, who took care of you.

TV moms might be a little odd or wacky, but always in a funny way. TV moms never curled up in bed with the lights off for days, or argued with voices that weren't there, or handed the car keys to a ten-year-old and cheerfully told him to drive himself to school. I was mad at my mother. Furious! I wanted to yell at her and demand that she be the mom I needed. To shout every single frustration I'd ever had with her.

But I couldn't.

Because my mother.

It wouldn't do any good. It wasn't her fault she was mentally ill, and there wasn't anything she could do about it that she didn't already do. All I would do was hurt her. I knew that because I'd done it. More than once. Mostly when I was much younger and didn't understand what was wrong with her. So, I bottled it up. I swallowed the rage and I forced myself to be kind even when I was hurting. Sometimes, I did it so well I forgot I was doing it. And that's why I'd ended up sitting on the roof crying and shaking. Because you have to let it out some way or you'll explode.

"Because my mother," I whispered.

"What?" Sparx looked confused.

"That's why I'm up here and why I'm not okay. Now that I can see it, maybe I can let it go again."

"Oh. Do you want to talk about it?"

"I think that maybe I do."

So, for the next hour, I sat on the roof of my house and told a magic rabbit all about how my mom made me feel as I watched the sun slide across the sky. It didn't change anything. Not really. But at least for today I had found a way to let the hurt out without exploding. I even ended up laughing a bit because of the ridiculousness of the situation . . . which was another way I'd learned to cope. If you can laugh at something, that reduces its power over you.

8

Spring Forward, Fall Flat

SUNDAY CAME AND went quietly. Sparx spent more time out and about and, reluctantly, I went back to Oscar's secret lair with a big sketch pad and did my best to copy the spell. The diagram on the floor continued to glow faintly, which was deeply alarming. Afterward, because it was bucketing cold rain and my brain had turned to goo, I wandered up to the attic and spent a few hours lying on my back and watching the water roll down the skylights while I half read a book.

The wait for the bus on Monday was damp and chilly, though the last of the snow had gone with the rain. It was also lonely, since Sparx was off looking for answers again. But by the time I got to school, a surprisingly bright sun had already started to steam the worst of the wet out of the ground. That meant spring cleanup after our morning advisory meeting—which I'd forgotten completely—was still on. Fortunately, I didn't really own any clothes but jeans and tees or sweatshirts, so at least I was dressed for mudding it.

I don't know if normal schools do this kind of thing, but at Free, we're big on community learning and service. One of our graduation requirements is a certificate for service to school, and another is for service to community. Every year in the spring, as soon as the snow melts, the whole school takes a day off classes and cleans up the surrounding area. We divide up the neighborhood and go out in our advisory groups with garbage bags and those pokey sticks for picking up litter, and we try to clear away all the trash that piled up over the winter.

There's a big hill behind the school that used to be a miniature urban forest with a ton of trees and low brush and all these little trails and hidden clearings. I loved sneaking up there to read a book or just enjoy the afternoon sun. It was one of my favorite places in the whole world. Then, when my fire powers were first coming in, I'd screwed up really bad and burned the whole slope bare. Since then, I've felt guilty every time I looked that way.

It wasn't too awful during the winter when the whole thing had been covered in snow and it all just looked white and clean. But now, with the melt, burned stumps and charred stone poked out everywhere. It was a punch in the gut at the best of times, and, *lucky me*, Evelyn's group got to clean it up.

The only good thing about the exercise was that I could focus on the physical task at hand—stabbing bits of trash and stuffing them in my bag—and ignore the fact that Dave had chosen to work on the opposite side of the hill. He was up above the court building while I was over on the east by a little spring-fed creek that carved a gully into the slope before vanishing down a culvert. By lunchtime, after three hours of working in the wasteland I'd created, I was covered in dirt and soot, and I wanted nothing to do with anyone.

I took the brown-bag lunch the school had supplied and sat on a rock by the creek—the damage was less visible from there. The sun on the water was dazzling, striking rainbows off a streak of oil and making my eyes tear up. Dave was off somewhere around the slope, though several other kids from my group found spots nearby. So did a couple from Tanya's class. They'd been cleaning the grounds of the apartment building which abutted the hill. I was just finishing up when I saw Tanya and decided I might as well catch her now.

"What's up, Kalvan?" she asked when I waved at her.

Once she got close enough to speak without being overheard, I described what we'd found below my basement and showed her my sketch.

"Hmm, I'd have to see it in person to be sure, but that doesn't look like anything I've ever studied." She looked it over carefully. "Are you sure you drew it properly?"

"I'm sure." I *really* didn't want her to come by the house. Not only would I prefer to avoid *any* of my teachers seeing the shape my mother was in, but I figured Tanya and my aunt should be kept as far away from each other as possible.

"I don't like the look of that thing one little bit. Did Sparx say what he thought it was for?"

"I . . . no." Why hadn't I thought this conversation through in advance?!? Of course Tanya was going to want to know what the spell did, and that led straight to my mother's problems, and from there on to anything from Child Protective Services to foster care. A pit opened in my stomach like the world's biggest sinkhole. "He didn't mention it. Something to do with the Crown of the North is all. He thought I should check with you if it looked familiar. It's nothing important, just curiosity."

She raised a skeptical eyebrow. "Maybe I *should* stop by your house. Just to take a look."

"I, uh, I don't think that's a great idea, but let me ask Sparx."

"All right. Speaking of which, where is he?"

"Oh, you know, out and about." I glanced at my watch—I know, I'm a dinosaur, but my mom won't let me have a phone yet—and thankfully realized lunch was almost over. I quickly got up off the rock. "I'll let him know you want to talk to him."

Tanya sighed, but let me off that hook for the moment. "All right." She traced a couple of the lines on my drawing. "Did you make any more notes? Let me see your spell journal."

"It's, um, at home."

The eyebrow went up again. "All right, but I'll want to see it tomorrow with extensive notes about that thing." She poked my sketch before looking around and raising her voice. "Come on, gang, it's time to get back to work." She headed out, and so did everyone else, either following Tanya, or—in the case of the kids from Evelyn's group—heading up the way I had come.

I held my breath until Tanya vanished around a bend in the gully with all of her advisory students. Man, this day just couldn't get any better, could it?

"That's a *very* interesting little drawing." Josh's voice whispered practically in my ear, just dripping with sarcasm and contempt.

I whipped my head around but didn't see anything. Then, the rainbow shimmer on the water twisted and Josh sort of faded into view. Before I could say anything, he pulled the sketch pad from my hands.

"Your technique sucks, Monroe. You can't draw a straight line to save your life, and someone needs to teach you how to shade. But the subject is *fascinating*. Mind if I borrow this?" He tore out the sheet without waiting for my answer and dropped the pad on the muddy ground.

I wanted to punch him in the nose so bad, but I'd gotten lucky last time and there was no one around to stop him from beating the crap out of me this go-round. I was angry enough I might have tried magic if we weren't standing in the middle of the charred mess that was the worst magical mistake of my life. Instead, I just picked up the sketchbook and cleaned off the mud before putting it away and getting back to work.

Tuesday, I woke up feeling sicker than I had in years. Fever, chills, stuffy nose, the whole works. So I unplugged my clock, crawled back under the covers, and decided the universe could live without me for a while. I woke again around noon to find Sparx snuggled against my side and snoring away, with tiny stutters of smoke coming out of his nose to go along with the snorfly noises. I slid out without waking him, wrapped a blanket around my shoulders, and staggered off to the bathroom.

On the way back, I stopped in the kitchen. I was thirsty, my throat felt gooey, and I really wanted some orange juice to clear out the gunk. But the only things in the fridge were half a jar of pickles, some butter, and a plastic container full of something green and fuzzy my dead aunt was probably saving for a snack. The freezer had nothing but ice cubes, and the cupboards weren't in much better state. I did finally find a thing of bouillon cubes, so I dropped one in a mug I fished out of the sink, ran some water over the top, and stuck it in the microwave.

Then, because I was hungry as well as thirsty, I went back to staring at the cupboards. They remained stubbornly empty. That shouldn't have been a surprise, because no one had done any real shopping in at least two weeks, but somehow it was. When I'd beaten Oscar I sort of expected the world to go back to normal, and there'd been a few weeks right afterward where my mother seemed almost "here and now" and up to doing things like grocery shopping. But that was well in the past. My mom was hanging out on planet ten these days and my aunt had seriously weird ideas about fresh food.

I'd brought home a few things picked up at the gas station or Doughboy, but had mostly been scavenging through the increasingly empty pickings without ever really thinking about the fact that no one was doing the shopping till now, when I was too sick to deal with anything. But, sick or not, it was all on me, and it would stay that way until my mother got better. The realization made my chills even worse, and I pulled the blanket tight around my shoulders. That's when the phone rang. I wanted to ignore it. But when I looked at the caller ID, I saw it was school, which meant not answering could make things go very bad very quickly.

"Hello?"

"Hello, this is Jan, the administrative assistant from the Free School. Is this Kalvan?"

"Id is," I replied, playing up my stuffy nose.

"You sound terrible."

"I'b sick."

"I'm sorry, dear. You know you're supposed to let us know when you're staying home sick."

"Oh, righd, I'b sorry. I'b sick. Mighd be a couple of days."

She laughed. "Not *you*, you, dear. You should be resting. We need a parent or guardian to confirm you're ill. Can you get your mother or stepfather for me?"

"Uh . . . sure. Hang on." *Now what?!?*

I set the phone on the counter and looked around frantically. I didn't dare put my mom on. There was no telling what she might say. If I didn't sound like someone had corked my nose shut I might have tried to fake her voice, but there was really only one option.

I hurried down the basement stairs. "Aud Noelle?"

"What is it, Kalvan?"

"I'b sick, and school wads do dalk with Mom or Oscar. Can you . . ."

"Do Genny's voice?" she asked, mimicking my mother perfectly. "Of course."

"Dank you. Der's a phone on da desk."

She quickly walked over and picked it up. "Hello, this is Genevieve Monroe."

I probably should have stayed to listen, but simply walking down the steps had left me lightheaded. So I dragged myself back upstairs, drank my bouillon, and crawled into bed. Food would have to wait.

The next time I opened my eyes it was dark. The only light in the room came from Sparx's fur—the dim red glow of his fires at their lowest. I glanced at my clock, but, of course, I'd unplugged it hours ago. I poked the hare gently. "Wad time is id?"

He stretched and his fires brightened. "A bit after midnight."

"I'b starving. I wad some soub and a grilled cheese."

The hare stood. "I'll see if I can get someone to make you something. I'd do it myself if I had thumbs."

I caught him by the scruff before he could take off. "Der's no food in da house. Nobody's been shopping."

"Oh. That complicates matters. If there's nothing here, I'm afraid you're out of luck."

I thought for a couple of minutes. "Pizza."

"What?"

"I cad order pizza onlide, and pay wid Mom's debid card." That would solve my problem for the moment but . . . "No, waid, dah's id!"

Sparx gave me a confused look. "*What's* it?"

"Domorrow I cad order groceries onlide, doo. Dave's mom does id dad way when she geds doo busy." I felt about a thousand pounds lighter as I reached for my laptop. "I jus need Mom's purse."

Wonder of wonders, it worked. Both the pizza and the groceries. It wasn't until the next day, after the grocery truck left, that I thought to wonder what Mom would have done if I hadn't taken care of the problem. She'd been in one of her lying-in-the-dark moods for a couple of days. She did pretty well some of the time, but what if she'd been in the place where she talked about conspiracy and the houseplants? I felt like an enormous dog had taken me by the collar and shaken me as a cold sweat broke out all over my body. This *couldn't* go on.

I *had* to find some way to help her get better, or find someone who could. Right after I felt well enough to put away the groceries without going through a box of tissues and taking three rest breaks, that is. I ate a half pint of ice cream for lunch—I'd ordered lots— and crawled back into bed.

By Thursday, I was probably well enough I could have gone to school. But without anyone to *make* me do it, I couldn't manage to get myself out of bed on time for the school bus. And I still wasn't in any shape to walk or bike, as I found out when I brought a sandwich to my mom—I was sweating by the time I reached the second floor.

For a mercy, she was doing pretty well. Not one hundred percent, but she happily took the sandwich and kissed my cheek after setting aside a novel by Georgette Heyer.

"Thanks, Kalvan, that was very thoughtful of you. I saw you ordered in groceries, too. I really appreciate it. I thought about shopping on Monday, but I, well . . ." She sighed. "You know I'm not myself, and there's no sense in pretending. I was too depressed to do anything. I'm feeling much better at the moment, but I don't know how long it will hold. My medications don't seem to be helping the way they should."

"I know, Mom. I'm sorry I can't do more."

"It's all right, honey. It's not your fault. Look, I don't want to put any of this on you, but I think you have a right to know. I'd go in to see my doctor, but I'm worried they'll want to have me committed for a bit. That's happened before, and it helped, but now, because of you, the thought terrifies me. After what happened with Oscar I know you can take care of yourself, but the state wouldn't see it that way, and . . ."

I took a deep breath. "If you really need to go to the hospital, Mom, I'm sure I can deal with foster care for a while." The idea terrified me, but if it would help my mom . . .

"I'm sure you could, too, but I don't want you to have to, and that's not the worst possibility."

"What? I don't understand."

"It's Oscar. Noelle tells me he's still alive and out there somewhere nearby. I can't tell much more than that he's not dead, but she has powers I never owned."

"I can handle Oscar, too. I've already done it once."

"No, you don't understand. I'm still married to him, and he formally adopted you. If I have to go into the hospital, he'll be your legal guardian."

"Oh." That hit me like an icy sledgehammer.

"I've been in a mental hospital before. Twice. The first time they diagnosed me with paranoid schizophrenia, the next with psychotic depression. They won't take my wishes about what to do with you seriously . . . and, well, they probably *shouldn't* when I'm in this state. But even if they did, what could I tell them: Please let my dead sister take care of Kalvan for me?" She laughed. "That'd make me look ever so much saner."

I had to smile, if only for a moment. "You might have a point there. But what do we do?"

"We keep making things work for as long as we can. That's all anyone *can* do, really."

In the afternoon, Sparx and I went back to looking over Oscar's big spell in the subbasement. My conversation with Mom gave the project a fresh urgency. Not that it helped. Sparx still didn't know enough about the magic involved to even be willing to cross into the glowing diagram, and I knew less. We needed to find somebody who understood this kind of magic.

Friday saw me get my butt severely chewed by Tanya for not bringing in my magic journal—I'd looked for it again Thursday, but it hadn't turned up and I was starting to really worry about what might have happened to it. If that didn't make me feel bad enough, Dave was still not talking to me for whatever reason. I was so desperate for *somebody* to tell me something that might help with the magic Oscar had used on my mom, I actually tracked Josh down in the theater shop to ask what he'd done with my sketch.

"I gave it to Herself, Monroe." Herself was Mississippi. "She thought it was a very interesting little spell."

"And?" I demanded.

"And She might have something to say to you about it later. But right now, you're irritating me. So buzz off before I push your face in." He turned away.

I caught his arm and tried to bring him back around. It was like tugging on a lamppost. "But, Josh, I need to know now!"

He spun then and slammed me up against the wall so hard it drove the breath right out of me—why did this kind of thing always happen on the days when Sparx stayed home? "Look, Monroe, you don't get to tell me when to do anything. And you certainly don't tell Her anything. If She wanted to talk to you today, I'd be taking you to see Her whether you liked it or not. But She doesn't. So, for now you're out of luck. I'll find you if She wants you. Until then, consider my not pounding you into a pulp as a huge favor."

I didn't like it, but there wasn't anything I could do about it, so I went looking for Morgan and Lisa. They were the only other magic people I knew, even if Morgan was air like Tanya. I found them sitting together on a couple of cushions in the library loft.

"Hey, Kalvan." Lisa smiled as I knelt on the other side of the low table.

Morgan's expression was more neutral. "Hi, Kalvan. You might as well cough it up."

"What?" I blinked at the older girl.

"Speak." Morgan rolled her eyes. "You obviously want something. What is it?"

"I . . . uh, there's this spell I found."

". . . and?" She twirled her fingers in a move-it-along gesture.

I grimaced—there was something about dealing with Morgan that made me feel like an idiot. "I'm trying to find out what it does."

"All right . . ."

"Oh, yeah. Sorry." I pulled out the sketchbook and opened it to the place where I'd made another drawing of the thing.

Lisa took one look at it and shook her head. "Not my kind of magic."

Morgan's expression was more thoughtful. "I might have seen something like that before."

"Really!" I leaned forward. "What can you tell me about it?"

"Nothing yet. Can I take this?" She tapped the sheet. "There's someone I'd like to show it to."

"Sure, I guess." I really needed answers and I could always sketch it out again. Sparx would even say it was good for me. I ripped out the sheet and handed it over. "Who?"

But Morgan shook her head. "Not my secret to tell."

I couldn't read anything from her expression so I glanced at Lisa, hoping she might know something. But if she did, her face didn't give it away, either. An awkward silence stretched out between us as I realized we didn't really have anything else to talk about.

Finally, I rocked back onto my feet. "Thanks. Uh, when do you think you might know something?"

Morgan shrugged. "Next week is spring break, so I should be able to see my . . . friend in there somewhere. I might have something for you the week we get back."

I'd forgotten about spring break, but there wasn't much I could do about it, any more than I could make Josh or Morgan get back to me, so I just nodded and left the sketch with her. Normally, spring break is something I look forward to, but the next couple of days were super frustrating. About the only good thing on my big list of life messes was that the delvers hadn't tried to kill me in weeks. Sparx thought that might be because the whole dragon thing had scared them off, which sounded great, but I had my doubts.

I really wanted to talk with Dave about everything, but both times I tried calling him he pretty much shut me down, and there wasn't anything I could really do about it over the phone. I spent a lot of time staring at Oscar's big spell, but we still didn't know enough to do anything useful with it. I also poked around in the magic books Tanya had lent me, but it was all basic stuff and none of it helped.

When I couldn't stand to think about incomprehensible magic anymore or the way time was racing past while I was stuck, I paced around the attic or tried to lose myself in video games. That worked about as well as you'd expect in a house where what food I didn't cook for myself was made by a dead woman and my mother kept going la-la land on me.

The Coyote That Didn't Bark in the Night

BY WEDNESDAY EVENING I was going completely bughouse. I'd just reexamined the big diagram of Oscar's spell for the forty-bajillionth time when I heard a knock on the door to my room. My aunt again, probably.

"Come on in."

My mother poked her head in. "Honey?"

"Yeah, Mom." I braced myself for what had become her usual series of sentences that made sense individually, but turned into brain-bending hash when you tried to put them together in paragraphs.

"Have you seen Nix around?"

"I . . . what? My dad?" That was so much worse than what I'd expected—I actually felt a little sick to my stomach.

"I can feel him sometimes, stirring deep within stone." She sighed. "It's both like and unlike what I feel from Oscar these days.

One is trapped, the other hiding. I don't have proper magic. Not like yours or theirs. That's not the way the fire within me burns, but I can *sense* power."

I didn't know what to say to any of that. "Mom, maybe you should get some rest."

But she either didn't hear me from whatever planet she was currently visiting, or didn't care. "Nix said his people came from another world, only . . ." She looked lost for a moment. "Only . . . they got there from our world by accident long ago, but then they were cut off from us for millennia. He said it was only in the last fifty years they'd been able to find the way back consistently, and that he was a part of that way back somehow. He was something like a prince among his people, only his title was Anixiarus. Well, not exactly that, but close to it. I never did learn to speak his language properly."

Greeeat, now my missing earth power father was a magical prince as well. Go, me. "Nix the Anixiarus?" I had a hard time keeping the skepticism out of my voice.

"No, silly." She shook her head. "Nix was *short* for Anixiarus. His people spoke a dialect that mixed earth tongue and whatever their original language was, and we had a miscommunication about names and titles. Later on, we got it sorted out, but I misunderstood at the beginning. I felt like a double idiot when I figured it out, since I'd been calling him Nix for three weeks by then. But he told me it sounded perfect to him and asked me not to change a thing."

Noelle spoke then, startling me, as I hadn't heard her arrive. "Men can be idiots when they fall in love. Nix more than most."

My mother turned to glare at her sister. "That's not nice."

"Is it wrong?" asked Noelle.

Her face fell. "We've had this fight before . . ."

I stepped between them, putting my mom behind me. "Don't."

But it was already too late. My mother swallowed audibly, pushed past me and her dead sister, and bolted for the back stairs.

I stepped in close to my aunt. "That—"

"—was stupid," she finished for me, her face sour. "*Really* stupid. I've been doing everything I can think of to try to reground her in this world, but I *know* better than to push reality on the subject of Nix. She never did want to hear the truth where it came to him."

"Reality like the part where he claimed to be some kind of alien from another world?"

"He *was* from another world, Kalvan, and not an alien in any way other than nationality. He's as human as you or Genny and far more so than I am these days. If he weren't, he could never have been your father."

"But was he really some kind of . . ." I trailed off as I tried to figure out how not to sound like an idiot while asking if my father had been some sort of other-dimensional prince.

"The Anixiarus?" She nodded. "Oh yes, whatever that means— it was never completely clear to me. Maybe he still is. It's hard to say with the passage to the otherworld blocked."

"I . . . there really is an otherworld?" I know she'd told me that before, but my mom had fed me enough nonsense over the years I couldn't help doubting her sister, too.

"There's more than one." Sparx hopped onto my bed—I hadn't told him about any of this yet, since I hardly believed it myself. "Where do you think all those tales of people appearing from faerie or the underworld or a land in the clouds come from? For most of human history the ways between worlds have been shut to your kind, with only the occasional crossing point opening for a brief time here or there. When those paths close again, groups of humans who have passed through from one side or the other often get stranded. It sounds like your father is caught on the other side."

"Oh no," said my aunt. "It's much worse than that. He was trapped *within* the gateway when it closed. He never made it through. That's why I want my sister to let go of his memory. He is bound deep in stone and forever beyond her reach."

It was good and dark when I climbed out onto the roof this time, but still quite a bit warmer than that first afternoon. Sparx met me by the chimney.

"That went well."

"Do you mean the part where I flipped out about my dad being trapped in stone? Or the part where I stormed out of the room?"

"To may-toh, to-mah-toh." Then he grinned. "But the stuff your mother and your aunt had to say was very interesting."

"So you believe all that about the Anixiarus and my dad being part of a gateway between worlds?"

"Actually, yes. I see no reason for your mother and aunt to lie, and it makes a fair bit of sense. I haven't been to any of the elemental lands since I came across the Atlantic to the New World a few hundred years ago, but I know there are crossing points here as well. I expect they're no more reliable than the ones back home where it comes to flesh-and-blood types like yourself. If your dad had some way of stabilizing a gate for humans between his realm and this one, that'd make him a pretty big deal."

"Really?" I was torn between wanting to believe and wanting to scoff at the idea.

I think every kid who doesn't know one of their parents makes up stories about what they're really like. Part of it is filling in gaps in your own story, but mostly it's about needing a reason for them not being in your life. Maybe you're super angry at your missing dad and you want a reason to hate him and feel like you're better off without him. Maybe you're pretending to be strong and self-sufficient, and that you don't really need your absent mom to care about you. Or, maybe—and I think this is most common—you want to believe your mom or dad loves you. That they wish they could be with you, and there's some really important reason they've chosen not to be in your life.

Usually, if I'm being honest with myself, I'm in that last group. But I've done all three at one time or another, and I've made up a lot of stories about who and what my dad was really like over the years. I do have a few faint memories of him. Mostly, I remember a dark, bearded face with a star sapphire shining on one earlobe, and a deep voice reading bedtime stories.

I don't remember the other language my mother mentioned. Not consciously, anyway. But I've told myself a lot of stories about my dad that involve him being an important man in some faraway country. That might come from him speaking something other than English part of the time. In those stories he usually got called home to do big, necessary things, like rescuing a whole town from some kind of disaster, and he really wants to come back to see me, but he's way out on the edge of the map and he can't come back to me until everyone is safe once and for all. I know it's kind of stupid, but if it's not something like that, then . . .

Well, no one wants to believe their dad just doesn't care enough to even write. Not unless they're *really* mad at him. Probably not even then.

The idea that my dad might *actually* be a big VIP among his people and the only reason he hadn't come back to see me was that he was trapped by magic . . . It's hard to even express how that made me feel. That was the fantasy version of my dad come true. It made my heart hurt.

Then another thought occurred to me—if my dad came back, he might be able to do what I couldn't and stabilize my mom! "We have to find him!"

Sparx sighed. "I figured you were going to say that."

"How could I not?" And, the sooner the better.

He nodded decisively. "We'd better get the fire bowl out and have another go at scrying, since I've no idea where to even start. It'll have to wait for tomorrow, though, as we've missed the midnight hour."

I nodded. I just hoped I could remember all the right ideograms and phrases without my missing journal.

"NO!" I kicked the bowl over, spraying burning gasoline across the muddy ground beside the railroad tracks. This time it was no accident. "Why does it keep showing Oscar turning into me or vice versa?" The idea still horrified me.

"Because you've both got rocks in your heads?" he said brightly.

"Not funny, bunny boy. Not funny at all."

The hare shrugged and I began to pace. I'd asked the bowl three different questions about my real dad and how I could rescue him and if that might help my mom. Each time the bowl had shown some variant on my face hardening into stone before blurring into my stepfather's—basically a reversed version of the vision I'd gotten the first time I tried this. The Corona Borealis, which had figured prominently in that earlier attempt, only showed up once in this set of images—when I asked my second question, resting briefly on my brow before my face twisted into my stepfather's.

"That is NOT going to happen," I whispered, and went back to pacing. "I won't let it. I can't." I raised my voice. "Sparx, do the flames ever lie?"

"Depends on what you mean by lying. I've never heard of the fire bowl showing someone a vision that was completely false, but it can as easily picture something you need to avoid as a course you must follow."

"So, the whole thing is basically useless?" I was so frustrated and scared I wished I had another bowl to kick over. "Why did you even make me look at the flames?"

"First, I didn't *make* you do anything. I suggested what I thought was a useful course of action. Second, the fire bowl usually shows a questioner what is most important for them to see. The question isn't whether your vision is true or false. The question is always: Why did the flames show *you* that particular thing?"

"So," I said quietly, "why *did* the flames show me turning into my stepfather? Because I can't think of a single thing I want less, and I *need* answers." With all my heart I wished for another vision, *any* other vision.

"I don't know," answered Sparx. "Maybe it's not about the who so much as the how. Maybe it's about earth magic and your mother and the Crown. Maybe you need to learn from Oscar's discipline—"

But whatever he was going to say next, I didn't hear. The last remnants of the gasoline burning in the mud suddenly flared high and bright with a sort of *foomph* that I felt through my feet more than heard. The smoke and flames shifted in color from red to a dirty brown-green as a fresh image formed. In it I was standing beside a grave surrounded by a circle of spellwork similar to the stuff we'd found in Oscar's secret subbasement.

A flash like lightning ripped the scene apart. The picture re-formed an instant later to show Dave standing beside the grave with me, my spell journal clutched tightly in his right hand. Another burst of lightning and the scene shifted again. Now I was using a blade of fire to slice off Dave's right hand. Blood fountained everywhere and Dave crashed to his knees in the dirt beside the suddenly opened grave.

Flash! Dave fell into the grave and darkness. *Flash!* My father was rising from the darkness that had devoured my best friend—his flesh cold and gray and unmistakably dead, Dave's severed hand clutched in his own. *Flash!* My mother danced along the edge of the grave in a torn dress, her hair wild and full of burning twigs. *Flash!* My father offering Dave's hand to my mother.

Another flash, the brightest yet. But what it portended I would never know because I turned and bolted. I didn't have a destination in mind. I just needed to get away from the horrible pictures in the fire, pictures of *me* and *my magic* destroying my best friend. I headed up the tracks for no other reason than that was the direction I ended up facing when I started running. I don't know how long I ran, or how far.

Eventually, when I saw moving lights on the tracks ahead, I turned in to a patch of scrub trees. There was a wrought-iron fence at the top of the slope, but someone had bent a couple of bars, and

I was able to slip between with a bit of effort. The small woods opened up soon after that, and I found myself in a graveyard. Remembering my vision, I almost panicked again, but this place felt nothing like that grave had. There was a peace here that drew me despite myself, and I wandered among the headstones for a long time before settling on the dead grass in the shadow of a small mausoleum.

More time passed, and I realized I was chilly. I shivered, and drew fire from my heart—warming myself from within rather than getting up and moving. I wasn't ready to go home yet. If I did, I knew Sparx would start being all reasonable and understanding at me, and I couldn't bear the thought of it. I forced my mind away from that . . . from thinking at all. I didn't want to deal with any of it.

For a long time, I simply stared into the darkness and tried to pretend Kalvan Munroe and his problems didn't exist. I think I might even have succeeded for a while—I'd had enough practice—because I had no idea when the coyote first arrived. I simply realized at some point that a pair of yellow eyes had been looking straight into mine for what felt like forever. With a little shake, I slid back into awareness of myself, at which point the eyes rose a few inches and started slowly moving toward me.

"Lisa?" I asked.

But the coyote neither spoke nor changed shape, simply continuing forward until it stood less than a foot away. It was certainly big enough to be Lisa in her animal form, but I had no idea how you told one coyote from another. I'd never had the chance to really *look* at one so close before. Though the dark hid many of the details, I got a distinct sense of beauty and restless energy.

"Hello?" I said. "Lisa?" Still no words.

Cautiously, I reached a hand out, palm down, to let the animal smell it. The coyote sniffed my hand several times and then moved forward a bit, bumping my fingers with its forehead. Its fur was much softer than I expected, and I very carefully traced a fingertip back to the lower edge of its right ear, where I tried a gentle skritch. The coyote turned its head into my hand and I scratched harder. With a quiet, happy, *whuff* sort of noise, the coyote dropped onto the grass beside me and put its head on my lap.

As I scratched the coyote's ears, I couldn't decide if it would be weirder if this *was* Lisa or if it *wasn't* . . .

I woke to sun in my eyes and a crick in my neck, and it took me several long seconds to realize there was nothing between me and the late morning sky.

". . . the heck?" I mumbled.

But when I started to sit up, my chin encountered fur, and the warm weight on my chest reminded me of the graveyard and the night before. I had vague memories of sliding down to rest my head on the stone lip of the mausoleum, and the coyote shifting with me.

"Lisa?" I whispered.

"What?" Sparx stood up on my chest and looked down into my bleary eyes. "Was Lisa here, too?"

"I don't know, maybe. There *was* a coyote." I lifted myself onto my elbows, noting as I did so that I felt a LOT better than I would have expected after spending a night sleeping on the cold ground. "When did you get here? Didn't you see it?"

Sparx shook his head and hopped down onto the frost-touched brown grass. "No, I didn't see anyone but you, and I got here not too long after you did. I followed you from the train tracks, but I didn't move in close until you'd settled down."

"Are you sure? Because I was here for a long time before I noticed the coyote, and it stayed with me until . . . well, until I fell asleep, I think. Unless . . . unless that was all a dream." If so, it was a weirdly embarrassing one—snuggled up with a . . . girl, even if she was in another shape.

Sparx's expression grew troubled. "I knew you were upset, and you needed to be alone for a while, so I settled in on top of the tomb over there where I could keep an eye on you without intruding." He jerked his chin toward another small mausoleum, maybe fifty feet away.

"When I first arrived, you were staring off into space," continued Sparx. "After an hour or so, you shifted position, crossing your legs and just kind of looking at your lap for a while. Eventually—much later—you slid down onto your back and went to sleep. That's when I moved in close to sit guard on your chest and keep you warm."

I didn't know what to say to that, as a much more worrisome thought had occurred to me while he was talking. My mother sometimes saw things that weren't there . . . I pushed myself fully up into a sitting position and put my back against the dark, sun-warmed stone of the mausoleum. I could feel its quiet strength, steady and comforting like . . .

I rocketed to my feet and leaped away from where I had been sitting. "AHHHH!"

"Spirits and shadows, child! What's wrong?"

I pointed at the mausoleum. "The stones! They were trying to make me feel better! And don't you dare say it's because I'm an earth power!"

Sparx made a zipping-his-lips motion, but it didn't really help. I wouldn't soon forget the way the stones had tried to ease my back and shoulders like the world's slowest and weirdest massage. Worse, perhaps, it brought back memories from the night before and the very edge of sleep. Memories of the tombstones making me feel welcome and the earth beneath me seeming more comfortable than any bed . . . almost as if it were shifting to accommodate my needs.

I started to walk away from the mausoleum but stopped abruptly when I noticed a narrow line of char running through the dead grass. It described a large circle completely enclosing the mausoleum where I'd been sleeping. A ring of protection perhaps, and not to be crossed lightly in any case.

I tapped the earth inside the circle with a foot and looked at Sparx. "Yours?"

For the second time in a few short minutes his expression went sour and worried. "It is not, and I should have noticed it before now. Be extra cautious."

He matched action to words, extending his nose very slowly to within an inch of the line. "I don't recognize the spell that went into its making—something much more complex than a simple warding, that's for sure. I am happy to see it's focused outward, and that protection for those within is the main purpose of the crafting. Someone besides me was looking out for you last night."

"*Main* purpose? What else does it do?"

"I don't know." He sniffed again. "It's not elemental magic at all, though the charring tells me fire was involved. It contains something of deception as well as protection." His gaze went far away. "Hmm, I wonder . . ."

"Wonder what?"

"When this was done. It involves a charm of concealment. If it was placed before I arrived, that might explain why you saw a coyote where I did not. You were within its protections and I was beyond them."

"But, wouldn't you have noticed the spell when you crossed the line to join me?"

Sparx snorted. "I would very much like to believe so, but even more I would like to believe no one could have set this around me without alerting me to their presence. *I* couldn't craft such a thing to conceal itself from me, but there are many with powers deeper or more subtle than my own."

I squatted to take a better look at the narrow burn. It was barely wider than a pencil's lead—almost invisible against the dead brown of the grass. "Can we cross it safely now?"

Sparx sniffed at it again. "Probably. Before we try though, I have a question. How did you notice it in the first place?"

"I . . . I don't know. I was about to step right on it when I . . ." How *had* I seen the thing?

"You what?"

A sick feeling started to churn in my gut. "Oh, crap. My toes itched like they did at the conservatory, only not so obviously or for long. I think the earth itself warned me to be careful . . ."

"I'm sorry, Kalvan, I know this is hard for you."

"It's more than hard. I don't think I can do this. At all. Is there any cure?"

"For affinity with an element?" Sparx shook his head slowly. "Not that I've ever heard of, no."

10

When One Door Closes

WE HAD BARELY started the walk home when something smacked the soles of my feet like the shock wave of some distant explosion transmitted through the earth. "Did you feel that?"

"Feel what?" Sparx gave me a funny look.

"It was a sort of *foomph* feeling, like when the fires flared up all green and brown at the end of our scrying session last night."

Sparx's expression went even funnier as his eyebrows rose and his ears cocked forward. "*Foomph*, you say? And green and brown?"

"Yeah, right before that vision of me beside the grave. The one that made me bolt."

"Pretend for a moment that I wasn't there with you, and describe exactly what happened."

"All right." I quickly talked him through the explosion, the visions that followed, and how scared I had been that I might somehow hurt Dave. ". . . and that's when I ran away." By the end, Sparx's eyebrows had nearly vanished over the top of his skull. "Why are you looking at me like that?"

"Because I saw none of that. Not the flare, not the weird colors, not the visions, none of it. Neither did I feel any *foomph*, as you put it."

"I . . . Wait, what now?"

"Exactly!" said Sparx. Then his face went very thoughtful. "That's a very different sort of vision than anything you'd gotten earlier. But put that aside for the moment and answer me this: What has really happened to your spell journal?"

I sighed. "I don't know. I haven't been able to find it anywhere, but I didn't want to admit I'd lost it."

"When was the last time you saw it?"

I thought back. "The night I turned into a dragon, I think. I reviewed the spell I was supposed to practice on the tracks and then tucked it into my bag before taking a nap."

"Don't 'think'; be certain. Was that truly the last time?" I considered it for a little while and then nodded. "You're sure?" I nodded again. "You're positive you put it away in your bag?" One more nod. "When was the next time you saw your bag?"

"When Dave handed it to me before school the next . . . oh no!" I quickly reviewed everything that had passed between Dave and me since the night he'd wished for magic of his own, and I suddenly knew that part of my vision from last night had been true. "Dave took my journal."

I should have been mad, but he wanted powers so desperately. Besides, I remembered with a sort of sick dread the vision where I'd cut off his hand—I couldn't bear the idea of that coming true. But maybe I'd interpreted it wrong last night and it wasn't me who was going to hurt him directly. Maybe it was my journal.

Sparx's face was grim. "I fear you are right."

"And the *foomph*? What was that about?"

"I felt nothing."

"But why would . . . oh."

Another piece fell into place. Sparx hadn't felt the blast just now for the same reason he hadn't seen my visions—because they had come from my earth powers. It wasn't a physical effect at all; it was the earth speaking to me. I hated the idea, but that didn't matter nearly as much as the possibility my best friend was in trouble, which both the explosion and the vision strongly suggested.

"We've got to get to Dave's!" I ran for home, where we stopped only long enough to try the phone. But his cell went straight to voice-mail and no one answered the landline.

With all the transfers, it could easily take two hours to get to Dave's on the bus, and even longer on foot. So it was a good thing I'd gotten a new bicycle for Christmas. The lean road racer with its twenty-one speeds was at least twice as fast as my old BMX-style kid's bike. My new helmet was a lot nicer than the old one, too, as was the heavy-duty U-bar lock mounted to the frame.

I pushed hard as I took the combination of park trails and bike routes that led to Dave's. The speedometer hovered around sixteen for much of the ride, and I broke twenty twice on the downhills. Sparx had a grand time, poking his head over my shoulder and grinning like a maniac, but I was out of breath and very thirsty by the time I got to Dave's house—like an idiot, I'd forgotten to fill my bottle.

I couldn't see anything obviously wrong as I locked my bike to the fence in his backyard, but that didn't mean everything was all right. No one had answered the house phone when I called, but I went around the side of the house to our secret entrance anyway. I didn't want to have to try to explain to Dave's mom or sisters why I was showing up unannounced on the off chance they *were* home.

For no obvious reason a toy phone lay near the base of the big old maple tree. I poked at it with a toe before climbing onto the fence. From there I was able to jump and catch the lowest branch and move up through the tree to a limb that overhung the screen porch. Lowering myself onto the roof left only a short scramble up a steep strip of shingles to get to Dave's attic window. Which was, rather surprisingly given the weather, open.

The lights were off and the room was dim, so I didn't immediately see my friend when I poked my head over the sash. "Dave?"

"Kalvan?" Dave sounded exhausted and worried, and even with his voice to guide me it took a moment to spot him. "Oh man, am I glad to see you and Sparx. I tried to call but . . ."

He trailed off as I slipped in over the sill and caught my first look at him. Dave was sitting on the floor with his back firmly wedged against the bedroom door and his feet braced against the leg of his desk. The family's small black-and-white cat, Meglet, was snuggled in his arms with her head tucked firmly under his chin. He was petting her with a sort of maniacal intensity. Their other cat, a huge black pillow of a thing named Jordan, was curled up against his hip. He was also wearing . . .

"Is that a dress?" I asked. "Not that I'm judging." We had a couple of trans kids at Free, and everyone was cool with that. "I'm just asking becau—"

He cut me off. "Yes, and just . . . don't. It'll be simpler if you let me explain the key bits first."

"All right."

"I'm wearing a dress for the same reason I'm wedged against this door."

There was a long pause. "I'm listening . . ."

"I did something stupid, and now I can't get anything to stay closed. Not the latch on my door. Not the window. Not even the fly on my jeans. This"—he tugged at the tight neckline of the blue sweater dress—"was the only thing I could find that wouldn't fall off. Well, my T-shirts stay on just fine, but they don't cover everything that needs covering."

"Oh." Sparx inserted himself into the conversation for the first time. "I think I may begin to understand what has happened."

"I'm glad one of us does," said Dave, "because I sure as heck don't, and it's me it's happening to."

I shook my head. "I know I'm lost."

"Tell me *exactly* what you did," said Sparx, "and we'll see if we can help."

"Okay, but please don't be angry." Dave looked at me rather imploringly. "Well, first, you *have* to know how bad I want my own magic."

I nodded. "I've gotten that sense, yeah, though I'm not sure I'd have opted into the whole business if I'd had any choice." I thought about the feeling of stone tugging at my heartstrings and shuddered.

"That's bullpucky, Kalvan, and you'd know that if you were being honest with yourself. Yes, the crap with your stepdad was awful, and so was what it did to your mom. But be real. You love all the cool stuff you can do with fire . . . and that dragon thing? That was AWESOME!"

"Incredibly dangerous," interjected Sparx.

"But still awesome." Dave looked me straight in the eyes. "Come on, if someone offered to take your magic away tomorrow, would you really say yes?"

I considered that. There were so many times in the last couple of months where I had wished for a normal life and the freedom to be just a regular kid with boring parents. But I couldn't deny how incredible it felt to pull fire from my heart when I was cold, or to shoot flames from the palms of my hands. Even the stuff that had been hurtful or dangerous was pretty amazing.

Finally, I shook my head. "No, I don't think I would let it go if I could." Not the fire stuff anyway. The earth magic was a whole 'nother story, and one that scared the devil out of me.

Dave took a deep breath and seemed to let go of some of the tension I could see in every line of his body. "Thank you for being honest. That's going to make this at least a little bit easier to tell. You know I've been down and kind of avoiding you, right?"

"Yeah. It wasn't exactly subtle." I wanted to ask him about my journal then, but I couldn't bring myself to do it. Not with the vision of me cutting off his hand so fresh in my memory. Whatever happened, I had to avoid that!

Dave winced anyway. "I'm sorry, man. It's not you. It's me."

"I know, that wasn't meant to make you feel bad." I held up a hand. "We're good."

"Thanks." He looked at his feet. "Where do I start . . . I guess with that thing Sparx said about being careful about magic and what I wish for because my involvement with all this means my wishes might come true. I've been going over and over that in my head, trying to figure out exactly what I would want to ask the universe to give me. I kept thinking about those stories where the genie gives you *exactly* what you ask for and it turns out horribly."

I nodded. It was a pretty common feature in the kinds of books we both liked to read. "So, you started writing down different variations and trying to come up with the perfect one."

"No. I wanted to, but I thought even writing down a test message might count as me asking the magical universe for whatever I happened to write down first."

"Smart," said Sparx. "That's very much the sort of thing my fellow spirits and the greater powers go in for."

"Good to know I did *something* right. Instead, I started trying to figure out the perfect phrase in my head, but I could never make it work right. So, finally I decided that maybe my best bet was to kind of throw myself on the mercy of the court."

"That sounds like it has about fifteen million ways to go wrong," I said.

"So did all the other options, and I was getting desperate. Especially after seeing you chatting with Lisa or exchanging knowing glances in the hall with Morgan, or even when I'd catch Josh staring cold death at your back. It seemed like everybody had magic but me. Finally, I cracked. I went down to the storeroom and drew a big magic circle like I've seen you make, climbed into the middle of it, and lit some candles. Then I asked any power out there that had my best interests and happiness at heart to give me whatever magic it thought I would most want or need."

Sparx put his face in his paws. "Oh, child, that was rashly done."

"Tell me about it. No sooner had I finished asking than the

candles all blew over and out, sending wax trails across the lines of circle. Two seconds after that, the door sprang open. When I jumped up to close the door, all my buttons and zippers popped at once and I landed on my face when my jeans fell down around my ankles."

"When did all this happen?" asked Sparx.

Meanwhile I bit my tongue to keep from laughing at the image. It *was* pretty funny to think about, but Dave was my best friend and it would have been cruel to laugh at him. Maybe, someday, if he came to see it as funny, too, but not now.

"A couple hours ago. I tried to pretend I had things under control for a little while, but I finally panicked and started trying to call you. That was a nightmare, too."

"What?" I asked. "Why? And where's your phone?"

Dave blushed. "It's in the storeroom in the basement with the sim card pulled out. Turns out this opening thing extends to connections between phone lines. Right after my pants fell down, my phone sprang out of my pocket and the screen lit up on its own. By the time I was able to pick it up, there was some dude on the other end speaking a language I'd never heard before."

"Scary," I said.

"Tell me about it. The cancel button wouldn't work and I was terrified my mom was going to get a giant cell bill for me calling Abu Dhabi or something, so I pulled the card and left it there along with my jeans."

"I thought you said you spent a bunch of time trying to call me? If you tossed *your* phone, how did that work? I can't imagine you sitting in the kitchen and calmly dialing the landline with a dress on."

Dave snorted. "Nope. I used my baby sister's toy phone."

I raised an eyebrow. "That doesn't make any sense."

"And you turning into a dragon does?"

I had to nod at that. "Fair point. What made you think of it?"

"I tripped over it in the basement and then it rang. When I answered it sounded like the guy from my cell phone again, but *it* hung up when I put the handset back on the hook. It rang again a few seconds later, but at least there was a different person on the other end. Later, I found if I hung up and then picked up again before it could ring on my end, it let me call out, though who I got was pretty random and I never managed to get through to you. Eventually, when I got sick of the ringing, I chucked it out the window."

Sparx hopped to the door. "We'd better look at this magic circle. It might tell us something about what's happened to you."

"Not that way," said Dave. "I don't want to try to explain the dress or any of this to my family. Not if I don't have to. We can go down the roof and in through one of the basement windows. They were painted shut years ago, but they open up just fine for me now."

"All right," said Sparx. "But aren't you worried your mom will have found your magic circle in the basement?"

Dave shook his head. "That's why I put it in the storeroom. We're not supposed to be in there. It's where Mom stuck all my dad's stuff when she first had to kick him out. It's been a couple of years, but he's still got a few things tucked away and she won't let us use it until it's empty."

"Isn't the door hanging open?" I asked.

"Nope. I used the drill gun to screw it shut and got clear before it could finish unscrewing itself. It should be good. Here, Kalvan, can you hold this door shut until I'm out the window? Once I get far enough away it'll stop trying to slam itself open."

I braced the door with the bottom of my foot as Dave set the cat aside and headed for the window. The dress clearly belonged to his older sister, who was about the same size as Dave, because it almost fit him and he didn't actually look half bad.

"What about sweat pants?" I asked as he stepped up onto the dresser in front of the window.

He shook his head. "No luck so far. They slide right off. I'm pretty sure the only reason the dress stays on is gravity and the fact it doesn't have any buttons or zippers or anything."

I cracked the door open for the cats as he slipped onto the roof, and I followed him out.

A few minutes later we were standing outside the storeroom. A padlock hanging off the open hasp twisted and dropped to the floor as we arrived. A moment later a pair of screws started slowly twisting their way out of the plank door. Dave's basement was dark and damp and creepy, with concrete block walls and a rough cement floor where patches of red showed here and there from when someone painted it about a million years ago. It had probably made the space more inviting when it was new, but now it looked rather like spattered blood.

The screws fell to the floor with a jingle and the door creaked open. Beyond was a small room walled with rough planks and lit only by a bare bulb. A carefully drawn chalk circle enclosed much of the freshly swept floor, though its perfection was marred in three places by spilled wax that had also wiped out several ideograms. Whatever magic had animated the circle was broken or in abeyance now. We slipped inside and closed the door behind us.

"Hang on." Sparx touched the door and said something fast in the language of fire. I didn't catch all the words, but it sounded like a spell of closing. "There. I don't know how long it will last in the face of Dave's newfound talents, but it should keep the door shut for a little while at least."

"I don't suppose it works on pants?" Dave poked at his abandoned jeans with a toe, shifting them off to one side of the circle.

"It might," replied Sparx. "Or, it might just start them on fire."

He sighed. "I guess I'll stick with the dress for a little longer."

Sparx snorted and then hopped around the circle, examining the ideograms one by one. "This isn't half bad, Dave. You must have had a good teacher." He tapped his foot on the nearest.

Dave blushed. "Yeah, about that. Kalvan showed me the journal where he keeps his magic homework, and I . . . kind of took it." He pointed at a high shelf. "It's up there. I'm so sorry, Kalvan."

"Dave . . ." Even though I'd known we had to get to this eventually, I didn't know what to say. The idea that my best friend had been riffling through my bag without my permission made me angry and a little sick to my stomach. But that wasn't half as bad as I felt about the vision of him losing his hand—I *had* to keep this from going wrong.

"I know," he said. "I'm not proud of myself, and I'm *really* sorry. It . . . I just wanted my own magic so bad."

"I guess I can understand," I said after a moment. "But that was super dangerous."

Dave actually laughed. "Yeah, I kind of figured that out. Are you mad?"

"No. Not really. Not being able to find the journal got me in a lot of trouble with Tanya, but it's okay, I guess."

Sparx coughed sharply. "Can we save the half-hearted recriminations and inevitable reconciliation for some later conversation?

We have more important things to deal with. Dave has already inflicted on himself a more appropriate punishment for opening other people's things without permission than any you or I could ever hope to devise. Don't you think?"

I had to nod. "True enough."

"More like too true by half." Dave glumly poked at his jeans again. "But yeah, I guess I earned the mess I'm in. I hope you can both forgive me someday."

"No worries, man." I turned to Sparx. "Have you figured out what he did to himself?"

The hare snorted. "I haven't even finished figuring out *how* he did it. Dave, why did you choose this set of ideograms? It's not quite like any spell I've ever seen, and that's not a good thing."

"Well, first, Kalvan takes lousy notes."

"Conceded."

"Hey!" I barked.

"Be quiet, child, I need answers." Sparx flicked an ear at Dave. "Go on."

"So I'm not sure which of these *ought* to go together. I mean, I was able to figure out a couple of combinations that looked like they might be attached to specific spells, but all I knew about the spells themselves was their names and some very cryptic and badly penned things: '*BIG boom, protects against* unintelligible garble,' or '*watch out for hellmites!*'"

"Hey!" I said again.

Sparx snorted. "Hush. I'm impressed he got that much out of your scribbles. What else?"

"A lot of the ideograms were labeled with two or three words, such as *ash* or *char*, and *summoning?* or *protects*. I know from what

Kalvan has said in the past that some of it is specific to his family, or to fire powers generally. So, I looked for things that might be more broadly applied, and for words that seemed like they might help in what I wanted to do. Things like *open* and *friend* and *safe.*"

Sparx inclined his ears forward in a gesture I'd come to think of as a combination of *huh* and *not bad.* "That's not actually as bizarre a method for creating this mess as I expected. So, you picked out things you thought might work, and then what?"

"Well, I can't speak the language of fire, or any of the other magical tongues you guys use, and I was pretty sure butchering the pronunciation wouldn't go well, so I just chalked them in and thought about what I wanted them to mean in my head."

Sparx's eyes widened. "You know, it's a miracle you're alive, human shaped, and in the right dimension."

Dave winced, but continued. "After that, I lit the candles. Then I gave a little speech asking whatever benevolent powers that might be listening to help a guy out. That's when everything went all 'Ali Baba and the Forty Thieves' on me."

"Wait, what now?" I was confused.

Dave grinned. "You know, all that *'OPEN SESAME!'* stu—"

Dave's voice started out deep and far away and echoey, like something from a movie with a serious sound budget and weird ideas about magic. But it cut off abruptly when the circle on the floor suddenly dropped away beneath us.

11

Well, That Might Come in Handy

WE LANDED IN a heap.

Hard.

I'm not sure how far we fell. It couldn't have been much more than ten or fifteen feet, because my skull stayed more or less in one piece when my forehead bounced off the floor . . . or possibly a wall—I kind of lost track of direction somewhere in there. In either case, it rang my bell pretty good, and the whole world went wobbly as my vision filled with flickering purple stars.

I was still trying to sort out which way was up when a wave of furry darkness broke over me. At least, it was dark and there were a lot of things with fur and I ended up on the bottom of the pile. It hurt and I cried out, only to be answered in the tongue of earth.

Delvers—and I understood them!

I spoke again, this time trying to weave a spell, but where my heart spoke in the tongue of fire, my mouth shaped words that flew heavy and hard into the air like stones from a sling. The ground beneath me seemed to heave and buckle in response, and I bit down hard on my betraying tongue. Something hot and vaguely sharp touched the injured place on my forehead and pain blurred my senses as a delver voice spoke a word of stillness.

After that, the world and I parted ways for a while. When we returned to each other, I was relieved to find that my sense of up and down had come back to me. It was a brief sort of triumph that ended as soon as I opened my eyes and took in the situation. The room was twenty feet across with a high domed ceiling. The light was dim and blue, and if it had any source, I couldn't see it.

I had been placed in a large stone chair with steel straps tight across my ankles, wrist, and throat—they blended into the chair with no visible locking mechanism as if they'd been bonded directly to the stone. Still, I felt strangely buoyant and cheerful.

Before I could even think about getting loose, Dave called out, "Don't try any magic!"

"What?" I croaked—I'd never gotten that drink after my ride, and I'd swallowed a lot of dust when the floor fell in. I licked my lips and tried again. "Why?"

I turned my head and saw Dave seated on the floor to my right with his back against the wall. Globes of some grayish stone flecked with red completely enclosed his hands and feet—granite maybe. The ones on his hands were the size of bowling balls, while those on his feet were perhaps twice as big.

"They told me the air in this room has a lot more oxygen than normal. If you summon any kind of flame, the air will start on fire and so will . . . well, me at least. They weren't as sure about what it would do to you."

"Oh." The extra oxygen explained that feeling of buoyancy, too. "Where's Sparx?"

"On your other side."

A huge transparent tank stood there, much like you might see at an aquarium . . . with a few modifications. First, a hollow glass ball floated in the exact center of the tank, completely surrounded by water and containing one very annoyed fire hare. Second, a ten-ton chunk of marble was perched atop the tank in defiance of at least a couple of laws of physics.

". . . the heck?" I said.

Dave spoke from behind me. "They said if either of you performs any kind of elemental magic, it'll disrupt the spells holding the rock up and then it's 'bye-bye bunny.'"

"That's ridiculous; he can move right through solid objects." But, when I took a closer look at the enormous granite block with my newfound sense of stone, I got the distinct feeling there was more to it than just mass. "Maybe . . ."

Sparx's mouth moved angrily at that point, like he was speaking—well, swearing really—but nothing came through the water and glass surrounding him. Eventually he subsided into an obviously frustrated silence and I turned back to Dave.

"All right then, barring desperation, neither Sparx nor I is the answer here. What have you got?"

He shrugged and nodded meaningfully at the stone globes. "As far as I can tell, there's nothing to open. Even if there were, I've got jack all control over this new power of mine. That's the first thing you and Sparx were supposed to help me with. Remember?"

"That could be a problem, since he's in the tank, and I've never even *heard* of anything like what you can do now. You may just have to start experimenting and hope."

Dave swallowed hard and shook his head. "I don't think that's going to work out so hot. I've had my power less than a day—I think, I was out for quite a while, too—and not a single positive thing has come from it. Given what it's done *to* me, messing around with it sounds terrifying. What if I open another giant hole in the floor, but this time the fall kills us all? Or something worse?"

I hadn't thought of that, and he was right about how frightening power could be. "I don't know, Dave. I wish I had answers for you, but all I've learned about this stuff so far is a tiny slice of fire magic. Even that's gone pretty seriously off the rails for me a couple of times. On the other hand, you might be our only chance of getting free."

Dave looked like what he really wanted to do was cry, but he kept it together and all he did was shake his head again. "I can't do it, Kalvan. I can't."

I didn't have any answer for that, so I shrugged and decided to shut my mouth for a while. Talking was only drying me out more. Time passed. A lot of time. I grew hungry, and thirstier than ever. I also slept for a while despite the steel bands.

When I woke, the first thing I noticed was that I'd need a bathroom soon. I also suspected I wasn't going to get one. I forced my head to turn on a neck that felt like it'd fused into a column of glass and might shatter if I moved. It hurt. I looked left first. Sparx had curled up in the bottom of the glass ball and appeared to be asleep. As I started to turn right, I heard a popping noise. At first I thought it might be my neck.

Then it happened again. This time I saw what made the noise. A faint glistening circle of darkness briefly appeared in the air about midway between me and Dave before vanishing with the sharp pop of a bubble bursting. Dave had his eyes closed and an intense look of concentration on his face.

". . . the heck?" I said.

Dave blinked and looked my way, his bloodshot eyes showing deep sunken rings underneath. It was only then I realized how tired and drawn he looked, with sweat visibly dampening the armpits of his dress.

"I take it that didn't work," he said after a long moment. He sounded even more exhausted than he looked, with a voice gone harsh and raspy around the edges.

"Depends on what you're trying to do." I had little doubt the funny circle originated with him. "If you were shooting for making baby UFOs, you're off to a pretty good start."

Dave chuckled ruefully. "Alas, no. I'm trying to get us out of here, and not having much luck."

"I like the idea, but what does it have to do with flying disks of weirdness?"

"If I knew that, I might be further along with my clever plan." He paused for several long seconds. "I'm guessing from the look on your face I should maybe back up a couple of steps in the explanation process."

"Yeah, that'd be great. I get enough conversations that start half-way through the middle with my mother." The practice of which made me want to scream and bang my forehead on things.

"So, my powers still scare the bejeezus out of me, but I fell asleep thinking about what you said. That, and the delvers telling me that any of that elemental stuff you and Sparx do could get us all killed. It made for seriously ugly dreams. Add in the stone balls holding me down, and I woke up about an hour ago feeling like someone had stomped all over me."

"You and me both."

"Anyway, I figured I'm the one who asked to get dealt in on this whole magic thing. Which means it's my fault we're stuck here and I'd better step up if I don't want us all to end up as worm food."

"I wish I could argue with you."

"Yeah, me too." Dave sighed. "Anyway, I've spent the time since I woke up trying to figure out how to focus my power."

"All right, and the black disks?"

"I don't know. There's nothing in here that looks like any kind of lock I've ever seen. Sparx is in that glass thing. Those steel bands on your chair look like they grew that way. And these"—he nodded at the stone globes—"are skintight all the way down. Given that, I didn't want to try experimenting real close to any of us. What if I opened up an artery instead of that band holding your wrist?"

The thought made the skin on my back feel cold and tight, especially given my earlier vision. "Oh."

"Yeah. I figured I'd start by sort of aiming my mind at a point in space and thinking about opening. For a long time, nothing happened. But I kept trying. About ten minutes ago I got the first one of those things: *POP*."

"What are they?" I asked.

"No idea. Clearly, I'm doing something. But what that something is?" He shrugged.

"See if you can make one closer to me. If I get a better look, maybe I can help you figure this out."

"Worth a try." Dave closed his eyes and his face took on an expression of intense concentration.

I heard a very quiet fizzing that ended in a popping sound as a six-inch circle of darkness appeared a few feet in front of my face. It was slightly above the level of my head and I got a pretty decent look at it. Or, rather, *through* it. From this close, it was clear the circle was some kind of hole into elsewhere. I could see a starry sky through the gap and a faint warm breeze blew out of the hole. It smelled vaguely metallic and sooty, like a train yard. Then, *POP*, it was gone.

"I think you're making little doors into somewhere else." I told Dave what I'd seen and felt.

"Weird. Let me try again."

This circle was slightly larger and I couldn't see anything but darkness beyond the doorway. I didn't smell anything either, but I thought I could feel air flowing around me and being sucked into the other space, like maybe the pressure there was lower than it was here.

"That's a different someplace else, I think."

Dave grunted. "Huh. I couldn't feel any difference on my end. Whatever I'm doing, I'm not consistent about it. Let's try one more."

The next circle wasn't dark at all. Instead, I could see sunlight on deep-blue leaves through a hole barely two inches across. "That one's really weird. I'm not sure it's even this planet."

POP. Quite close this time, and leading into some kind of industrial space. A thought occurred to me and I shifted my head. "Weird. It only exists in one direction. From the back, there's no *there* there."

"But where does it go?"

"Maybe a furnace room? Someplace with lots of concrete block in any case."

"That's nothing like what I was trying for, and I don't seem to have much control on size, either. They range from two inches up to about a foot, more or less at random. I'm not sure what good this . . . wait a second. I have a really stupid idea."

I didn't like the sound of that, and I tried to catch his eyes. "Tell me about it."

"No, if I think about it too much, I'll chicken out. Here goes nothi—AIEEE!" He screamed as the stone globe enclosing his right hand suddenly dropped through a hole in space, dragging his hand with it.

I jerked helplessly at the steel bands holding me. "Dave!" I couldn't see much of what lay beyond the hole because of my angle, but this looked like the weirdest space yet, with purple flashes jagging lightninglike through a sea of red goo.

"It's too heavy, I can't pull it back up!" Dave's eyes remained squinched tight and I could see the strain building on his face, but there was nothing I could do. "No! No! Ahhhhhhhhh!"

POP.

The stone was gone along with Dave's hand and several inches of forearm. Horror shocked through me as Dave slumped to the side and I waited for the spraying blood I had seen in my vision. But no blood came. Dave's scream subsided to a whimper, and I thought I could hear him swearing under his breath.

"Dave?"

No response. I tried to throttle down my own panic. Dave needed me to buoy him up right now, not drag him down.

"Dave? Are you all ri . . . no, stupid question. Of course you aren't. Your hand is gone. Don't be an idiot, Kalvan." Still no response. "Can you hear me, Dave? Can you tell me what happened, because . . . well . . . um, your hand is gone but you're not bleeding." *Thank goodness!*

"I'm not?" Dave's eyes flickered open, though he kept them focused on me and didn't even glance at the stump he had tucked against his hip. "You're not just saying that to make me feel better, right?" He sounded scared and desperate. "Because I'm really, really close to completely losing it, and I need you to be honest with me. Honest, but reassuring. Okay?"

"Sure. Honest and reassuring. I can totally do that." *Right . . .*

"Thanks, man. You're sure I'm not bleeding?"

"That's about the only thing I'm really certain of in the whole world. I don't know *why* you're not bleeding, but you are definitely not bleeding."

Which meant this wasn't my vision. Well, that and the fact that *I* hadn't been the one to cut his hand off. This was a totally different future that coincidentally also involved my best friend losing a hand. *Hold on to that thought.*

Dave took a deep breath. "Good. Good. That's good. I think. I hope. Maybe. Because I—I can still feel my hand."

"You what?" That didn't make any sense, unless . . . "Ghost pain? I know amputees sometimes . . ."

Dave shook his head. "Nope. I don't think that's it. This feels like . . . well, exactly like my hand is still stuck in that big stone ball. The only difference is I can feel a sort of weird tingling on my wrist, like cold rain. Wait, what if I am bleeding, but it's just that

I'm bleeding into wherever my hand went and . . . I . . . okay, I'm going to lose it. Yep. Any second now."

"Hang on, Dave. This is magic, and that can get really weird really fast. Can you hold your arm up so I can see the stump?"

"Sure. No problem. Don't lose it. Don't lose it. Don't lose it."

Dave closed his eyes and lifted his arm so the stump was pointed straight at me. It looked like someone had replaced his missing hand with a glass plate. I could see the smoothed-off ends of his bones, and . . . I shuddered and suppressed the urge to throw up.

"I can see into your arm, man. It's . . . well, gross really. But you're definitely not bleeding into this world. I don't think you're bleeding into another world, either."

"Are you sure? Tell me you're sure and why not." Dave sounded desperate to believe me, and I couldn't blame him.

"If you were losing that much blood, I'm pretty sure you'd have passed out by now."

"That's a good—eep!"

"What?!?"

"Something touched my wrist. I mean the part of my wrist that isn't here. It felt like . . . you ever have a little fish nibble on you? Not an I'm-going-to-eat-you kind of nibble, but a sort of hey-what's-this kind of nibble. Happens all the time if you go swimming in the lakes and . . . am I babbling? Because I think I might be babbling."

"Maybe a little, but that's better than losing it. Right?"

"Yeah. Good. Babbling is goo—eep! There it is again."

"The nibbling?"

"Yeah. I . . . This isn't ghost pain. My hand is definitely still attached somehow. That's possible, isn't it? With magic? Like, maybe it's in another dimension where that's totally a thing."

"Sure." I had no idea, but I really wanted to reassure my best friend. "Heck, I was a dragon for a while. Next to that, a still-attached hand stuck in the wrong dimension seems completely reasonable."

"Thank you. I *really* needed to hear that. So, next question. Do you think I can get it back? You know, if I open up a door to that dimension again."

"I don't see why not." Except for the fact that he didn't seem to be able to hit the same place twice. But, what else could I say?

"All right. I'm going to do that now."

"How?" I hadn't intended to ask, but the word just kind of fell out of my mouth.

"I have no idea. But that's definitely what I'm going to do. I have to." He took a couple of deep breaths. "Maybe I could ask the powers that gave me my magic for a little help. What do you think? I mean, I know asking outside powers for help is how I ended up in this mess in the first place, but how much worse can it get?"

Lots! This time I managed *not* to say what I was thinking, though I wondered if maybe I should have.

"All right," continued Dave, "let's do this! Dear benevolent powers, or mischievous powers, or whatever kind of powers you are. You gave me this whole opening-things magic without a manual, and I've really screwed it up. So, if you could maybe help a guy out and make this next door into elsewhere be the one I need right now, that'd be seriously appreciated."

Dave looked at me and mouthed, "Was that okay?"

I had no idea, and that was the weirdest sort of invocation I'd ever heard, but I just nodded and gave him the thumbs-up with my bound right hand while I crossed the fingers on my out-of-sight left one. There wasn't really a lot else I *could* do.

Dave kept his eyes open as he concentrated, focusing all of his attention on a spot about five inches to the right of his face. When the circle showed up, I could barely see more than a line because my angle was edge on. Dave reached upward, pushing his stump into the opening. I held my breath. A moment later a look of profound relief spread across Dave's face.

"I think I've got it." He pulled his arm back and . . .

POP.

I felt a moment of relief to match Dave's expression as he flexed the fingers on . . . wait a second. It was *a* hand, yes. But it sure as anything wasn't *Dave's* hand.

12

The Fickle Fingers of Fate

THE SKIN OF Dave's new hand was slick and reflective, covered with slithering rainbows, like gasoline floating on dark water. To say nothing of the extra finger . . .

I spotted the differences a good second ahead of Dave and had time to look up and watch his expression as he realized what had happened. It made my heart hurt as he went from the beginnings of melting into a puddle of relief to openmouthed horror.

"AAAAAAAAAAAAAAAA . . ."

"Dave."

". . . AAAAAAAAAAAAAA . . ."

"DAVE!"

". . . AAAAAAAAAAAAAA . . ."

"DAVID HOWARD HARRIS! You stop that screaming this instant!"

". . . AAAAAAAAAAAAAA . . ."

That's when the hand slapped him.

". . . AAAAAAAH!"

Dave paused, probably more because he was out of air for screaming than anything. But he didn't start right up again, which was hopeful. "I . . ." He drew a couple of gasping breaths. "That wasn't cool, was it?"

"Maybe not," I replied. "But I can't say I'd have handled it any better. I . . . uh, this is a delicate question, but I have to ask. Did *you* slap yourself? Or was that . . . the hand?"

"I . . . I'm not sure." Dave held the hand up so he could look at it more closely, flexing each of the fingers and the thumb in turn. "I don't *think* it was me, but the . . ." He took a deep breath. "But *I* felt it on both ends. This palm stings as much as my cheek."

He looked at his new hand wonderingly and closed it into a tight fist. "From the inside, it feels like it's all me." He pressed the palm to his cheek. "Feels pretty much the same from the outside as well. I wish I had my other hand free so I could . . ."

Dave's voice trailed off as his right hand reached down to the place where the granite ball encased his left. Touching a point on the ball with all six finger- and thumb-tips, he flicked them apart in the kind of gesture you might use to expand a window on a touch screen. In response, the gap around his wrist suddenly opened wide and he was able to pull his other hand loose.

He immediately used his left hand to seize his right wrist right above the place where human skin met . . . whatever. "Okay, that *definitely* wasn't me." His words came out a full octave higher than normal. "Nope. Not me at all. Welllllll, not brain me, anyway. Because, I could totally feel it. I could feel *all* of it."

The way he said "all" sounded distinctly odd. "All of what, exactly?"

"Everything! I could feel the tug as my hand pulled my arm down to the ball. I could feel the stone against my fingers. I could feel the pulse of *garble* that released the . . . Wait a second, did I just say *garble*?"

I nodded as much as my neck band would allow. "Yeah, you did. I mean, I don't recognize the word or the language, or anything, but whatever you said the first time, you definitely repeated it. I . . . There's no good way to say this, but whatever that word was, it didn't even sound . . . well, human."

Dave's expression had gone deathly still, and he spoke now with a positively eerie calm. "Excellent. That's good to know. I'm glad. Really. I thought I might be hearing things—well, or speaking them—or maybe going like my dad, but nope, I'm possessed. That's really much better. I think I might go back to screaming here in a minute if that's all right with you."

"Sure, go ahead, I'll wait." I had an idea.

Seconds ticked past. Finally, Dave said, "Wait for what?"

"You to finish screaming."

"Huh? Would you care to explain that?"

I shrugged. "Well, obviously, you can't go on screaming forever. At some point you'll have to quit freaking and get back to dealing. Just like I did when I started speaking fire tongue. You're my best friend. Least I can do is wait it out. I mean"—and here I tugged at my bonds—"it's not like I'm going anywhere this side of you getting your shit together."

"That's cold!"

"It worked, didn't it?"

"Say what now?" Dave looked confused.

"You're thinking again instead of panicking." He blinked at me, so I continued. "I asked myself how Sparx deals with me when I'm flipping out about magic."

"And?"

I grinned. "He keeps poking at me until I'm too irritated to do anything but argue with him. I figured it might work on you, too."

"You're a jerk, Munroe. You know that, right?"

I nodded. "A smug jerk, even. Just like my bunny buddy. Now, if you're done with the freak-out for a bit, let's talk this through. Because I've got an idea."

Dave glared at me. "You're still a jerk, but I'm listening."

"Well, for starters, I think your magic did exactly what you asked the powers for."

"Your lips are moving, but you're not making any sense." Dave stuck his right hand out and waved it back and forth. "Does this look like my freaking hand, Kalvan?!? Does it?!?"

I shook my head. "No, but you didn't ask for the powers to give you your hand back. You asked them to help you open the door you *needed*."

"That's nonsen . . . oh." Dave glanced at his now-freed left hand. "You're thinking if I'd gotten my hand back, it'd still be stuck in a ball of rock and we'd be back at square zero."

"Pretty much, yeah. Am I wrong?"

Dave bit his lip. "No, I don't think you are. But what about my real hand? I can't feel it anymore. Am I ever going to see it again?"

"I don't know. Magic is weird and about half the time it doesn't do what you want it to even when it solves your problem. Maybe you can get it back later, but I sure wouldn't count on it."

Dave held the six-fingered hand up in front of his face and flexed the fingers. "This isn't going to be easy to explain to Mom. To say nothing of what it's going to do to my glove budget."

It wasn't much of a joke, but it made me think Dave might get through this. "You may also want to keep one wary eye out for anyone named Inigo Montoya."

That got an actual laugh. "Good point. I guess I should try this thing on my feet next."

"Probably. You might want to see if you can do it more as yourself this time. Tanya is always saying you need to control your magic and not let it control you."

"Okay. I want to do this right. Or, at least, better than *you've* been doing it . . . which actually shouldn't be too hard if what I hear from Sparx is true."

"Thin ice, man, thin ice."

"Says the guy who's stuck in that chair till I decide to cut him loose."

"All right, I'll let it slide. This time."

Dave leaned forward and placed his fingertips on the ball holding his right foot. Then, with a look of careful concentration, he flicked them open. There was a sharp *BANG* and shards of granite flew everywhere. One particularly nasty piece nailed my jaw hard enough to make my eyes water, but there was nothing I could do about it, and I was more worried about Dave anyway. He'd been much closer to the blast and now a huge cloud of dust blocked my view of him.

"Dave! Are you all right?"

There was a sharp cough. "Yeah, fine. Nothing big hit me." Another couple of coughs. "Well, except for all the dust. I think I might be starting an asthma attack." He coughed some more. "Yeah. My asthma definitely hates this, and my inhaler is in the pocket of my jeans." That last bit came out a little panicky.

"I don't suppose the delvers brought them along and left them in here with us?" I asked hopefully. Talking made the spot where the stone had struck my jaw feel like it was on fire.

Dave just coughed in response. When he finished, there was a wheezing undertone to his breathing. Not good, and there was nothing I could do about it. The dust settled, but that didn't seem to help. Dave was looking distinctly purple around the lips. More coughing, more wheezing.

Then, "Wait a second . . ." Dave's voice came out weak and raspy. "Asthma is *wheeze* basically airways closing. Maybe I can *wheeze* open them up again . . ."

I realized what he was about to try. "Dave, that might not be such a good idea." Again, speaking aggravated the pain in my jaw.

"Better than *wheeze* suffocating." He closed his otherworldly hand into a fist, looked briefly skyward, then slammed himself in the chest. For what seemed like forever, nothing happened. Then Dave let out one sharp hacking cough and drew in a long shivery breath that sounded deep and clean. "Booyah!"

"I take it that worked?"

"Holy hogrockets, but that feels better. I don't think I've ever been able to breathe this well in my whole life. Hang on." He bent to the other stone ball and did the point-and-flick routine. This time the ball split neatly in half, freeing his foot. "Still not what I was shooting for, but no explosion this time. That's a plus, right?" He stood and limped toward me.

"Yeah. The one that went bang didn't do me any favors." The

burning sensation on my jawline hadn't gotten any better with time, though I'd mostly been able to push it aside while I focused on Dave.

Dave's eyes suddenly widened. "Oh man, I am so sorry."

"Don't worry about it. I'll be fine." A lie—if anything, it was getting worse.

He leaned in close. "Dude, you do realize that you've got a two-inch-long shard of granite sticking out of your face."

"I do?"

"Yeah."

"Oh." I swiveled my eyes as far to the right as I could, trying to get a look at the stone. No luck. "That'd explain why it hurts so much. Am I bleeding?"

"Barely at all, but I expect that's going to change rather a lot once I pull that thing out of there."

"Are you sure that's a good idea?" I asked, rather weakly.

"Well, it's kind of a cool look as piercings go, but if we have to do any running away, you really don't want to have it stuck there ready to bang into something."

"Fair enough. Why don't you pull it now, before you work on these steel bands."

"Why?" Dave looked puzzled.

"Because if it hurts half as much coming out as it did going in, I'd probably punch you if I had a hand free."

"Good point." He chuckled, then his eyes went far away. "*Hmmm*, you know . . ."

"'Hmmm' what?" I didn't like the sound of that *hmmm*. Not at all.

"Got an idea." Before I could argue with him, he reached up

with his new hand, took the stone firmly between his fingers, and yanked.

"Son-of-a-sonic . . ." I trailed off as I realized it hadn't hurt nearly as much as I expected. I felt blood trickling down my neck, but there didn't seem to be a lot of it. "What did you just do?"

"Magic!" Dave grinned that amazing grin I hadn't seen in weeks. "Apparently I can exert *some* control over how much of an opening I leave behind, too. Who knew?"

"You magicked my jaw?"

"Kind of, yeah. I'm pretty sure I can't do closings, but I focused really hard on making the hole I left behind as small as possible. Then, when I pulled out the stone, I could feel the magic doing something. Since you're bleeding a lot less than I figured you would, Ima call that a win. Here, you want the souvenir?" He held out the jagged piece of granite—it looked a bit like the spear point that had melted into my hand when I did the Dragon's Wings.

"Dave!"

"Oh, right. You're still locked up. Hang on a tick while I see if I can't get you out of there."

"Please don't blow anything up while you're doing it. I like having all my bits attached."

"Yeah, smart boy, so did I. I'll see what I can do."

The right cuff left a band of blisters across my wrist as it heated sharply before falling to the floor with a clank. "OW!"

"Sorry about that, man. I'll try something different on this next one." The left cuff got very cold, but not quite cold enough to leave a frost burn. "Okay, so maybe that's not it, either."

Both of the bands across my ankles tightened somewhat before coming free—the right one hard enough to bruise. That left only my neck. I braced myself for the worst as Dave slipped two fingers between the steel and my skin. A moment later, with the faintest of pops, like a soap bubble bursting, I was free. Dave started to extend his new right hand to help me up, then froze halfway through the gesture.

I'll admit it; that hand scared me. But I could see his heart in his eyes and I reached up to catch his hand before he could pull away or be hurt by my fear. "Thanks, Dave, you're a lifesaver."

The skin felt cool against my own, and unnaturally smooth—like the surface of a Teflon frying pan. It did have some of the give of flesh and it felt . . . I don't know . . . alive? Real? Not quite human, but not like a human-made thing, either. I wanted to make sure he knew we were still good, so I squeezed his hand between both of my own.

"I'm sorry, Dave. This never would have happened if I hadn't dragged you into my magical hassles. I owe you—"

Dave cut me off sharply. "No, you don't. This is on me. You didn't drag me into anything. I jumped in with both feet because my best friend was in trouble, and I'd do it again tomorrow even if I knew this was coming." He pulled his alien hand free and held it up between us. "I chose to ask for magic, and this is what the universe gave me. I may have some problems with the details, but I'll deal. You got that?"

"Yes, but—"

"No buts. No backs. No secret guilt. I've got magic now. It's weird magic, and kind of scary. But how boring would it be if I just got a second helping of the same stuff you have?"

"You're sure?"

Dave nodded. "I'm sure."

"Then let's go bust Sparx out."

That turned out to be easier said than done. When Dave reached his otherworldly hand toward Sparx's glass prison, it hesitated, then started to shake—halting some inches from the surface.

"What's wrong?" I asked, while Sparx flicked his ears back and forth impatiently.

"I'm not sure, but I think the hand doesn't know what to do with this one. Give me a second." Dave leaned in and pressed his forehead and both palms against the tank.

Several minutes ticked past while my impatience built. There was no way to know when or if the delvers might come back. We desperately needed to get Sparx free and move on to the next step in our escape. Finally, Dave pulled back and shook his head.

"I don't think I can do it. The whole thing feels like one single piece to my new powers. The water is somehow part of what's holding the stone up. I can sense that if I open a hole in the tank and it starts to drain, the stone will shatter the tank and crush Sparx. If I do anything to move the stone, it will unbalance the load, the tank will break and Sparx gets squished. If I open up the globe, it will change the pressure in the tank and BAM!" Dave smacked his fist into the palm of his human hand.

"We can't just leave him there!"

Dave winced. "I know, but I've got nothing. Compared to this"—he tapped the tank—"the stuff they had us bound up with was like breaking out of a paper bag."

Sparx had canted his ears forward as though he was trying to hear us. When he caught my eye, he tapped his right ear with a paw as if to say, "Tell me." I pointed at Dave's hand and then at the tank and made an opening gesture. Then I mimed the stone dropping, shook my head, and spread my hands wide in the classic *I'm-stuck* pose.

Sparx nodded, then pointed at Dave before drawing a circle in the air. Next, he put his paw through the imaginary circle and made a chopping-it-off motion. Finally, he mimed the circle again and pretended to climb through it. His meaning was pretty clear, but I didn't like it.

Dave clearly didn't, either. "No way! First, I'm not sure I can get one precisely located enough for him to climb through. Second, I have no control over where those things go. What if I accidentally make a door into some kind of hell?" He shook his head emphatically at Sparx.

The hare responded with a nod that was just as emphatic. Then he touched his chest and pointed at the bubble beneath his feet, before pointing to the stone above him and making a squishing motion.

"He's got a point, Dave. If he stays here, he's in constant danger of being crushed. We have to get him out."

Before Dave could respond, Sparx waved his paws to catch our attention. Then he drew a circle in the air, looked through it, and shook his head. Another. Another shake of the head. A third. This time he nodded.

"I suppose he's right." Dave sighed. "If it looks like the gate leads to a bad place, he doesn't have to go through it. I guess I can give it a try."

Dave closed his eyes and began to visibly concentrate. As he did so, the six-fingered hand made a series of small complicated gestures, seemingly of its own accord. A few seconds later, a circle opened inside the globe that held Sparx. The hare leaned forward and looked through before hopping back away from the gateway as far as his small prison would allow and shaking his head violently.

I touched Dave on the shoulder. "That's a bad one; let it go."

Sparx didn't leap away from the next one, but he did shake his head. He did the same for the three that followed. By then, beads of sweat had broken out along Dave's brow line and it was obvious he was fading.

"I don't know how many more of these I can manage." He used the shoulder of his dress to dab away some of the sweat. "Hitting the mark for location is brutal, and even without that, I can feel something go out of me with each gate I open." But then he braced up, took a deep breath, and tried again.

Disaster.

The edge of the circle touched the surface of the sphere that held the hare. In the first instant, water started to jet in through the hole thus created. In the next, cracks spread across the surface of the sphere. Without even looking to see where the gateway went, Sparx leaped forward through it, vanishing as the globe imploded. I barely had time to register that before the walls of the tank bulged suddenly outward.

I threw my arm up to cover my face as the tank burst into a million pieces, sending water and shards of glass everywhere, while the gigantic stone block plunged toward the floor like the biggest hammer the world had ever seen. Sparks flew as stone met stone, igniting the too-rich air in a giant burst of flame.

BOOOOOOOOOOOM!

13

The Flagon with the Dragon

DAVE MIGHT WELL have died in the first blast of the flames if we hadn't been thoroughly drenched in the split second before they hit. As it was, he was protected just long enough for me to reach out from the place in my heart where a matching fire burned and draw the flames into myself.

It wasn't something I'd ever tried before—though I'd seen Sparx do similar things—and it made my whole body feel like a wool sock into which someone had stuffed a burning log, terrifyingly hot and heavy, and horribly stretched out. I knew it would rip me apart within seconds if I tried to hold it all. I simply couldn't contain that much fire. But I had no way to release it.

Not in that shape anyway.

This time when I became the dragon, it was an act of desperation, with no conscious thought or preparation. I cast no spells and I set no wards. My body and my magic simply did what they had to do for me to survive by taking the form of something that could hold the expanded fires within, a form that had written itself into my bones back on that night at the rail yard.

One moment I was plain old Kalvan Monroe, ready to burst from a surfeit of my own element. The next, with a wrench and a twist in the fabric of reality, I became a firedrake, huge and angry, armored in scales, and far more alien than Dave's new hand could ever be. A shape given strength by the mighty flames I had drawn within myself rather than the meager candle of my own human magic. Because of that, the transformation was deeper this time, and *I, Kalvan,* faded into *dragon other.*

Dragon's eyes saw things Kalvan's would have missed, like the place where magic swirled through the wall from repeated openings and closings. Flames could not touch such a gate, and Kalvan's new-found human connections to stone were still too weak for the fire-drake to use. But one smashing strike of his snakelike head made an opening big enough for a body grown long and sinuous, and he slithered through an instant later.

The passage beyond was ten feet across and five tall, barely big enough to allow him passage, and he was forced to go slow. Vaguely, in the tiny part of his brain that was still Kalvan, he registered the other human boy following him and felt that it was good. But the dragon's desires did not flow in the same channels as Kalvan's. So, when he came to a forking of the way, he sniffed the air and turned in the direction where he scented a greater concentration of his delver enemies instead of following the path that smelled of outside air.

He wanted . . . no, needed, *to rend/burn/devour the ones who had tried to cage him. They would pay with their lives for such effrontery, fuel for the living furnace that burned at his core. He would gobble them down, and in so doing, he would complete his transformation, just as some mortal travelers who wandered into fairyland committed themselves forever to its boundaries by eating of fairy food.*

A deep sniff brought the scent of fresh delver blood from around the next bend. The rich and complex smell carried a bonanza of information for one with a dragon's senses. There was the message of numbers—ten delvers made up this group, warriors all, armed with stone, driven by anger and reeking of self-righteous arrogance. The dragon surged forward, pressing against narrow walls that dragged at wings and hampered the free movement of his shoulders.

THERE!

Eyes that provided their own light fixed on a small group of the badgerlike enemy, pinning them with a lantern gaze. He smelled their surprise and sudden fear as they froze in place, and he savored it. They carried spears and axes with stone blades and razor edges, weapons that would turn and break on the armor of his scales as he would break those who wielded them.

Their leader was thickset, stronger and taller than most of his fellows, and the dragon recognized him . . . no, I recognized him. Cetius! The delver who had served the dragon's stepf . . . no. No. No!

Oscar. Not the dragon's *anything.* Oscar was *my* stepfather. My own personal monster. The man who had controlled my mother with his magic. The man who had tried to do the same to me. His stink was all over Cetius—aftershave and soap and a dozen other smells that I recognized from the bathroom of my own house.

For one brief instant, the pure rage I felt at the man who had done so much harm to me and mine drove the dragon out of the head we shared. But I could feel it fighting to assert itself again, to use my present shape to push me aside and resume control, and I knew if I let that happen, I would never truly be Kalvan again. I had only this one brief moment to act.

Opening my mouth wide, I let the flames that I had taken into myself pour forth to engulf the delvers. My conscience twinged as I watched them run burning down the tunnel away from me or plunge deep into the stone to put out the flames, and I was glad when one last breath sucked deep into a dragon's lungs brought no stench of death. They were hurt, many of them badly, but the children of the earth are as tough as the stones they come from, and I did not think any of them would die.

Then, with the fires that powered my transformation exhausted, I fell back into myself, and darkness filled the deep places under the earth once again. I didn't pass out. Not quite, though my knees buckled and smacked into the stone floor hard enough to bring tears to my eyes. The smell of burning delver—which had been so sweet to dragon senses—hung heavy in the air. I probably would have thrown up if I'd had anything at all in my stomach, but it had been a very long time since I had eaten or drunk.

"Kalvan?" Dave's voice came from somewhere behind me, quiet and cautious. "Are you, you again? Is that why the lights went out?"

"Yeah." I forced myself back to my feet with an effort that left me blinking spots out of my eyes. "I—oh hell, Sparx!" It was only in that moment I remembered the predicament of my familiar. "Dave, do you have any idea where he went?!?"

A reaching hand touched my back, quickly sliding up to squeeze my shoulder. "I'm sorry, Kalvan. Truly. But no."

"Crap. Crap. Crap. You're sure?"

"Honestly, I'm terrified of where I might have sent him, and I was hoping you'd be able to tell me something on that front. I'd have asked sooner, but you were a dragon."

"Sorry. It's the only way I could keep the explosion from killing us."

"Oh." Dave sounded nonplussed. "Good to know. Why'd you change back?"

"There were delvers—Cetius, and some of his lot. They smelled of Oscar and I . . ." I drew in a breath full of the stink of burned fur and flesh—hurts I had caused—and shook my head though Dave couldn't see it. "I—I really can't talk about it right now. I don't even want to think about it. Let's just say, Lisa's warning that taking a shape defines you didn't tell half of it, and leave it there. Okay?"

"Sure." There was a long pause. "I don't suppose you know the way out?"

"Not exactly. But I know this isn't it. Man, but I wish I knew if Sparx was all right."

"I'm really sorry, Kalvan. Isn't there anything you can do? I thought you had some sort of deep magical connection, what with him being your familiar."

"I, uh . . . huh. You might have something." I thought back to my first meetings with the fire hare. "Could you plug your ears for a second?"

"Sure, why?"

"I'm going to try to summon him, and I need to use his real name."

"Oh." Dave put a world of hurt into one syllable.

"It's not like that. I trust you completely, but I promised Sparx I'd never tell anyone, and I can't bear the thought of breaking my word to him. Especially if he's . . ."

"*Oh!* Yeah, absolutely. I'm doing it right now. There."

I took a deep breath and spoke clearly and carefully in the tongue of fire. "I conjure and abjure thee, *sprths*al*erarha. By fire and smoke, by ash and oak, by the flame in the darkness and the powers it awoke. Come to me now, no matter where you are. Ash and char, sun and star, wind and smoke, ash and oak!"

Nothing happened. Well, nothing physical, at least, but I had a sudden sense of sharp connection. I could feel the hare in my heart, like a sliver, and I turned in the direction it pointed. He was to the left and down from where I currently stood. He was terribly far away, thousands of miles at the least, but I could tell he was already on his way back. I felt something loosen in my throat, like I'd had a big piece of ice caught there and only noticed it in the moment it melted away.

I reached out to find Dave, and tugged his hands away from his ears. "Sparx is a long way off, but all right. We need to get out of here before any more delvers show up."

"Sounds good to me, but how do we manage it? Now that you're no longer the world's biggest night-light, I can't see anything. I'm not even sure which way is which."

"I think I can manage a bit of light on my own behalf." I reached into my heart and drew on the fires there. Bright flames blossomed from the upturned fingers of my left hand . . . and then immediately went out. "Hang on a tick." I tried again, and failed again. Sigh. "One more time." *There!*

Dave blinked in the ruddy light. "Okay. That's the creepiest thing I've seen you do yet. It looks like something from a bad horror film—one of those hand-of-glory things."

I chose not to point out he was a fine one to talk about disturbing hands. "Would you rather try to find our way out of here in the dark?"

"Not so much."

"Then zip it and let's get moving."

It was easy enough to figure out which direction was back the way we'd come, given the charring on the walls ahead. A few minutes of brisk walking brought us to the forking of the way where dragon me had smelled fresh air, and we turned into it. Not long after that, things started to get complicated when we came to another junction with three possible routes.

"Well?" asked Dave after several long seconds of staring down each of the paths in turn. "Which one is it?"

"I don't know. The dragon smelled a way out in this direction, but I have no idea how far it is or which one."

Dave grimaced. "It looks to me like the right path trends downward, so that's probably not it. Your turn."

I sniffed the air, but I was no dragon, and I couldn't smell any difference. I hesitated to guess, but the only other idea I had for making a distinction—using my new connection with the element of earth—scared me more than getting lost did. Finally, I just pointed left and started walking.

Maybe fifteen minutes passed before we came to another junction. This time, there was a spiral stair leading down, a path that angled slightly left, and another that turned steeply to the right—almost doubling back along the side of the one we'd taken to get there. Again, with the exception of not going down, there was no obvious choice. Dave pointed left and left we went, but we hadn't gone far before we found another multiple forking of the way. The yawning emptiness in my stomach transformed itself into a feeling of churning doom.

"We're lost." I pitched my voice as low as I could in case there were listeners nearby. "I really don't like the fact we're getting more and more branches. That seems like something you'd expect as you got closer to a delver village, not farther out toward the edges."

Dave looked troubled as well. "Yeah," he whispered, "about the only thing I'm sure of is the way back to our cell, and that's no good."

I was about to answer, when I heard a faint scuffing noise from somewhere behind us. I nodded toward the nearest passage and we both hurried that way. But it quickly narrowed so that we had to go single file, and then narrowed again, forcing us to edge along sideways until we finally hit a place where the walls came too close together for any further progress. I swore bitterly but quietly.

"Hush," said Dave. "Whatever made that noise might not be following us. If they aren't and they know the tunnels, they probably didn't head into this dead end. Let's not give anyone an excuse to come looking. Better put the light out, too."

He had a point. I closed my fist, snuffing the flames, but I doubted the noise had been a coincidence. That doubt was reinforced a few moments later by the sounds of claws clicking on stone somewhere in the dark behind us.

"Back up," I hissed. "If we have to face delvers, we'll need room to fight."

We started toward the junction, moving as quickly and quietly as possible. We'd gotten to a point where the passage widened enough to accommodate my shoulders, when a series of sharp, animal-like sniffs sounded in the darkness ahead. It was hard to judge in the echoey confines of the stone tunnel, but if the noise had come from more than fifteen feet away, I'd have been shocked. I ran into Dave as he stopped moving.

There was no more point in hiding, so I raised my left hand high and relit the fires on my fingers. This time I fed them more fuel from my heart, intending to blind as much as illuminate. With a sudden flash, the passage filled with light, and I saw . . .

"Lisa? Is that you?"

A huge coyote stood blinking in the sudden brightness just this side of a slight bend in the tunnel.

A moment later, Morgan came into view as well, though she didn't seem nearly as dazzled by the light. "It's about time!"

"I . . . uh, what?"

Morgan shook her head disappointedly. "We can't stop here. There's too much chance of the delvers finding us. Let's talk and walk."

"Great idea," said Dave. "Do you know the way out?"

"Not really, but Lisa can backtrack *our* trail, and that should get us to the place we came in."

The big coyote nodded and slipped past Morgan to take the lead. Dave quickly followed, but Morgan waited for me to come up beside her before she started walking. If she had any thoughts on Dave's dress, she didn't share.

As we fell in behind Dave and Lisa, Morgan started talking. "You know Lisa's been keeping an eye out for you, right? Ever since that day at the conservatory."

I nodded. "Sure, but why . . ."

"Because I . . . uh, we owe you one, obviously. Who's been teaching you about magic?"

"What's that got to do with anything?"

"Principle of reciprocation. It's a bit like the principle of sympathy, but at a larger scale. When one practitioner owes another a debt that involves magic, it can create an imbalance in the debtor's harmonic resonance."

I blinked at her rather stupidly—even by my own estimation. "Say what now?"

Morgan's lips pinched tightly together, but then she took a deep breath. "You saved my life in a magical situation when you didn't have to and when we didn't have any other form of connection. That means my magic is going to be out of balance until I repay the debt and I'd prefer to manage it sooner rather than later."

"But you saved my life right back by blowing that delver bolt off course," I protested.

Morgan shook her head. "Doesn't count because it was part of the initial event. That was just me helping you to save all of us."

"Are you sure?"

"Very. I can still *feel* that the forces are out of balance. I'd hoped busting you loose from the delvers would put us back to even, but by the time we got here, all there was to find was an empty cell and a lot of burned badger hair. We can still even things a little by leading you out, but that's hardly enough to balance the scales." She sounded positively grumpy about it.

"How did you even know we were in trouble or where to find us?" Dave asked over his shoulder.

Again, Morgan looked annoyed. "When the two of you didn't come back out of Dave's basement in a reasonable amount of time, Lisa slipped in through the window you left open and sniffed around. Your trail went into the storeroom, but it didn't come back out. That was weird enough to make her check with me."

"To say nothing of the giant hole in the floor," Dave added.

"What hole?" Morgan sounded genuinely confused. "All there was in the storeroom was a pair of crumpled jeans and the cleanest basement floor I've ever seen."

I was momentarily startled, but then I remembered what delvers could do with stone, and realized that might hold true for concrete, too. "Was there any red paint on the floor? Or wax?"

Morgan shook her head. "No, nothing. It pretty much looked like someone had poured fresh concrete in that one room."

"That still doesn't explain how you knew where to look for us," I said as we turned into a bigger tunnel, moving back along the track Dave and I had followed.

There was a pause, and I noticed Morgan's jaw briefly tense before she shook her head and said rather acidly, "We didn't know for sure till we got down here, but barring your vanishing completely, delvers seemed the obvious answer."

Dave chuckled but didn't say anything. In response, I glared at the back of his head. I'm sure it hurt him deeply.

"Well, yes, but there are lots of places the delvers could have parked us, aren't there?"

Morgan sighed. "Kalvan?"

"Yes?"

"I'm going to explain this with one word because it's clear you need things explained simply. Now, your current behavior suggests you might not be aware of it, but there's this thing called 'magic' and it involves lots of secrets that practitioners only share with their students or closest friends."

Ouch! I could feel myself turning bright red. "I . . . uh, but—"

She held up a hand. "Magic. Period. Full stop. That's how we found you. Nothing more nor less and it's all you get. Magic. Magic. Magic."

14

Crashing and Burning

MORGAN IGNORED EVERY other thing I said till we reached the surface, which wasn't all that far, fortunately—Lisa led us along a couple more passages and up a spiral stair that ended in an old hollow oak with a door hidden in its trunk. The stair was so narrow, we had to go single file. We emerged in a wooded area where it was pitch dark, though I could make out a line of streetlights in the distance.

"Where are we?" I asked. "And what time is it?"

"Close to three a.m. and the Highland golf course," replied Morgan.

Dave groaned. "That's like two miles from my place and this ground is *cold!*"

I remembered his newfound magic had left him with possibly permanent bare feet and winced at the thought of him having to walk any distance. I could *probably* conjure some heat to keep his feet warm without cooking them, but there were a million and one nasty things to step on in any city.

"Yeah, and that's not exactly the warmest dress I've ever seen," said Morgan. "Though, I have to admit, it looks surprisingly good on you. Someday you'll have to tell me why you're wearing it."

"Thanks," Dave replied drily. "But it'll have to wait. It's a long stupid story and I'm freezing and completely wiped. So, as much as I appreciate the rescue and all, if you two don't happen to have a warm car tucked away somewhere, we need to get walking."

Morgan sighed. "Sadly, no. My folks aren't big on fifteen-year-olds with no license borrowing the car, even if I am only a week away from taking my test and legal. We're going to have to hoof it, too."

Lisa, still in coyote shape, yipped once, short and sharp.

"Or paw it, as the case may be."

Lisa yipped again.

I thought I saw Morgan nod. "That's true. As Lisa just reminded me, it's late and we've got a long way to go. I wish we could stay and talk this all out, but if my mom happens to notice I snuck out, I'll be grounded for life. We'd better continue this at some later time. Good-bye, Dave, Kalvan."

I was still trying to figure out how to handle the older girl, especially given the way Lisa had warned me about her. "Morgan . . ."

"What is it, Monroe?"

"Thank you, and . . ." But I couldn't think of what I should say, and finally went with, "just, thanks. Good-bye."

It took Dave and me more than an hour to walk the two miles since we were both utterly exhausted and we kept having to stop so I could use my magic to warm him up. It wasn't a big or dangerous magic and Sparx could have done it in two seconds, but Sparx was who knows where, and managing it without starting Dave on fire took way more out of me than it should have. I was practically seeing double by the time we reached his block. Dave hoped to sneak in, but as soon as we came around the garage, we see could every light in the house was on.

"I'm so dead." Dave looked like he was going to puke. "I'm not even sure what day it is or how long we've been gone."

"Sunday morning, maybe, and about a day and a half?" I shrugged. "That's just a guess given how much time I was out of it. I'm sorry. Do you want me to help you sort it out?" I dreaded the idea, but I couldn't leave him hanging.

"Not your fight, man. You're better off grabbing your bike and sneaking off into the night."

I nodded, though what I wanted more than anything was simply to fall down and sleep for forty hours.

The ride home was surreal, filled with weird lights and long seconds of blank space in which I had no memory of making a familiar turn. Late in the trip I thought I spotted the crowned beggar, who might or might not be Oscar, peering at me out of a sewer grate. But when I stopped and went back to look for him, there was nothing there, not even the grate itself. Since I also saw what I could have sworn was an enormous marble birdbath in the middle of the bike lane at one point, I decided I wasn't a reliable witness.

I woke from bizarre dreams, in which I was a light-rail train intent on eating the ticket machines at each station I passed, into an even more bizarre reality. As I started to stretch, my bed and blankets shifted under and around me with a series of metallic clinks.

Clinks?

". . . the heck?" I blinked my eyes open.

My first thought was that the room had somehow rotated around my bed. I could see the ceiling of my bedroom with the gaming posters I'd put up there, but they were all 180 degrees from where they ought to be. I was still trying to sort that out when I noticed the coins. When I tried to sit up and figure out why everything looked so wrong, the clinking became a steady metallic cascade, and I realized I was almost entirely submerged in gold dollar coins—thousands of them. Only my eyes and nose broke the surface, rather like an alligator waiting for passing prey.

As I forced the rest of my head up and out of the giant pile of coins, I realized why all my posters looked out of place. I was at the wrong end of my bedroom. The coins were in my own bedroom closet . . . well, under it, really. Judging by the jagged edges of the oak flooring, either the floor in the closet had collapsed from the weight or, as looked more likely, something with big claws had dug right through the hardwood to expose the concrete floor of the crawlspace beneath.

In either case, the concrete was a much better bet for supporting such an enormous pile of metal. When I got one arm free, I realized that while the coins were cold to the touch, *I* felt as warm and well slept as if I'd spent the night under a down comforter. In fact, I'd rarely felt better on first waking or more inclined to simply roll over and drowse the morning away, which was hella weird given the coin bed.

Still, it was Monday, which meant school, and I started reluctantly moving in that direction. It took several seconds and some real effort to flail free of the pile. In the process, I realized that the me who had climbed *into* that pile hadn't bothered with pajamas—or even underwear—which was quite embarrassing. It also made the climb up into my bedroom a bit of a challenge, as I had to take extra care not to catch anything delicate on the jagged flooring.

The complete lack of smartass commentary on the process reminded me rather forcefully that my faithful fire hare was off I knew not where. Which triggered that splinterlike tugging at my heart again. This time it pointed off to the right. If I was reading the feeling properly, he was a good bit closer than he had been the last time I checked, but still a long way off.

With a sigh, I pulled on my robe and started toward the bathroom, only to come to a sudden stop when I glanced at my alarm clock. Someone or something had reduced the hated thing to splintered wreckage, which made me smile. It was an impulse I'd had to suppress on numerous occasions. *So, what time was it?* I glanced at the window where the thick curtains glowed with bright sunlight. With a sinking feeling, I realized I'd probably missed my school bus. Possibly by a lot. Someone who woke up easier might have figured it out faster, but mornings are soooooo not my skill set.

That's when I normally would have panicked about getting to school late, but somehow I couldn't find it in me to care. I had a million and one serious problems, starting with what to do about my mother. By comparison, missing a few classes hardly registered. So, instead of throwing on clothes in a hurried rush and racing out the door, I headed for the bathroom and took a leisurely shower. The next stop was the kitchen where I discovered it was a bit past nine. As I made myself a sandwich and settled in to eat it, I had one of those realizations that is simultaneously wonderful and terrible:

There was no one in the house who was going to make me go to school if I didn't want to.

My mother loved me but she was in no shape to take responsibility for herself, much less for me. My dead aunt had a very different set of priorities from the living. Sparx, once he got home, was, well—when you came right down to it—a magic rabbit. Eventually, if I stopped going to classes there would be consequences, possibly pretty severe ones if Child Protective Services ever figured out the condition my mom was in. But, on a day-to-day basis, the only person who could or would make me go to school was me.

No one would punish me if I took my sandwich and watched movies all day. I wouldn't have to deal with a single one of the things that were stressing me out or confusing me. I could do it for a day. Or a week. Or even more. Part of me wanted to let go of it all. Oh yes. I don't think I'd have been human if it hadn't tempted me.

I might even have done it if it was only me I had to take care of. But, my mother. If I didn't look out for her, there was no one else who would. Not in the long term. My dead aunt was a stopgap. She said so herself—that she couldn't resist the pull of the grave forever. If I failed my mother, that was it. All the responsibility for my little family was on my shoulders, and in that moment I could feel it settling like a wooden yoke.

It wasn't fair. It wasn't fun. It wasn't just. It just *was*. And I would have to deal with it. It was that or let the world break me as it had broken her. So, instead of settling in front of the TV and grabbing a bit of blessed oblivion, I straightened my shoulders under that terrible, invisible weight and I got ready for school.

Once I got my bike out of the garage, some of my worries shifted to Dave and what might have happened once he got home. The sooner I found out how he was doing, the better. Maybe we could sneak in a quick chat during our joint math class.

I went straight to Evelyn's room to check in as soon as I got to school. She smiled when she saw me. "Ah, excellent. That's one theory shot."

"Huh?" I had no idea what she was talking about.

"Why, the two Musketeers, of course. I don't suppose you happen to know where your comrade-at-arms is this morning?"

"My who now?"

"David Howard Harris? About so tall? Charming smile? Quite a decent young actor? Often seen accompanying his boon companion, the somewhat belated Kalvan Monroe?" And that was my drama teacher to a T.

"Oh, Dave hasn't come in yet?" I figured I had a pretty good idea why not, but that wasn't my story to tell

"I see the light has dawned like Juliet at the balcony window. No, Dave has not come in yet. Nor have he or his mother called. Given that was also the case with you till some short moments ago, I had thought the two of you might have sorted out whatever argument you were having and headed off on another of your extracurricular jaunts to cement the renewed friendship. Since that's apparently not the case, I shall have to give you a very stern look and a different lecture about getting to school on time than the one I had prepared in case of a joint venture."

"I'm sorry, Evelyn. My alarm clock gave out on me today, and I didn't wake up till just a little while ago." All true, if not for the implied reasons. "Then, my mom wasn't around to drive me, so I had to bike." Truish, but not so much because she was *physically* absent, more like she was spending half her time in the eighth dimension. "I'll try not to let it happen again." Very, very true. I never wanted to wake up like that again. "Is it okay if I head for class now, Evelyn? I'm late already, and I'd hate to miss any more of the lesson than I already have." Half truth. I *was* late to my pre-algebra class, but I would have loved to skip the whole thing.

Evelyn raised her eyebrows and looked skeptically at me over the tops of her reading glasses. "Of course, be off with you. I know how *very* much you love your math."

Okay, so maybe I laid it on a little too thick. Whatever the case, I simply nodded and ducked out the door before she changed her mind, mentally noting that I needed to give Dave a call as soon as I possibly could. I made it halfway across the building and down one flight of stairs on the way to class before I caught it between the eyes. *It* being a blunt-nosed paper airplane that hit with surprising force before falling directly into my open right hand.

". . . the heck?" I looked down and saw the plane had two words scrawled on its wings: *OPEN ME*.

Unfolding the plane revealed a brief note written in green ink with a big looping hand. As soon as I saw the signature, I ducked back into the stairwell and down to the basement. There was a narrow space between the base of the stairs and the big metal grid-work gates that led to the cafeteria. At this time of day, the gates were closed, which was perfect, as no one else was likely to be there. Not when there were so many better places to hide out if you were skipping classes.

> *Kalvan,*
> *I have some information for you in regards to that*
> *drawing you showed me. Can you meet me at lunchtime*

so we can discuss it? Off grounds would be best. Y/N
Circle one and fold the airplane back up.

Morgan Shears

I quickly dug a pen out of my bag and circled Y. No sooner had I refolded the plane than a gust of wind brushed across my hand, lifting the airplane up and away. Gliding just below the ceiling, it flittered up the stairs and away. It was such a cool thing to watch, I was half tempted to follow it, but I suspected trailing it back to Morgan would only annoy her.

When I got to my math room, I opened the door as quietly and narrowly as I could, sidestepping my way through in the hopes of avoiding notice. Much to my relief, our teacher, Scott, was working a problem at the board, and he didn't immediately see me. In fact, the only person who saw me slip in was a younger girl—Yvette, or something like that.

I didn't know much about her except she was super smart and five kinds of teacher's pet, but I touched my finger to my lips in a "shh" gesture and then put my palms together and mouthed "please." She nodded, smiling shyly, and I started to ease the door closed. At which point, another paper airplane skipped off the top of my head and a table before crashing to the floor in the middle of my classroom.

Before I could do anything about it, Josh Reiner, who was sitting in the chair closest to the crash, leaned down and scooped up the plane. The older boy might be two grades ahead of me, but he liked math even less than I did, which is how we ended up in the same class. Given his connection with the Rusalka and how much he cheerfully hated my guts, I couldn't think of a worse person to read any note from Morgan. As he started to unfold the plane, I swore silently.

Then several things happened more or less all at once. The first was Scott turning toward the door, his attention apparently drawn by the white flash of the paper airplane. The second was Josh letting out a sudden yelp and tipping over backward in his chair because of the third—the plane vanishing in a sudden ball of bright flames.

I was still trying to figure out how to react when Josh bounced to his feet and came straight at me with his hands balled into tight fists and a furious expression twisting his features.

15

A Storm in the Lull

"THAT'S IT, MONROE!" Josh lunged across the distance between us, catching me by the front of my shirt and lifting me off my feet.

I should have been scared. Instead, I felt a deep rage uncoil in my gut like scaly death and the world suddenly acquired extra colors and depth. My mouth opened and I drew a deep breath, only to clamp my jaws shut an instant later as I realized I had been about to pour flames down on the older boy. I swallowed them back with an effort that felt like swallowing hot coals. Rather to my surprise, an alarmed look slid across Josh's features and he carefully set me on my feet.

Letting go of my shirt, he hissed, "Later."

I stepped back, raising my open hands between us. "Whoa there, big guy!" I spoke loudly but also gently, forcing myself to calm as the extra colors slowly leaked out of my world. "We're cool. I had nothing to do with *whatever* that was. It looked like . . . maybe a paper airplane?"

My main reason for playing sweet and friendly when I kind of *wanted* to breathe flames all over Josh's face was that Scott had pretty much teleported across the room from his place at the board. After he stomped the smoking ashes of the plane out, the teacher moved to stand immediately behind Josh.

"Is that so, Kalvan?" Scott leaned forward and gave me a very hard look. "Because that'd be a mighty big coincidence."

I put on my best confused look—I tend to overdo it when I go for innocent. "It's true, I swear. I was trying to sneak in without getting noticed when that thing bounced off my head." I didn't go for silvertongue because I didn't know what Josh might be able to do to counter it, and that could go badly wrong. "I was still trying to sort out what it was and why when it went all *FWOOSH!* And then Josh was in my face."

Scott turned to the room at large. "Did anybody else see what happened?"

I held my breath as something really ugly hit me. An exploding paper airplane was the kind of dangerous stunt that could get a person in epic levels of trouble even at the Free School. The last thing in the world I wanted was to have the school call my mom in for a parent-teacher conference about something that would sound to her like fire magic. There was no telling how she'd handle it in her current state.

Then Yvette put her hand up. "I did, Scott. Well, a lot of it anyway. I happened to notice the door opening when Kalvan came in. I didn't see who threw the paper airplane because it came in from the hall, but it actually clipped Kalvan in the head before Josh picked it up."

Scott looked skeptical and for a couple of long seconds I expected him to send me down to the principal, but he finally nodded. "All right. Kalvan, I'll let that go for the moment. It was a really dangerous stunt on somebody's part, but if the plane's not your fault, I don't see why you should get roasted for it."

Relief washed over me. "Thank you, Scott."

His expression remained stern. "We still need to have a talk about your tardiness. But that can wait until after class. I'll also need you to try to remember anyone you might have seen in the hall on your way in. Even if it's not your fault, Aaron is going to want to know everything about this incident."

Next, he turned to Josh. "Let's see your fingers."

"Huh?" The boy looked confused.

"I need to know how badly that thing burned you."

"Oh, I'm all right. Really. I dropped it pretty quick." But Scott turned the same hard look he'd used with me on Josh, who quickly extended his hands. "See?"

I don't know what *Scott* saw beyond the lack of obvious burns, but I noticed traces of Josh's own bitter-water magic all over his skin. I couldn't tell whether it was from healing himself or some sort of protective charm that had prevented the burns in the first place—and even a couple of months ago I'd have missed the signs completely—but the magic was there, as plain to my eyes as if he'd circled the marks in ink.

Finally, Scott nodded. "All right, Josh. That's good. I'll want you to tell Aaron what you saw as well, but I'm not going to ding you for going after Kalvan. You definitely shouldn't have done it, but I know the fire must have scared you, and you realized it was the wrong move before you went too far. So, you're clear, too. Now, in the ten minutes we have left of the hour, I'm going to try to finish up this problem."

I sat down at the only open chair—next to Josh—and pretended to pay attention. At least until Josh slid a scrap of paper in front of me. It was a quick sketch showing a pair of eyes and a nose. Only, there was a wisp of smoke trailing from one nostril, and the eyes had a pair of interlocking spirals where the irises ought to have been. I don't know how he managed it with only a pencil and white paper, but the spirals showed very clearly as fire and stone. Underneath, he'd written "dragon's eyes" and I suddenly knew both why the world had taken on added depth with my rage and why Josh had seemed so alarmed. I soooo didn't need this on top of everything else.

At the end of class Scott waved for me and Josh to follow him out of the room. Which meant that instead of sneaking off to find Morgan as planned, I spent half the next period in the principal's office pretending I didn't know anything about the paper airplane. At Scott's insistence, I spent the other half writing a brief statement acknowledging my tardiness, promising to do better, and outlining specific steps I would take toward that goal, like replacing my alarm clock. It was a typically Free School kind of punishment that had to be taken home and countersigned by my mother and then returned the next day. Whee!

That was followed by my drama class, which was a lot less fun than usual with Dave missing. Later, Morgan and Lisa both ignored me as we passed in the hall on the way to our brief afternoon advisory meetings, but when I got out to my bike at the end of the day I found a paper airplane wedged in the spokes. *Wednesday, then? Y/N* I circled Y and sent it on its way. When I was about halfway home another plane dove into the open collar of my jacket. *Outside Doughboy, Wednesday lunchtime, don't be late. M.*

As I parked my bike, I tried to decide if there was any point in talking to my mom about the note for Scott, or if I should jump straight to seeing if my aunt Noelle could do my mom's signature as well as her voice. But I was greeted by two surprises when I went in the back door. The first was Sparx, looking somewhat the worse for wear, but basically himself. I immediately knelt on the floor to give him a hug.

"Man, am I glad to see you in one piece. Where did you end up?"

"Indonesia. I'd have been here sooner but I can't cross broad stretches of wild water on my own, and it took a fair bit of island hopping for me to get someplace where I could catch a trans-Pacific flight. I just got in about five minutes ago. Speaking of which, your bedroom closet is looking a bit . . . broken."

"Oh yeah, the coins. I—"

Before I could try to explain that I had no idea how it happened or where the coins came from, I got my second surprise of the afternoon when I heard my mother call, "Kalvan?"

"Hello?" I responded warily.

"Hi, Kalvan." My mother stuck her head out of the kitchen. She looked a little pale, but other than that, fine. Her hair was clean and brushed and she was wearing jeans and a sweater. "How was school?"

"Okay, I guess . . ." I felt . . . winded. Like I couldn't get enough air to breathe or even think straight.

"I'm making lasagna. It should be ready to eat any minute. Go wash up and I'll dish out a plateful for you."

I dropped my backpack in the middle of the hall, went into the bathroom with Sparx at my heels, and latched the door. For several minutes, I busied myself with washing my hands and face.

"Are you all right?" asked Sparx.

"Huh?" It wasn't until then, as I glanced in the mirror while drying myself off, that I realized I was crying. "Oh. It's fine. I'm fine." But the towel began to smolder in my hands.

"You don't look anything like fine. In fact, you look three-quarters of the way to a complete flip-out."

The towel burst into sudden flame, burning away completely in an instant, and I could feel the tears still running down my cheeks. "Okay, maybe I'm not fine." I sat down on the toilet and tried to catch my breath—it felt like I'd just run a brutal sprint or someone was squeezing my lungs. "It's Mom."

"What's Mom?" asked Sparx.

"You saw!" I half shouted, though I couldn't understand why I was so upset. "She made me dinner, and now she's acting all normal!"

Sparx nodded sagely. "That *would* explain it."

"Explain what? Shouldn't I be happy?"

He sighed and looked at me with deep sympathy. "Why?"

I blinked at that. "Uh, because she's acting like herself."

"For how long? Will it last through dinner? Till tomorrow? A week?"

"I don't know."

"Exactly." Sparx nodded. "You know it won't last, and you have no idea how long you've got to breathe. It's like life has been hitting you in the face over and over for weeks, and now, suddenly, the beating has stopped. But you know it's not going to stay stopped and you don't know how bad it will be when it starts again. All the lull does is give you time to realize how much it's hurt so far, and how much it's *going* to hurt again later. You don't feel any relief because you know it's not over."

"Oh." That made a lot of sense.

"Worse, the fact it doesn't hurt right this instant lets you compare what not hurting feels like to the pain you've been dealing with and that you know you'll be dealing with again. It makes you realize exactly how much you've been through already."

"So, what do I do?"

Sparx sighed. "I don't know. If you've got it in you, you could try to treasure this moment of peace and make the most of it. But no one would blame you if you can't. I don't think I could do it, and I've had a lot more years to build perspective."

I glanced at the locked door. "I more than half want to pretend I'm sick and stay in here for the rest of the night."

"I can fetch you some snacks if you decide to go with that."

"You wouldn't judge me?" I asked.

"No. Not on this. Not ever. The main thing you need to do right now is survive. If you think hiding out is what's best for you, I'll support you one hundred percent."

"Thanks, Sparx. That helps . . . a lot."

I closed my eyes and tried to force myself to breathe easier, but I kept picturing my mother in the kitchen waiting for me to come to dinner. Waiting and waiting and waiting, and I imagined how that would make *her* feel. It hurt my heart, and, finally, I shook my head and stood up, quietly unlocking the bathroom door.

"You going out there?" I could hear Sparx's concern for me in his voice.

"I have to. If she had diabetes or cancer, I wouldn't lock myself in the bathroom and refuse to deal with her while she was fighting it off. What she has isn't any less of a disease because it's affecting her mind instead of her body."

"You're sure?"

I smiled then, though it hurt to do so. "You talked me into it."

"Huh?"

"You pointed out that it's only a lull and that it's almost certainly going to start again. That it could actually get worse."

The hare looked even more confused, and it was kind of nice to be ahead of him for a change. "I'm not following you."

"This might be the last chance I get to spend time with my *real* mother, the woman she is when she's not crazy. In two hours she might be gone forever, or she might get so bad *I* have to call Child Protective Services. If that happens, if I do lose her forever, I'd never forgive myself for missing this moment right now."

Sparx nodded. "You know what, kid?"

"What?"

"I didn't think I'd ever say this about any human, but you're turning out to be an exceptionally fine Accursed Master."

"Thank you, Sparx, I appreciate it."

Then I opened the door and went out to have dinner with my mom. And, for an hour or so, it was almost like living in a normal home. We chatted about school and my grades and nothing at all. I even admitted to the trouble I'd gotten into with my math teacher and got both a short lecture and my note signed. I won't go into the details of the evening. Not because they're boring, though they are, but simply because they're mine and precious. For one brief meal, I got to be a kid again, or almost, anyway—you can never unknow things aren't really all right, or that they could end at any moment, but you can pretend. And, sometimes, pretending is the best deal you're going to get.

But like every precious thing, it had to end, and it did, with Mom giving me a kiss on the cheek and shooing me off to do homework. I wanted to prolong the moment, to make that window of relative peace and sanity last forever, but I knew that wouldn't—couldn't—happen. So, I smiled, gave her a hug, and went to do my homework, knowing there were so many worse ways dinner could have ended.

As soon as I'd closed the door to my room, Sparx cleared his throat and pointed at the hole in my closet floor. "What's up with that?"

I shrugged. "No idea, honestly. It was like that when I woke up." I quickly explained how my morning had started with me playing alligator in a sea of coins.

He hopped over and peered down at the pile. "That's not good."

"Oh, and there's this." I handed him the drawing Josh had done and told him about my math class. "Any idea what I should do about it?"

"Nope. I don't do dragons or windows."

"What?"

"Sorry, it sounded funnier in my head. I've got nothing. I guess I'll add it to the pile of mysteries beside the gigantic spell of doom in the basement."

"Oh, hey, speaking of which, Morgan might have something for me there. I'm supposed to meet her at lunchtime Wednesday to find out what she knows."

"How would Morgan know anything about that spell?" Sparx asked, his voice stern.

"Oh yeah, I might have forgotten to mention I showed her and Lisa my sketch of the spell and asked them if they knew anything about that sort of magic."

"You what?!? How do you even know you can trust them?"

"Morgan said she owes me because of the . . . what was it? Oh yeah, the principle of reciprocation."

"She might actually have a point there." Sparx sounded surprised.

"Besides, after Josh listened in when I told Tanya about it and then stole the first sketch of that spell off me for the Rusalka, I figured the cat was out of the bag big-time."

Sparx put his face in his paws. "You are going to be the death of me, child."

"What? *You* told the selkies about it."

"*Carefully*, with much hemming and hawing and obscuring of facts and places." He sighed. "I suppose it's too late to do anything about it now but hope that whatever forces of Luck or Fate have picked you out as their special project tilt this one for us instead of against." He gave me his best grumpy-teacher look. "Is there anything else you've done without telling me that I ought to know about?"

"Did I mention I turned into a dragon again right after you left for Indonesia?"

"NO YOU DID NOT! ARRRRRRRRRRGH!" His face went back into his paws.

I chuckled and bent in close. "Breathe. In. Out. In. Out. Again."

He did that for several long minutes, before finally looking up at me. "Tell me all of it. Every single thing that you have done involving magic since your aunt arrived. I don't care if I was there or not. Just talk."

So, I did. Then, while Sparx wandered off to, quote, *"Think dark thoughts about Accursed Masters and catch up on my screaming,"* unquote, I got my homework done. Sparx hadn't yet returned when I finished, so I went out to the kitchen. My mom had gone upstairs, which was just as well given the phone call I needed to make. Dave's cell went straight to voicemail and I didn't bother to leave a message. Chances were it was still somewhere in the delver tunnels beneath his house. Next, I tried the house phone.

"Hello, is this Kalvan?" I recognized Dave's mom's voice when she picked up. She did not sound pleased.

"Hello, Veronica." Most Free School parents preferred to be called by their first names, the same as our teachers. "Yes, it's me, Kalvan. I'm calling to see how—"

She cut me off. "He's in pretty rough shape, actually, and I blame you for getting him into this mess!"

"I . . . I'm sorry." That was hard to argue with and it gutted me. "I . . . it's just he wasn't in school today and I was hoping to—"

"I don't want to hear it, Kalvan! If I'm understanding the story correctly, you got him into all of this awfulness to start with. I'm keeping him at home for a few days while we . . . sort things out. In the future, I'll thank you to stay away from my son. That's if I let him go back to Free at all." Then she hung up.

The words *if I let him go back to Free at all* rang in my ears as I put the phone down. I crawled into bed after that and spent a long time staring at the ceiling and wishing Sparx would come back from wherever he'd gone this time. Having him curled up next to me is very reassuring. Eventually—sometime well after midnight— I felt him drop into his usual spot and some of my worries eased.

"Goodnight, Sparx."

"Goodnight, Kalvan."

My dreams were filled with rivers of gold and the taste of crunching bones. Somewhere, down deep, I knew that should bother me, that I should fight against it, but I didn't know how.

This time, the tinkling of the coins when I woke rang in my ears like the sweetest music. For several long blinks I wanted nothing more than simply to go back to sleep. But then I thought about what Dave's mom had said. My stomach filled with acid and I was no longer sleepy. I figured I might as well get moving and started to dig myself free of the giant heap of coins. I had neglected my pajamas again, and I should have been embarrassed, but somehow the feeling of the coins sliding against my skin made me forget any possible shame.

About halfway through the process, I noticed Sparx sitting on the edge of the broken floor above with a rather bemused look on his face. "What's up, bunny boy, you look like someone poured ketchup on your oatmeal."

"I'm trying to figure out when and how you moved from your bed to the coin pile without waking me. I didn't know it had happened until I heard the clinking as you woke a few seconds ago, and I don't like that at all."

I didn't know what to say, so I shrugged and got on with getting up. A glance at the window showed nothing but darkness, which meant it was early. With a sigh, I put on my robe and stomped off to the bathroom, though I half wondered if there was any point in getting dressed for the thirty-foot walk. I hadn't seen my aunt in the morning for a while—she was probably off doing dead-people stuff, whatever that might be. And if past experience was any guide, my mom was staring at the ceiling or muttering to the houseplants.

After showering and having a couple toaster waffles, I was still almost an hour ahead of the bus's arrival. Which was okay. Biking would be cold, but it would also keep me from having to deal with people.

16

Muddy Waters

THE ONLY PERSON around when I got to Free was the custodian who waved cheerily at me as I went upstairs to the big theater and my favorite chair under the stage. There, with Sparx curled on my chest, I fell asleep again.

"Kalvan, *hsst*, wake up." I blearily blinked my eyes open and found Dave crouched beside me. He was wearing some kind of long, elaborately patterned robe-thing that pooled around his feet, while his right arm was tucked into a sling that concealed his alien hand.

Sparx hopped down and I twisted in my chair so I could hug Dave. "Oh, hey, man, it's great to see you! After I talked to your mom last night, I really didn't expect you today."

"It was a close-run thing. For a little while there, I didn't think Mom was going to let me come back to Free at all."

"I'm so sorry I got you wrapped up in all this! It was my fault that—"

"Don't!" Dave's voice came out hard and sharp. "This"—he lifted his otherworldly hand free of the sling—"is on me. I wanted magic. Bad. And I got it. Real bad." Now he laughed. "Actually, I'm already starting to get used to it and sort out some of my new powers. I can even get a few things to stay closed for me."

I tugged on the robe. "So, why this?"

"It's part of winning the fight with my mom."

"I think you maybe skipped a step in your explanation there," I said.

"Part of my argument for coming back to Free was that I could wear my dad's old dashikis here and totally not get hassled for it, unlike at a regular school. Mom dug them out for me once she saw the dress and I explained why I was wearing my sister's clothes. I'm pretty sure she'd ultimately be okay if I *wanted* to cross-dress, but she was still seriously relieved the dress was all about wearing something that would stay on."

"What about your feet? It's only April and it still gets cold out there."

He tugged up the hem of the dashiki, exposing a pair of high-tops with the laces knotted about seventeen ways from Sunday. "I have to retie them all the time, but they're mostly staying on."

"And the sling?"

"Gotta keep the hand out of sight until I can figure out a solution or a good story, and I still can't keep a glove on. Not even by holding it in place with my other hand—the seams unsew themselves when I do that."

Sparx spoke then, "I wonder if we might be able to make an illusion of some sort work. Let me see your hand."

Dave dropped to sit cross-legged on the floor so Sparx could have easier access. The hare started by sniffing along Dave's fingers and thumb before carefully looking at the hand from a number of angles.

"Hmm, tricky. I don't know where you pulled that thing from, but it's a very long way from our plane of existence. It's quite unlike anything I've ever seen."

"Which means what?" asked Dave.

"Which means I don't know. Illusion isn't a primary power of fire, though there are a few exceptions—say, for example, you needed to look like an oasis in the desert. But that wouldn't help here. I know the two of you don't get along with him, but it might be worth talking to the bitter water boy. His Rusalka friend could certainly do it. That's a mighty power of water, and water rules illusion, but I don't think approaching Mississippi is the best idea."

"It certainly wouldn't be my first choice," said Dave. "But I really do need to get this thing covered up."

"What about us?" I asked. "I mean, is your mother cool with me now?"

He shook his head. "Not even a little bit. We're still friends here at school where she can't see us, but I'm not supposed to be hanging around with you at all. That means no phone calls or e-mail until I can talk her down, and absolutely no out-of-school visits. Sorry, man."

I shrugged. "It is what it is. I'll miss hanging out after school, but we'll make it work. By the way, what time is it out there? Am I late for checking in with Evelyn, or early?"

"Early. My mom didn't want to make me take the bus with this on." Dave pulled at the sleeve of his dashiki. "Not the first day back. Not with the way things have been going with the country lately. She brought me in on her way to work. Morning advisory isn't for another forty minutes. But enough about me; what's happening in the Kalvan saga? You know, that whole *delvers are trying to kill you, your mom is getting worse, dead aunt* end of things. I cut you off pretty hard the other day and we really haven't talked since."

"It's complicated." I quickly filled him in on the details he'd missed.

Dave glanced over at Sparx, who nodded and added, "The boy is a lightning rod for weirdness."

I raised an eyebrow at him. "Said the weirdness his ownself."

Dave laughed. "He's got you there."

"Actually, to be fair," I said, "Sparx is only about the tenth strangest thing in my life at this point." I put the faintest spin of sil-vertongue into my words—just enough to really sound sincere. "I told you about the lizard people, right?"

"Lizard people?" Dave's jaw dropped and Sparx gave me a hard look.

"Yeah, they wanted to make me their thane, but I couldn't han-dle the diet."

"The diet?"

"You know, live mice, frogs, all that."

"I . . ." Dave blinked and shook his head, then absently rubbed one ear with his alien hand. It was like flipping a switch. His eyes narrowed sharply and his expression went skeptical. "Wait, you're pulling my leg now. That was silvertongue!"

"Maybe a little."

"Jerk."

I laughed and he punched my shoulder. Then he laughed, too. It felt good to have my best friend back and I wanted nothing more than to take the morning off and hang out, but the first bell would be ringing any moment and that meant I had to get moving if I didn't want to get in real trouble.

"Look, after check-in I've got to drop this note off with Scott." I waved it in the air. "Josh'll have to stop in there, too. I'm not his favorite person, especially right now, but do you want me to ask him about an illusion for your hand?"

"I don't know, Kalvan. What if he wants to take me to the Rusalka? She kind of scares me."

"That's because you're sane and have a reasonable sense of self-preservation," said Sparx. "Unlike the Bad Idea Kid here."

"Come on, Sparx. I know Mississippi can be bad news, but she's helped us in the past. Dave can't wear that sling forever, and a glove's no real solution. The sooner he gets it fixed, the better. Besides, Josh might be able to handle it himself."

Sparx rolled his eyes, but he finally nodded.

Dave did as well. "All right." But he looked dubious.

Dave reached out with his six-fingered hand and touched the door marked EMERGENCY EXIT. It swung silently open—a particularly useful piece of magic, that. "I can't believe Josh offered to take us to Mississippi so soon."

"I was a little surprised myself."

More than a little, but Josh had just shrugged when I brought up the idea of illusions and said, "I can't handle it, but She wanted to see you anyway and it's your funeral." I didn't share that part with Dave, only, "Meet me at the bridge, lunch hour."

With Dave along, we took a more cautious route down to the river. Under normal circumstances, he draws three times as much of the wrong sort of official attention as I do simply by being black. With his colorful robes on top of that, we wanted to be super careful not to get stopped. That meant staying on low-traffic side streets, but out of alleys and other shortcuts that might make us look suspicious. It took half again as long as it would have taken me alone.

Josh was waiting on the other side of the railroad bridge we used to talk to the Rusalka back in the deeps of winter. When we reached the far shore, he ducked between two bushes and silently led the way to a small muddy flat masked by trees. There was still a lot of snowmelt coming down from up north, and the river was high and angry—a snarl of brown ripples and whorls ready to devour anyone who came too close.

"I can't believe I let the two of you talk me into this. I don't like the look of it," said Sparx. "Not even a little bit. Perhaps we should come back another time."

"She already knows you're here," replied Josh. "If you leave now, She might take it as an insult. Your choice, but I'm staying."

"Point taken, but I think I *will* make myself as unobtrusive as possible. Water does not love fire." Sparx slid into the depths of my pack.

"You ready?" asked Josh.

I wasn't, but I nodded anyway and he picked up a big chunk of rock, tossing it into the madly swirling waters. For several long seconds nothing happened. Then, just when I was beginning to think we weren't going to see Her, a surge of water rolled up the shore, drenching us to mid-calf and nearly pulling us into the flood. Josh's face went deathly white and he fought his way to the edge of the flat where he grabbed on to a small tree.

"She's wild today!" he yelled as Dave and I followed his example. "Dangerous because of the flooding. I was wrong. We shouldn't have come."

But it was already far too late to change our minds. As the wave slid back into the main body of the Mississippi, there was a great splash and a broad brown waterspout rose in its wake, rising a good fifteen feet above the surface of the river. For a long moment, it hung there, angry and elemental, like some huge snake preparing to strike. Then, slowly, it began to change—taking on the shape of a woman.

That much was similar to my previous meetings with the Rusalka, or Mississippi, as She was more properly called—though neither human-given name accurately represented the language of the waters, according to Sparx. What was very, very different this time was the scale of Her. Her arms were as big as tree trunks and Her hands the size of basketballs.

Her features were rougher as well. In the past, She had reminded me of some beautiful queen of faerie, elegant and cold, with skin like a clear window into deep waters. This time, She was an angry giant, as muddy and opaque as the river itself—more ogress than princess. White rills rippled wickedly across Her surface, suggesting hidden snarls and deadly undercurrents. Her fingers bore long, cruel talons, and a pair of tusks jutted from Her lower jaw.

"What do you want?" Her voice held the roughness of floodwaters clawing at a riverbank.

What I *wanted* was to get as far from Mississippi as I could as quickly as possible. What I was going to get, on the other hand . . .

"Or have you only come to waste my time?"

She glared directly at me and I realized the only thing in common between this form and Her earlier appearances was the eyes—those terrible, drowning eyes. I'd intended to ask her about the spell in my basement as well as Dave's stuff, but there was such an obvious threat in the question I decided to keep it short and simple. My problems would have to wait.

I hurried to answer, running my words together in my rush. "No-not-at-all! We-wanted-that-is-Dave-wanted-to-ask-your-advice! This-is-Dave-go!"

The Rusalka turned Her massive head, focusing an angry glare on Dave, who practically wilted. Finally, with an obvious effort of will, he lifted his alien hand out of its concealing sling. "I came about this." His voice sounded surprisingly calm.

A tiny flash of surprise rippled across the face of the great elemental, and She bent to look more closely at Dave, whose grip on his small tree tightened. "Interesting, if not unprecedented. Why should it matter to me?"

"I . . . I don't know," said Dave. "I was hoping you might know some way I could make it look like a normal hand."

"I know many ways to do such a thing. I see no profit in any of them."

Dave nodded, looking resigned now as well as frightened. "I'm deeply sorry we bothered you."

She dismissed him with a glance and turned back to me. "Why did you bring him here on such a foolish errand?"

I shrugged. "You've helped me in the past."

"Only because your needs flowed between the same banks as mine for a time. That time has ended, child of stone."

"I don't think—"

Her voice cut across mine with a roar. "Do not believe for an instant I am a fool, boy. I know what you are by the mark on your forehead, Summer's Prince. And I know what you wish to do. My disciple showed me the spell you would master—a tool fit only for the hand of a Season King. That alone would give me reason to doubt you. Add in that you are the law-son of the last Winter King— even if you opposed him for a time—and that you now share in his powers . . ." She shook Her head. "I regret the help I gave you, son of stone and Winter."

"I am not the Winter King's son!" I was terrified but I flat refused to be tied to Oscar. I stepped away from my tree and walked forward to glare up at the Rusalka. "I never was. Not in any way. I was only ever a means to an end for him."

"You may not wish to own him. But in all the ways that matter most, you are his bond son and natural successor, and not merely where it comes to the Corona Borealis. I should destroy you now, but for past services I will spare you to seek destruction in your own way. Do not approach me again unasked, if you value your life."

"Gosh, thanks. But if I'm so dangerous to you, or might be in the future, why don't you go ahead and get it over with?" It was a dumb thing to say, but my mouth gets away from me at the most inopportune times.

"Uh, Kalvan, ix-nay with the aunts-tay!" Dave called from behind me.

The towering figure of water bent down so those drowning eyes were inches from my own. "Child, I have given you my main reason for sparing you. But here is a second. I am Mississippi, and you are mortal. Even if it were possible for you to wholly become what your law-father was and hold the Corona Borealis for more than a single season, you are a danger mostly to my peace of mind. That is not a small thing, but it is a fly's bite when measured against the long years of my span. No, I said I would spare you this time for past favors, and I stand by my word."

I had more to say about Oscar, but my sense of self-preservation belatedly kicked in then. "Come on, Dave, let's get out of here."

Mississippi laughed. "Run away, child. It is the wise choice. But, in the end, it will avail you nothing. Reach out your hand to take the Crown and it will destroy you utterly. You have not the years to hold it."

It was only as we started to walk away that I realized Josh had gone already, choosing some earlier moment to make himself scarce. Behind us, I heard the giant form of the Rusalka fall back into the river with a mighty splash. Icy water spattered my head and shoulders, but I didn't look back as we hurried to put distance between us and the river.

Once we'd gotten a few blocks up from the banks, Dave caught my shoulder and pulled me to a halt. "Kalvan, what was that all about with you getting in Her face? You realize you could have gotten us killed, right?"

I sighed. He wasn't wrong. "Yeah, I'm sorry about that. I don't know. My mouth got ahead of my brain."

Sparx poked his head out of my bag. "There's a surprise."

Dave turned his attention to the hare. "You were on the chopping block with the rest of us. Why aren't you madder about this?"

"Because I understand what drives Kalvan in moments like that.

I understand it in my bones. The boy is a child of fire, just as I am, and fire is never temperate. It flares and sparks and reaches too far. Always. Fire will not stop of its own accord. It will burn every ounce of fuel if it is not checked."

"And then?" asked Dave.

Sparx shrugged and his expression held no hint of humor. "And then, fire dies."

Dave looked me square in the eyes. "From the horse's own mouth, my friend. You have got to get yourself under better control."

I didn't have any comeback, so I simply started walking. The rest of the journey passed in uncomfortable silence as I spent more time staring at my feet than looking at Dave, while Sparx retreated to the privacy of my bag.

When we finally got back to Free, we headed for the same fire door we'd used to slip out. With Dave's magic to quietly open the way, it was the best and most protected route. Since we still had a bit of time before the afternoon round of phys-ed classes, we were golden.

Dave used his alien hand to open the door and we both stepped through . . . only to find Tanya waiting for us on the other side with her arms crossed and a very grim look on her face. "Munroe, Harris, my office. Now." Without another word she turned and started walking, and we fell in behind.

"Tanya," I began, but she simply held up a hand in the universal stop gesture.

Once we got to her office, she pointed me at the little darkroom where I had so often gone to practice magic. "Kalvan, you wait in there. I know how good the two of you are at concocting a plausible story when you have time to put your heads together, so I'm dealing with you individually. Go."

I went. As soon as the little airlock door closed behind me, Sparx poked his head out of my bag. "Do you want me to talk to her?" He sounded like he'd much rather pretend not to exist for the moment.

I couldn't blame him. "No. You tried to talk us out of it. This is on me. I'll take the heat.

"As you wish." He disappeared back into the bag with a relieved look.

At which point, time seemed to screech to a halt. I tried pressing my ear to the metal of the door, but all I could hear was a gentle whooshing that told me Tanya was using her powers to prevent being overheard, so I moved away from the door. I didn't want to get caught eavesdropping, especially if it wasn't doing any good. I kept glancing at my watch, but someone had clearly magicked it to move at one tenth speed, and it wasn't until after several hours—or fifteen minutes by my watch—that the door rotated again to reveal Tanya.

"Your turn."

I left my bag behind. As soon as I came out, Dave went through into the darkroom. We didn't get the chance to so much as exchange a meaningful glance, and I had no idea what he'd told Tanya. My mind spun in mad, useless circles as I followed the teacher back to her desk.

I'd never seen her look grimmer as I took the seat across from her, and her first words were a gut punch. "Can you give me one good reason why I shouldn't have you suspended?"

"I . . . uh . . ." *What did she know? How could I spin this so I didn't get in a world of hurt? What if she wanted to talk to my mom?* That last was what decided me on my next words. "No, I can't." If there was ever a time to throw myself on the mercy of the court, this was it. "Not one. I'm incredibly sorry for my behavior, and I hope you won't have me suspended, but I take full responsibility for my actions."

If anything, Tanya's expression became grimmer. "That's a very nice tactic, Kalvan. It sounds like you're sorry and that you understand why you should be sorry, but it's completely empty of content. You're going to have to do much better if you want to get out of this without a suspension, or even being expelled."

At the word *expelled* my heart pretty much bricked itself. "I . . ." *What had Dave told her?* "I . . ." *I couldn't know the answer to my own question and I had to assume he'd told her everything.*

For one brief second I considered trying to shift the blame and throw Dave under the bus. That made me feel even sicker—that I would so much as consider betraying my best friend like that . . . ugh! No. Like I'd said to Sparx, this was on me. I took a deep breath and tried to force my brain to work. This wasn't simply about skipping out of school. I'd done that lots and only gotten in the more routine sorts of trouble for it. No, this was Tanya, which meant it was about the magic. But that wasn't all of it. *Come on, Kalvan, think! Think like an adult! Think . . . oh.*

"Is this because of the Rusalka?"

Tanya's jaw tightened briefly. "Getting warmer."

"I thought she could help Dave hide his new hand. I know it was stupid."

"Nearly fatally so!"

"I . . . maybe, yes. I should—"

"Do you have any idea how dangerous it is simply to go down to the shore of the Mississippi when it's this high? Even without the magical component of the thing, you were on a mud flat on the edge of the most dangerous river in North America. It could so easily have been undermined by the waters without you ever knowing about it. Even without bringing the Rusalka into it you could have gotten yourselves killed and your bodies lost for weeks or forever. Three students could be dead without any of us here at the school or your homes even knowing about it!"

"I'm . . . I didn't think about that." She'd said three students, which meant Dave had told her about Josh, but maybe not Sparx. It also sounded like he'd told her it was all my idea—so, the truth, as much as I might hate to admit it. "You're right. I just wanted to help Dave out, but it was pretty stupid."

"Add in the Rusalka, and I can't imagine what you were thinking! Dave says you actually got lippy with Her. Do you have any idea how . . ." She trailed off abruptly, possibly because of the look on my face, which had to be awful.

It wasn't until that very instant that I recognized—really recognized—the implications of what I'd done. I *could* have gotten us all killed. And this was different than the stuff with the delvers or my uncle. For one, that was mostly *my* life I was risking. For another, it was adversarial. *They* had come at *me*. Yes, I'd had to fight to survive, but I hadn't gone looking for the fight. But this . . . I'd risked Dave's life and, to a lesser extent, Josh's for a bit of cosmetic magic. And it hadn't so much as occurred to me at the time what I was doing.

Tanya nodded. "Yes. I can see it's actually sinking in. Here at Free we give you an enormous amount of room to make choices and to make mistakes, even big, painful mistakes. Failure is one of the most important ways we learn the big lessons. But we have to keep you alive in order for you to do that." And now, for the first time since we'd come through the door, she gave me the ghost of a smile. "That's not always easy with teenagers, but we do try."

"I'm so sorry, Tanya. I was a fool and I take full responsibility for my actions."

"And *this time* I think you mean it. More important, I think you understand it. All right, Kalvan. I'm going to hold the suspension in abeyance for the moment, but it's not off the table."

"Thank you." My heart started to beat again, slowly and stiffly as though it were pumping molasses instead of blood. "Is there anything I can do to make amends?"

"There are several things you're *going* to do as part of acknowledging the mistakes you made today. Once those are done, *and* you have met my expectations well enough to keep suspension from coming back into the mix, then we will begin to talk about amends."

I nodded, but didn't say a word. I deserved this, and I knew that even now I was getting off lightly.

"To start with, I want you to write me a paper explaining exactly what you did wrong, and *why* it was wrong. Once I have that, and I decide it is adequate, we'll discuss what comes next."

"How long should it be?"

"As long as it needs to."

"I deserve that."

"You do. Speaking of which, when you pick up your backpack, tell Sparx I want a few words with him. He should have known better even if you didn't, and he's on my list, too."

"I'll let him know."

"Good." She slid a sheet of paper over to me—another acknowledgment of responsibility form. "There's this as well." She took a deep breath. "Oh, and, Kalvan . . ."

"Yes."

"I know your life is not a normal one. Even more than most of us who have the gift of magic, you are in an unusually dangerous position. I don't expect you never to take risks. I don't even expect you not to take some that will put your life in jeopardy—because those are the cards you've drawn. But that makes it all the more important that you don't take *unnecessary* risks. There are so many things you will have to face that might kill you, it's critical you avoid giving chance any more shots at you than you must."

17

Ashes, Ashes, All Fall Down?

FOR THE SECOND time in as many days, I brought home a note for my mom to sign. This time, she wasn't in the kitchen when I got in. Instead, I found her in her bedroom with all the lights off. She was lying in bed half propped up on the pillows, her eyes wide open and staring at the ceiling. Her window of normality had lasted less than a day.

"Mom?"

Nothing.

"Mom, it's Kalvan."

Still nothing.

"I need you to sign another note for me."

Silence. She was barely even blinking.

"Mom, it's pretty important. I'm in trouble again, and I have to bring this back tomorrow signed."

Finally, with what looked like enormous effort, she turned to look at me. "What?"

"I need you to sign something for me, Mom. I messed up big and Tanya had me write a letter acknowledging my responsibility." I waved the paper at her.

"Oh." She went back to staring at the ceiling.

"MOM! This is important! If I don't get it signed, they might call and . . ." I trailed off as I sickly imagined what would happen if they tried to talk to my mother in this state.

"Let it go, Kalvan." A cool hand landed gently on my shoulder— my dead aunt arriving with her typical eerie silence and a pair of very dark sunglasses. "I can sign it." She took the paper. "I do Genny's signature better than she does."

What I wanted to do was cry and scream and rage at my mother. What I did was nod and follow Noelle out of my mom's room. "Thanks. I probably should have come to you as soon as I saw the way she looked, but she was so much better yesterday and it's hard."

Noelle gave me a long, searching look as she signed the paper. "So, what have you done about it?"

"What?" I couldn't have been more shocked if she'd slapped me.

"I told you that with Oscar and Nix gone the only person who can really help your mom is you. What have you done about it?"

"I've only known I'm an earth power for a couple of weeks and I still don't even know *how* Oscar helped my mom."

"So, nothing, then?" She raised her eyebrows challengingly.

"No. I found that big spell in the caverns under the basement and I'm trying to find out how it works. I don't know the first thing about earth magic." Yeah, it sounded like crap even to me, and my heart started to hammer in my chest while my stomach did a triple backflip. I soooooo didn't need this on top of the stuff with Tanya.

"Kalvan, the clock is ticking and you really don't have a lot of time. I won't last long after the coming of the Summer Crown and that's only ten days from now."

"I can't handle this. I just . . . can't."

"I'm sorry to hear that, Kalvan, because no one else is going to handle it for you." Shaking her head, she turned and walked away.

Noelle was right, but that didn't mean I had any clue what to do about it. My eyes fell on the coatrack and I decided that maybe what I needed to shake up my sense of the possible was some fresh air and a change of scene.

I didn't really have a goal when I started walking, but I eventually found myself at the Como Park bonfire pits. It was a sunny afternoon in mid-April and the weather was very fine by Minnesota standards, so there were people everywhere and the fires were active. I watched the dancing flames from a distance, hoping for some sudden inspiration. I could feel the fire in my own heart responding, but I couldn't get any closer without joining a party I hadn't been invited to and I still hadn't found what I needed.

After a bit, I walked into the nearby woods. The growth was sparse along the edges of the trees, but there was a deeper and wilder place at its heart, and I wormed my way inward, ducking and twisting to get through the thickest growth, looking for . . . there! A limestone ridge sheltered a tiny hollow where someone had scooped out a shallow firepit.

I arranged deadwood into a loose cone, then settled on the ground. Calling fire into my hand, I leaned forward to touch the wood alight. At first, I pulled my hand back, but the fire kept calling me. I took off my jacket so I could reach both arms deep into the flames without worrying about burning my clothes.

I began to work with the stuff of fire, spinning red and gold streamers into brief flowers or the shapes of animals, soaking myself in flame. This was my *true* element, and even though it hadn't shown me a solution for my problems, giving myself to the fire eased my heart and I began to believe a solution was possible. Later, after the sun had faded from the sky, I looked up and noticed a coyote staring at me across the flames.

"Lisa?"

With a shrug, she flowed from one shape into another and I was suddenly sitting across from the girl, though her eyes remained the eyes of a coyote. "That's not the smartest thing you've ever done."

"Huh?"

"Sitting here in the wooded deeps playing with magic in the most obvious way imaginable without any hint of caution or awareness of the world around you. If I were one of the Stogari, you could be dead now."

"Stogari?"

"The delver clan your friend Cetius heads." She shook her head sadly. "I have no idea how you've managed to live this long when you can't be bothered to sort out all the players."

"I didn't even know there *was* more than one kind of delver until you mentioned it. I haven't had a lot of time to figure things out lately."

"For a smart guy, you make a lot of dumb choices."

"What's *that* supposed to mean?" Coming from Lisa, the question made me more curious than angry.

"Not watching your back. Returning to the dragon again and again. Trusting Morgan."

"I thought she was your best friend."

"Yes and no. It's complicated. But then, most things are with people . . . if you look deeply enough."

"You don't seem all that complicated."

Lisa laughed, a short bark of a sound, and her expression shifted enigmatically, becoming much less human and much more coyote in a way I found hard to describe. It was the first time I'd seen a human face do anything like it and I suddenly remembered her comment about bodies shaping minds. How much had the coyote shaped Lisa's personality?

"Maybe that's because I'm not entirely human, or maybe appearances are deceiving. Maybe I'm the most complicated person in your life and you just haven't figured it out yet."

I wanted to ask her if she was really in my life now, but that seemed too personal. Instead, I asked, "So, why are you here?"

"I was hunting and I happened on your trail. When I saw you weren't keeping an eye out for trouble, I figured I'd better hang around and do it for you. Now that you're paying attention, I should probably get going." She rose to her feet in one fluid motion.

I quickly scrambled upright as well, stepping through the fire to touch her elbow. "Wait, I'd like to talk more."

She paused and arched an eyebrow. "What would you like to talk about?"

"The Stogari, for one. How long have you known there were factions among the delvers?"

She moved away from me, turning toward the darkened wood. "Not factions, clans. And that was the wrong question."

"I don't understand."

"No, you don't." This time, her voice sounded almost bitter.

"So, help me out. What's the right question?"

"I'll let you know if you ever ask it." Before I could say another thing, she leaned forward. As her palms touched the dirt, she became a coyote once more, bounding away into darkness.

I turned back to the fire, though the flames no longer drew me as they had earlier. "I am *never* going to understand girls."

A voice spoke from the deepest part of the fire. "Not if you think of them that way, no."

I more than half jumped out of my skin. "What the . . . Sparx?"

The hare shaped himself out of flames and nodded. "You didn't really think I'd let you out of my sight for long, did you? Not with the way things have been going."

I felt a bit put out that everybody seemed to think I needed watching, but I had a more pressing question. "What do you mean I'm not going to figure out girls if I think of them *that way?*"

"As girls first, and not simply as people. Obviously."

"Huh?"

The hare rolled his eyes. "Don't be an idiot, Kalvan. I've been to that tree-hugger colony you call a school. How many times have your teachers stressed that you need to see people as individuals and not as categories?"

"I . . . um . . . lots. But that's not about girl and boy stuff . . . is it?"

"You tell me."

"Oh."

He leaned back and crossed his forelegs. "Now that you're done sulking in the woods, are you ready to head home?"

"I wasn't sulking, I was thinking. And honestly I don't know what I want. Nothing is going like it should anymore. This time last year, the most I had to worry about was if my mom and Oscar were going to have another big fight over the way I was slacking off in class."

"And you want to go back to that? Knowing what you know now?"

I shook my head. "No. That life was a lie. I can't go back there. But I don't know how to go forward, either. Truth be told, I'm not really even ready to deal with this." I reached into the fire and scooped out a tongue of flame, holding it on my palm. "I can't begin to handle the earth stuff on top of it, to say nothing of my mother."

"Can't do it or won't?"

"Both? I don't know . . ." I turned away from Sparx and the fire. More than anything in the world, I wanted to walk away. To point my nose in a random direction and keep going until I couldn't go any farther.

"Kalvan, you're better than this. What's *wrong* with you?"

I rummaged around in my head, desperately trying to find an answer that would make him stop asking me questions, until, suddenly, I found the truth instead. "I'm scared. No, that's not quite it. I'm freaking terrified!"

"Of what, the delvers? They're a—"

"I'm scared of trying and failing, all right? My mom is . . . broken. She's always been a little bit broken, but it's worse now than I've ever seen it."

"Doesn't that make you want to help her?"

"Of course it does. But what if I can't? What if I get it wrong?"

Sparx shook his head. "Then she'll be no worse off than she is now. How is that—"

"It will all be *my fault!* Don't you see? I've spent my whole life dealing with a mom who has problems and isn't always there for me, who is . . . broken. I hate that. I want her well, more than anything. I do. But, as broken as she is, that's just my mom. That's the way she is, the way she's always been. Ask Noelle. It started before I was born. Now it's up to *me* to fix her. Before, she was broken because she was broken, even if my fight with Oscar made things worse. But now, if I try to fix her and I don't get it right, or make her even worse, then . . . then it really will be all my fault."

Sparx sighed. "Your first mistake is thinking in terms of *fixing* your mother. You fix cars or broken toys. People you help, and only to the extent they want or need it."

I didn't know how to process that. "So what's my second mistake?"

"We are defined as much by the choice not to do something as we are by the decision to act. The world has put you in a place where this is your burden to bear. If you have the chance to do something for your mother and you choose not to, that is your responsibility, too. You can't get away from it by burying your head in a fire, and pretending not to understand that's also a choice."

Heat blasted across my back then and the tiny clearing suddenly flared with a light as bright as day when the remaining wood in the pit flash-burned in response to my inner anguish. The darkness that followed was complete, blotting out the world around me at the same time it slithered in through the cracks in my heart.

Because, of course, Sparx was right.

Sparx hopped along beside me during the long walk home, but I hardly noticed him and I simply couldn't find it in me to answer his attempts at conversation. I knew I had to find a way to help my mother, but I still didn't know how. Maybe Morgan would be able to give me something when I met her at lunchtime. It was nearly midnight when I climbed into bed, but I wasn't the least bit sleepy.

I spent the next hour staring at the ceiling and pretending to know what I was going to do when the sun came up. Sometime around one, I crawled out of bed and tried to bury myself in the heap of coins under the closet. But whatever happened when I went there in my sleep didn't work when I was awake. The cold metal leached all the heat from my body and I quickly found myself shivering.

Morgan was waiting outside Doughboy when I arrived. "About time you got here, Monroe. Come on." She started walking.

I fell in beside her, once again aware of how much taller she was. "Where are we going?"

"Nowhere. Walk and talk for privacy. I'll bend the winds around us so no one can hear what we say and few will even see us."

"All right. What did you want to tell me?"

"Each thing in its proper time." She was walking fast, and I had to half run to keep up with her longer stride as we headed off in the direction of the hospital—not an area I'd ever explored that much. "Tell me about that." She pointed at the mark the Crown had given me.

"I . . . uh . . . it's complicated."

She laughed then, a bitter, silvery sound that set my teeth on edge. "Then you don't fully trust me. Good. That's smart. You can't trust anyone in the world of magic. Not your best friend. Not your family. Not even yourself. Not entirely."

"Oooookay." Because *that* wasn't creepy at all. "Are you going somewhere with this? Or, are you just trying to scare me?"

"Neither. Speaking a truth, because every so often that amuses me. The mark on your forehead is a scar left by the forepeak of the Corona Borealis. It was given to you by your stepfather, the stone-shaper and Winter King, Oscar Dalterre, though that's not his real last name."

I felt a pressure against my back as Sparx let me know he was still with me, though he didn't reveal himself to Morgan. "I—how do you know . . . any of that? I know I didn't tell you."

"You dueled with Oscar at the crescendo of the Winter Carnival and defeated him. An impressive feat and a great surprise. But even though you won, you also lost. In breaking the Winter King's power you broke the spell that helped your mother keep her wits."

I stopped walking. "You are seriously creeping me out, Morgan." The only people who knew the whole story were me, Sparx, and Dave. "I'm not sure this was such a good idea, and I'm not going to take another step until you tell me exactly how you know all that and why you're suddenly telling me now."

"Oh, Kalvan, I thought that *was* what I was doing. Look." She reached into her jacket and pulled out my drawing of the spell. "You brought me this because you didn't know what it was or how it worked. I have answers for you, answers that might save your mother, but you have to come with me if you want to get them. Leaf and feather, hawk and heather, as I am a power of air I swear that you shall end the day free and unharmed if you follow me now."

"Sparx?" I said quietly.

The hare poked his head out of the top of my bag. "I don't like it, but we have very little time, and that's a binding oath with grave consequences for breaking it. Up to you."

"All right." I gestured for Morgan to lead the way. "I guess it's your show."

"Thank you." She shook the drawing as we skirted the edge of the hospital grounds angling toward the far side of the hill behind the school. "This *is* the key to alleviating the worst of your mother's symptoms. You were right about that."

"But not to fixing her?"

"No." Morgan shook her head. "It would be incredibly dangerous to even attempt that. Your mother's mental illness has shaped her entire life. Removing it completely would effectively carve away a huge part of her mind. She might survive that, but she would become a different person in the process."

I winced. "I guess I've never looked at it that way." Morgan had a point—not quite the same one Sparx had made, but definitely related, and I realized I had to learn to change the way I thought about my mother's illness. "So, what does the spell do?"

"Many things. The magic is rooted in the Corona Borealis. For your mother? It gives her the tools to sort the real from delusion and it helps her medications keep her from sliding into despair or mania."

"You still haven't answered how you know all this."

"Momentarily. Here we are." She gestured at a blank rock wall.

"Where? I don't see . . ." An arched opening sort of faded into existence as I started speaking—though whether it was an illusion being pulled aside or the shape of the stone actually changing, I couldn't say.

"After you."

I had rarely wanted to do anything less than pass into the shadows beyond that gateway, but I remembered Morgan's oath and went forward. A narrow passage took us perhaps twenty feet into the hill before another archway led out into a larger room shrouded in deepest darkness.

As we entered, the way back vanished completely and Morgan spoke again, "I know all about the spell because I spoke to the man who built it, my uncle Oscar."

Light bloomed from a dozen huge crystal globes set around the edges of the great room, and I found myself facing a high stone dais, where a bald man in rags and a silver crown sat upon a throne shaped from a single block of onyx.

"Hello, Kalvan. Welcome to my temporary abode."

Oscar looked much the worse for wear. In addition to his ragged clothing, his bald scalp was covered in rough and twisted scar tissue and I hissed in surprise as I got a better look at his "crown."

"Do you like it?" he asked, touching a finger to the center of his forehead and the ring of bright silver that mirrored both my own new scar and the inside of the Corona Borealis. "It's your work, a burn born of fire magic and the Crown of the North."

I whipped around to glare at Morgan. "You promised!"

"That you would be unharmed and walk away free," said Oscar. "Just as I told her to, and just as things will play out. I have no intention of either harming or binding you, dear boy, however much I might prefer to deal with you so."

"I . . . don't understand. If you don't plan on hurting me . . ."

Sparx slipped out of my pack, dropping to the floor beside me.

"Obviously, he wants something from you, and it's not a thing he can force."

"Ah, yes, the k*tsathsha." The firetongue word sounded heavy and harsh in Oscar's mouth. "So perceptive and so fierce in defense of his master. I approve. Yes, I need something from you, boy."

"Well, you can't have it!" I snapped. "I hate your guts."

"The feeling is quite mutual, but immaterial. Morgan, leave us. Why don't you hunt up Cetius and tell him that whatever he's plotting against the boy this time, he needs to drop it until I tell him otherwise."

"Of course, Uncle. Whatever you say." Morgan bobbed a deeply ironic curtsy and walked forward to pass through an arch that appeared briefly behind the throne.

Oscar shook his head. "That girl is going to cause me endless hours of trouble. She's even more willful and headstrong than you. That school of yours is to blame."

"I'm not sure what the point of this is," I said as angrily as I could manage—if I couldn't hold on to being angry I was pretty sure scared half to death was the next thing on the menu. "I've got no interest in helping you."

Oscar smiled—a cold and terrifying expression. "Oh, I think you'll change your mind once I've explained. But if you don't, I will at least have the pleasure of knowing your imminent death will be excruciating beyond all measure and that your soul won't survive the failure of your body. Though I am most definitely not looking forward to the catastrophic headache the whole thing will give me."

"What are you talking about?" demanded Sparx.

Oscar spread his arms wide. "The Corona Borealis, of course. It wasn't my intent to make you my heir when I threw the Crown in your face, but intentions and results are not always a perfect match. In ten days, that scar on your head will draw the Crown to you as a flame draws a moth, and with equally fatal results. You are too young to contain the power of the Summer King and it will burn you away from within, consuming even your soul."

I glanced at Sparx, who made a balancing gesture with his paws. "It's a possibility."

"No, k*tsathsha, it is a certainty. There is no greater expert on the Crown than me, and I know for a fact the boy can't master it. It will destroy him unless I prevent it."

"Why would you do that?" I asked. "And how?"

"Because I want to continue as I have, the Winter King eternal. As to how, I will show you the way to shift the coming Crown to another of my choosing."

"Morgan!" It couldn't be anyone else.

"Sadly, yes. I had hoped she could convince you to give it to her in such a way as to keep my hand invisible in the thing. But every time I set her up to rescue you and win your undying trust, you rescued yourself instead. Beyond that, she is only barely mature enough herself, and maddeningly independent to boot, but I've no choice. Because of your scar and mine the Crown has become bound to our bloodlines."

"Are you saying no one else can take the Throne now?"

"Not quite. Neither you nor I can *give* it to anyone else, and the only way for *you* to be free of it short of death is to use the spell under your house to pass it along to Morgan. Before you ask the tedious question, yes. You could also give it to your mother, but without me stabilizing her through the spell, it would destroy her as surely as it would you, if not as quickly. To say nothing of the damage a mad Queen of Summer could do."

"Maybe I could learn to stabilize her!"

"Doubtful, seeing as you lack both earth powers and the knowledge available to one who has mastered the Crown."

I almost blurted out that I did too have earth powers, but Sparx kicked me in the ankle as he leaped to put himself between me and Oscar. "So, if the boy agrees, what's in it for him?"

Oscar held up a finger. "First, he survives." Another. "Second, I will swear an oath to leave him and his mother alone in the future and to prevent the Stogari from seeking their own revenge. Third, I will create spells that stabilize Genevieve and renew them each year going forward until she dies or Kalvan figures out how to take care of her himself."

"In exchange for that, you get to go back to being the Winter King?"

He nodded. "A small price, I would think, given the alternative. But don't answer me now. Take a couple of days to think it over. No more than that, of course. The deal won't be on the table forever and I'm only offering it because it's the simplest and surest way. Also, the spell takes some time to prepare and Coronation Day is less than a fortnight off. At which point, the boy of fire will become a brief torch brightly burning and end in ashes."

18

The Queen of Air and Duetness

"WHAT AM I going to do?" Sparx and I covered half the distance back to school before the shock wore off enough for me to start thinking again.

The big hare didn't answer at once and I couldn't see his expression, but I felt his tension in the grip of his paws. He was wrapped around the back of my neck like a collar of living fire, with his hind feet on my left shoulder and his front on my right.

"I don't know."

There was a swirl in the air and words spoke themselves out of nowhere in Morgan's voice. "To do? Why, what my uncle asks, obviously."

"Morgan!" I looked around angrily, but the older girl was nowhere in sight. "Come out where I can see you!"

"Where's the fun in that?" Again, the voice spoke from thin air.

Sparx leaned forward so I could see his face out of the corner of my eye. "You can stop looking for her, Kalvan. She's a windweaver and words are mostly air. For all we know, she could be half a mile away." But even as he spoke he pointed silently downward.

I followed his direction with my eyes and saw we were standing on a steel grating in the sidewalk with a deep well below. "Oh." We were passing the hospital, and slats in the side of the well suggested it was part of their heating and ventilation system—a natural amplifier for air powers. I quickly tilted my head up and pretended to look for her. "Wherever you are, Morgan, I don't want to talk to you. Not today. Not tomorrow. Not ever again."

"The feeling is so very mutual, but you're my problem until dawn comes on the twenty-first and gets you out of my life one way or the other."

"I'm not giving you the Crown, and no one can make me."

"Oh, Kalvan, you're smarter than that. Of course someone can make you, and that someone is *you*. Because, if you don't, you die. And then your mother slips over the edge of madness never to be sane again. We all know you're not going to let that happen, so here are my uncle's first instructions."

A paper airplane came drifting down out of the sky to land in my outstretched hand. It was heavier than expected, and when I unfolded it I saw that it was actually a half dozen sheets of tracing paper covered with notes and diagrams in a spider-thin hand.

"Sparx—"

But the hare shushed me with a paw and pointed at the grate again.

I nodded and tucked the sheets into my jacket pocket. "Right. Morgan, I know you're still listening. I got the package, but don't think this is over." *How could I have ever thought she was cute?*

"Not till the twenty-first, Kalvan. Not till the twenty-first."

When we got back to school, Sparx pointed to an enormous square vent across from the back doors. I'd never really thought about the vents before, but the shadows beyond the grillwork took on a darker cast now that I imagined the entire duct system as an enormous spiderweb with Morgan at its center. I desperately wanted to talk to Sparx about everything, but it couldn't be here. A second later, it occurred to me that I couldn't tell Dave anything, either. Not at school, and we weren't supposed to see each other anywhere else. I paused and quickly scrawled a note before heading to my next class with him.

Dave, need to talk soon, but can't do it at school—magical ears listening. Will figure out someplace we can go—maybe tomorrow. In the meantime, don't ask about magic or anything.

I passed Lisa as I hurried to class and she waved, but I barely nodded. She *had* warned me about Morgan, but I had no way of knowing whether that meant I could trust Lisa or if it was all part of some ploy. Hooray, another thing for my list of stuff I had to figure out in the next couple of days if I didn't want to die horribly.

"I think we can talk here free of Morgan's ears." Sparx looked around the cavern immediately below the house. "I'm sure Oscar sealed this space against any power of air when he created it."

"But what about Oscar himself?" The cavern made me deeply uncomfortable, an effect heightened by the papers I clutched in my right hand—instructions Oscar had written. *Oscar!*

"The wards we put around the house *should* keep him and his delvers far away."

"But? I definitely heard a 'but' at the end of your sentence."

Sparx flicked his ears back and forth in a bunny shrug. *"But I'm no kind of earth master. When we talk, our words bounce off the stone around us. I have no idea how far that sound will carry through stone, especially if someone like Oscar is doing things to make it travel farther, though I'm sure there's an answer to that problem."*

I gave my companion a hard look. "And? This time I heard a silent 'and' at the end of *that* sentence."

"Follow me." Sparx hopped through the arch leading from this cave to the next and onward, and I reluctantly trailed behind. "There." He pointed at the stone altar where Oscar had once laid me out like a sacrifice.

"There what, bunny boy? I still have nightmares about that altar and Oscar's stone dagger. I don't want to go anywhere near it." And I hadn't, though I'd been in the other caverns several times over the previous weeks—the whole room gave me the screaming creepies.

"I was thinking of the throne next to it, actually. I'm guessing it answers to the Crown of the North."

I ran a finger along the edge of the Crown—a necessary adjunct to entering the cavern. "I hate this idea sooooo much."

"But you're going to do it anyway. I can tell by the pitch of your voice. That's your Idonwanna-but-Imagonna whine."

"I should never have given you that dratted muffin."

"Yeah, because I totally started hanging out with you on account of half a stale muffin and not that whole summoning-and-binding-me thing."

"Hey now, that was an accident."

"More like a train wreck. Now, are you going to do this thing or what?"

"Fine." I climbed up into the great stone chair and settled myself in place.

BAM!

I felt like lightning had struck the point of the Crown. Huge, heavy stone lightning that crushed me to a pulp even as it electrified my soul and filled me with the blinding light of knowledge. Through the throne and the Crown I could feel the whole weight of the earth beneath me. Above me. All around. I *was* the cavern but still Kalvan.

No. That's not quite right. I was the stone of the walls and floor and ceiling for many yards in every direction. The throne and its altar were a part of me, each riddled with a slow and heavy sort of magic that ran through the rock like the hidden filigree running through the Crown. I couldn't imagine the time and effort it had taken to do that. The spell carved into the floor of the other room was a crude thing by comparison, like a brand burned into my flesh, hot and aching and still full of fire. The greater cavern was a void within me, a hollow place in my heart I could only sense as a stress on my arches and domes. I wanted to crush and bury it, to fill it and be whole, and in that instant I knew exactly how it could be accomplished.

Without thinking, I started to reach out to the pressure points that would bring the roof down. There, and there, and . . . wait, what was that? I touched a vein of harder stone running down and away toward the river, a vein with a ghost of magic running through it. Oscar! Now that I touched his presence there, I felt him everywhere in the cavern. His magic had shaped every curve and angle. But in most places he was a background presence. In the vein I could feel his active will, though he had not yet perceived me.

My first impulse was to twist the walls and utterly crush that thread of magic, but then he would know I was aware of him. No. Perhaps I could . . . there were no words for it in English, but the Crown guided my will with the help of the throne.

"Yes!"

"What?" asked Sparx.

My primary awareness returned to my body and I touched a finger to my lips. "Ah, no, I was wrong. Bother. Let's head back upstairs. This place gives me the creeps."

I moved most of my awareness back into the surrounding stone and pushed ever so gently with my mind. The sound of footsteps started at the throne and moved quickly off toward the exit. Sparx gave me a silent round of applause but I held up a hand. The next bit was super tricky and it took all my concentration to simulate the effect of a boy and his companion sliding up through stone to the basement above.

Then, one more twist, and . . . "We're good. He can't hear us now unless I let him. Not here and not in the basement above. If we stuff a blanket or something in the duct running up to the house from the furnace whenever we want to talk there, we should be able to block Morgan, too."

"Very slick. Now I can give you the silent 'and' I didn't speak earlier. *And* you *are* an earth master."

I shook my head as I climbed down from the throne. "*Child of earth*, maybe, and that reluctantly. But a master? Not even close. I could never have done any of that out in the real world. For that matter, I'm pretty sure I couldn't have done it here without the Crown. It . . ." I paused to think about what had just happened. "It interacted with the throne somehow to do the thinking for me."

"All right, that's the opposite of reassuring, but I guess it worked out this time. So, now that we can talk without being heard, what do we say?"

"I don't know. We can't let Oscar regain control of the Crown, but if we don't give it to Morgan, I die and my mom loses what's left of her sanity."

Sparx nodded. "Now, I mention this only to outline all the possibilities and not as a suggestion. Oscar also said you could transfer it to your mother."

"Who it would also destroy!"

"Which is why I didn't make it a suggestion, O Accursed Master."

I barely heard him. "We need a . . . wait. I might have an idea." I thought back to what Oscar had said about the Crown being bound to our bloodlines. "What about my father? My real father. If I can pass it to my mom, why not my dad?"

"Aside from the fact that we have no idea where he is and— according to your aunt Noelle—that he is buried deep in stone and beyond any reaching?"

"Yes, aside from that."

"I have no idea. I've been over Oscar's instructions half a dozen times, and they don't give any explanations, just orders. I can make some educated guesses about the whys, but they're only guesses. This a big, complex, time-intensive spell. We need an expert and the only one available is Oscar."

I took a deep breath. "I bet Mississippi would know."

"That would be extraordinarily dangerous. She told you not to seek her out again unsummoned on pain of death."

"I know. And Josh hates my guts. And Tanya will have me expelled if she finds out. I still think we should do it, and none of that is even the best part."

"There's more?" Sparx pasted a huge false grin on his face. "Oh, goody."

"Yes. If we see Mississippi we have to make sure neither Morgan or Oscar finds out what we have to say. Which probably means a boat."

Sparx's ears seemed to wilt. "On the Mississippi. In spring flood. With an angry river goddess beneath."

"Yep."

"Stupid, dangerous, and with a very low chance of survival or success. I love this plan so hard."

"Me too, bunny buddy, me too."

I was slow getting out the door the next morning and a few minutes late to school, which wouldn't have been a problem if it had been a normal Thursday, because I have an open period first thing on Tuesdays and Thursdays. Unfortunately, it was an OLC Joint Advisory morning, and I had forgotten it completely. JAs are one of those uniquely Free School institutions I should probably explain for those who go to a normal, sane sort of school.

Our teachers and administrators feel it's important for every student to understand what's happening in their education and have a voice. Whenever there's big news—like the shift from trimesters to semesters back when I was ten—everyone gets together so the principal can tell us what's going on and get input from all the students and teachers. There's a couple of microphones that get passed around to whoever wants to speak.

Sometimes it's something we don't have any real control over, like the school board deciding we were shifting to match our schedule to all the other schools. But sometimes it's more like when we were offered a chance to start up a football team. A couple of students who had done a big project on head injuries helped convince the rest of us to vote against that one and the principal ended up telling the school board "thanks but no."

When I arrived at school, I was immediately struck by the complete lack of older students in the halls. The school has big, wide hallways and they're a favorite place for kids with a free period to hang out. You have to be quiet but not as quiet as in the library, so a lot of board games and study groups happen there. So does the occasional round of bouncepong, which is sort of a hybrid of Ping-Pong and dodgeball, with a side of light parkour—another uniquely Free School institution. But that's only allowed in a few halls and at certain times of day because it is NOT quiet.

I quickly waved down the nearest sixth grader—the top end of the Early Learning Center kids. "Jada, where is everybody?"

She rolled her eyes at me. "OLC's in the gym for Joint Advisory. Started right after breakfast, duh."

"Oh, he—uh, bother. Thanks!"

Evelyn had mentioned there was going to be one at yesterday's afternoon advisory, and I should have remembered. I raced for the gym, sparing a guilty mental "my bad" as I passed the charred patch on the wall where someone—read: me—had accidentally melted one of those security key light switches. That was a couple months ago and the lights in the pass-through from the main school building to the gym had been on ever since—school system maintenance does not move quickly.

When I got to the gym, I found the main doors closed. They wouldn't be locked, but they opened noisily and I didn't want to draw attention, so I raced to the end of the hall where a pile of old office furniture let me climb up into the ceiling and drop down to the locker room beyond. From there it was a short distance to the door that led out under the left side of the bleachers—a much subtler entrance. Even better, I saw Josh and a couple of other rougher boys hanging out in the shadows there playing some game that involved dice.

I headed that way instead of out to where most of the students were listening to what sounded like my student mentor Aleta speaking about some decision from the school board meeting Wednesday night. She sounded pissed about whatever it was, and I'm sure I should have cared, but it would have to wait till I found out if I was going to survive the next eight days. On the upside, a pissed-off Aleta is loud enough to cover a lot of quiet whispers.

"Josh." I leaned in close and spoke very quietly. "Come with me for a second."

Josh, on the other hand . . . "Go away, Monroe. Before I push your face in."

"It's about Herself, and you might get to see me die. But it's got to be quiet and it's got to be now."

That got his attention. "What's up?"

"Not here. The *air* has ears."

"You finally figured that out, did you? Come on." He headed toward the locker room and I followed. Once inside, he pointed. "Showers."

"What? Why?"

"Showers or we're done."

I didn't want to go because Josh could beat the crap out of me back there without anyone hearing. It was probably a stupid worry considering I was about to ask him to arrange something that might get me killed, but that didn't stop my brain from spinning away as I complied.

Josh quickly turned on two of the showers and led me to the booth between. "All right, Monroe, now we can talk."

"I don't get it."

"I wouldn't brag about that if I were you."

Sparx poked his head out of my bag. "He's a bitter water sorcerer, Kalvan. Notice how very much louder the showers are than they ought to be."

"Oh."

Josh shook his head. "For a teacher's pet, you sure can be dumb as a bag of bricks. So, now that you've figured out Morgan is nine types of bad news, what do you want?"

"I need to talk to Mississippi."

"You really are a moron. She told you not to come back unbidden."

"I know. I'm hoping you can arrange for me to get bidden. I need to talk to Her about the Crown and I need to do it where neither air nor earth can hear. I'm thinking a boat."

"That's a tall order and incredibly risky while She's in flood even if She agrees to see you in advance. How soon would you want me to work this miracle, assuming you convince me I should?"

"As soon as possible. Today even."

"You are way too eager to die, Monroe. Today's not going to

happen. Neither is any other day if you aren't all kinds of convincing. It's dangerous to approach her at all this time of year, and doubly so on something that's already made her angry, even for me. Talk."

So, I did, quickly telling him everything I knew about Oscar and the Crown and Morgan and what they wanted to do.

At the end he nodded. "You're right, She probably will want to see you. I'll talk to Her, but remember, if you live through this, you'll owe me."

"My life, yeah, that hasn't escaped my attention." I didn't like that any more than I liked the rest of the game, but nobody had given me the option to quit while remaining in one piece.

"Good. I wanted that crystal clear and . . . uh-oh."

"What?" I asked.

"A breeze just stirred the showers."

"Morgan?"

"No, Tanya. I think. We need to get out of here since we're both already on thinnest ice there. Hang on." He spread his arms and every sink and shower except the one where we stood suddenly turned on full and hot, filling the room with steam.

"Come on." Josh grabbed my wrist and pulled me over to the corner where he braced himself against the wall and made a stirrup of his hands. "I'll give you a boost, then you can pull me up after. Hurry."

A moment later, we were both in the ceiling, me with the arm I'd used to help Josh up feeling like it was half out of the socket. There was also an unnatural amount of steam up there considering how quickly we'd closed that tile.

Josh spoke again, his voice barely louder than a breath, "Hold perfectly still and don't make a sound. Don't even breathe." The steam that followed us slid in tight around us like a blanket, taking on a weird sort of sparkle as it did so.

Seconds later, a ceiling tile blew into the air and fell to the side. More steam poured through, then flowed away as a wind whistled through the open space and stirred the dust around us into a thick cloud. The edges of our own steam blanket were tugged and tattered, but it held together. After a time that seemed very long indeed, but couldn't have been much more than a minute, the winds caught the tile and dropped it back into place before fading to nothing.

Josh let out a long-held breath with a sigh and a whisper. "Definitely Tanya."

"How can you tell?" I whispered back.

"Morgan would have broken my illusion. If she gets curious about what Tanya wanted, she might yet, which means it's time to be gone. I'll let you know what Ms. Sippi says. Until then it'd be better if we weren't seen together outside of class."

"But tomorrow's a school holiday and then it's the weekend."

"That's okay. I know where you live."

Least reassuring reassurance EVER!

I wrote another sentence and then let out a long sigh. Tanya's paper seemed incredibly pointless when I stood a good chance of dying within the next week or so, but I still had to do it to keep from getting thrown out of Free in case I lived. So, after my morning's adventures with Josh and two exciting hours of class, I slithered off to a study carrel in the library instead of heading to the cafeteria for lunch. My stomach hated me, but I had to get this done.

I'd just bent back to my paper when I heard a faint popping sound. "Psst, Kalvan."

"Wha—oh." A circle not much bigger than a baseball had appeared in the air above the carrel's shelf and Dave's left eye peered at me through the gap. I quickly glanced around to make sure I was alone. "How are you controlling that?"

"Poorly, and I can't hold it long. Only reason I'm managing it at all is because I'm pretty much directly above you."

Reflexively, I looked up.

"Not like that, you goof. I'm in the theater. Back row, left side. I saw you go into the library and figured you'd be in our favorite carrel."

"I—that's pretty slick, Dave, but what's up?" I'd started to say more but then remembered who might be listening. "We shouldn't talk like this for long."

"Yeah, I know. But I had two minutes alone and I needed to let you know we're still cool even though I have to stay far away for a bit. My mom completely blew a gasket about the thing down by the river and now she's got all three of my sisters taking it in turns to spy on me. I'll check in again when the heat's—oh, gotta-go-bye."

POP

The knock on my window came around ten a.m. on Saturday, waking me. I blinked and tried to move, only to be greeted by the gentle tinkling of coins.

Great. Again. Super. Yay.

"Sparx, who's—"

"Bitter water, finally. I'll let him know you'll be along in a minute."

I quickly extricated myself from the heap of dollar coins and pulled on the clothes I'd taken to storing there. *Weird thing number seventeen about that: Whenever I woke up there, every single coin in the crawlspace was part of the heap despite the fact they tumbled every which way as I crawled out.* Weird thing number sixteen was Sparx never saw any of it happen.

I opened my window to find Josh standing in the rain outside. Before I could speak, he waved for me to lean out farther and made a gesture that evoked the falling rain.

I did as asked, poking my head into the wet. "Hi, Josh, what's the word?"

"She wants to see you. Now, while it's raining."

"Did She?" I pointed into the sky.

Josh laughed. "No. That's beyond even Her. We got lucky."

"Okay, we'll be right out."

He shook his head. "It's not a we. It's a *you* and *me*. Bunny stays here."

"Hey!" Sparx hopped onto the window ledge beside me and spatters of rain flared into steam as they hit his fur. He hissed and glared at the sky. "Okay, that's a problem, but I can ride in the pack."

Josh shook his head. "There's a much bigger problem, and you staying here is part of the solution."

"I don't understand," I said.

"Again, not something you should brag about, Monroe." He pointed at me. "You have a LOT of scrying eyes looking your way right now. I can cover us both with illusion in this rain easily enough, but it's a thin protection and not hard to break. Especially if there's a lull."

"Not sure how that affects bringing Sparx along."

Josh rolled his eyes. "Well, for starters, it's much easier to cover two than three. But, more important, thin protection is all you need if everybody is looking elsewhere." He pulled a glass jar full of muddy water out of his courier bag. "This is a charm Herself made. Sitting with it'll make someone who shares the right magical sympathies look like you. Fire magic, in the case of your rabbit buddy."

"Hare," said Sparx.

"Like I give a rip. But this is all taking time we don't have. If you want to make this work, toddle on up somewhere near that spot on the roof you like so much and park the jar. Then, swap places with Peter Rottentail and hustle back double time so we can get on the road. I'll wait ten minutes. After that, deal's off. Before you start to argue, remember She made the charm and She will be very angry if you made Her waste time and power."

"Hang on." I closed the window. "Sparx?"

"If we're not going to call the whole thing off, there's little choice. It's up to you. You could still go forward with Oscar's deal."

"It really is that stark, isn't it? Okay, come on. We need to do this quick."

19

Water Way to Go

"SHUT UP AND keep paddling," Josh growled over his shoulder. "This isn't as easy as it looks."

The older boy was lying on the bow of the short kayak with both hands in the river a few inches apart. A vee of calm water expanded back through the wild churn of the flood from those points of contact, collapsing in again a few yards behind us.

"I just asked when—"

"I said 'shut it,' Monroe!"

I felt a sudden tugging on my paddle. Glancing along its length, I saw a hole about the size of my palm open in the water to my left. For about one second the dark patch reminded me of Dave's new-found magic, but then, as it grew, I realized . . .

"Whirlpool!"

"In that case," said Josh, "the answer to your earlier question is 'now.'"

The whirling hole in the water grew rapidly, pulling the kayak sharply down and to the left as we began a slow spin. "Are we going to die?"

He shrugged. "I sure hope not."

Within seconds, we were a yard below the surface of the river and the top of the whirlpool was fifteen feet across. Between the spinning and the terror, I had to fight not to throw up. We continued to sink until we were ten feet down. At that point, the mouth of the funnel above began to close, though both the spin and size remained constant down where we were.

"That's new." Josh didn't sound happy as he rolled over onto his back to watch the waters shut out the sky.

Soon, the aperture above had dwindled to a tiny circle no bigger than a dime, enclosing us in something very like a giant bubble. The spinning slowed, though it never quite stopped. A stripe of foam more than a yard across appeared in the wall of water, shaping itself into a mouth—a grim smile teasing its white lips as they kept pace with our circling progress. A pair of huge catfish slid forward into the place where eyes should have been, their barbels making tentacled lashes around their widely opened mouths. The face had no nose.

"Uh, hi?" Feeling like an idiot, I waved at the enormous face. "I could use some help." A soon-to-be-dead idiot, at that.

"Tell me why I should not simply destroy you, boy."

I shook my head. "Nope. We did that one before. If you haven't destroyed me yet, it's because you have a good reason not to. I'm not playing that game."

"You are arrogant."

"Probably, given how many people have said so. Also, if you

believe my teachers, stubborn, sarcastic, and unwilling to apply myself. None of that has anything to do with the fact I need your help, or that you have reasons of your own for giving me a hand. Otherwise, why are we here?"

The paired catfish shut their mouths with an almost audible snap and the white foam lips grew darker as turbulence swirled mud through the water. Up front, Josh gently but repeatedly smacked his head against the plastic bow of the kayak.

After perhaps a minute, the mouths snapped open again. "I will aid you, but do not speak again if you wish to live, boy. My tolerance rides the edge of a breaking wave.

"What you wish to do cannot be accomplished with any structure built by the Winter King, nor in a place of his power. Your father is buried deep. Perhaps too deep for you to reach. But only in the attempt can the possibility of the thing be realized one way or the other. The verses I gave you in the heart of winter were a test you passed. Have another.

> *"Find the father, bound in stone.*
> *Seed of power, tied to bone.*
> *The key, a Crown high and fair*
> *The lock, silver bright and rare*
> *Patterns carved in ancient rite.*
> *Seal the bond with fire bright."*

The catfish turned in the water, pointing their mouths at Josh. "Hide him as he needs, my disciple. But do not guide him. The riddle's answer is his to find. Now go."

The waters opened suddenly wide and our whirlpool spat us out with a sound like the roar of a mud-drenched lion.

"Maybe it's simpler than that." I turned to where Sparx sat between the model of the capitol and the circle containing the Crown. "Maybe this time I need to stop thinking so hard and just *do* it."

We'd been hashing over the riddle, what it might mean and how to address it, for hours. Given Oscar's note, Sparx thought he could probably reverse engineer much of the necessary spell structure, but none of that mattered if we couldn't figure out where my dad was trapped.

"Do what?!" The hare threw his paws wide. "Because I'm not seeing it."

"Use the Crown, obviously. If it's the key, then maybe my scar is the silver lock."

Before Sparx could argue, I raised the Corona Borealis and set it on my brow. It felt cool against my forehead but not cold—more like exposed skin on a breezy fall day than the pressure of a thing of metal and adamant. I could sense its power rising as the spring fallow came to an end.

"Well?"

I sighed. "Nothing. It feels stronger now but . . . wait a second." I thought back to my experience on Oscar's throne below, about how it felt like the stone was doing the thinking for me. "The patterns in the Crown . . ."

"What about them?"

"What if they're like the lines of a magical circuit? A really complex one, like a magical computer core."

"I'm not following you, kid. Computers aren't really my thing."

"When I was on the throne, it worked with the Crown to let me do more than I could by myself. It sort of . . . thought for me. Like a computer. And, it had all these lines through it like the Crown does, or like a circuit. What if part of the way the Crown amplifies power is by acting as a magical computer? Letting you think through spells and stuff much faster than you could on your own."

The hare blinked. "Interesting theory, but how will you use it? You aren't the Summer King yet. Well, and we're trying to prevent that because it's going to destroy you."

"No, but I have the scar and I am the . . . I don't know, Crown Prince. Maybe I can tap some of that. Let me try." Guided by a sudden impulse, I reached up and pressed the place where the Crown rested above the scar on my forehead. "Yeah . . ."

"What?"

"I can feel a connection, but it wants something more. I . . . think I need to go outside. Come on!" I dashed up the stairs and out into the backyard where I looked at the stars and . . . "YES!" I turned to see Sparx waving frantically and making zip-your-lips motions. *Oh, right. Oops.*

I let him lead me back to the basement where he hopped onto a table. "Now, talk."

"Once I got outside I could feel the Crown sort of reach out to the real Corona Borealis, the constellation. It was a weak contact, but I think I can steer by the stars."

"All right, but I see a few problems."

"Like the fact that if we don't want Morgan and Oscar to find out what I'm doing, we'll need Josh again. Also, I need to leave you behind to play decoy."

"Yeah, those'd be big ones. Since I can't come with you I'm going to have to go there myself as soon as possible after you find the place." He sighed. "I wish you could get Dave to do this stuff instead of Josh."

"You and me both, but even if he had the right powers, I'd hate to run the risk of getting him into any more trouble with his mom." I sighed. "Besides, we don't have a lot of choice, and Mississippi did tell Josh to help me. When we parted ways this afternoon, he gave me his cell number. Let me give him a call."

Josh wasn't any happier to hear from me than I was to have to call him, but he did promise to be there in an hour. A bit after midnight I stood in my backyard with Josh beside me, the Crown on my head, and a watery shimmer of illusion all around us, while Sparx perched on the rooftop above, pretending to be me.

"You look awfully pretty in that shiny hat, Monroe, but I had plans for the night. Can we maybe speed this up?"

"Working on it." The problem was, while I could feel a link and the stars definitely wanted to help, they were being pretty vague about where exactly to steer me. I was beginning to think I'd been premature in believing I had this.

So, what was I missing? I started to run through the riddle again:

Find the father, bound in stone.

Seed of power, tied to bone.

Oh. Of course.

Reaching inward, I tried to touch the place in my heart where stone lived. But all I could find there was fire. Disappointing, but not unexpected. I hated the whole idea of having earth within, and reaching for something I didn't want to even exist was never going to be easy. So, find a different angle. But what?

Find the father, bound in stone.

Seed of power, tied to bone.

Well, I *had* written a new shape into my bones when I cast the Dragon's Wings, if only semi-intentionally, and that was because of my earth magic. Maybe that was my way in now. I concentrated on my bones, on the feeling of ideograms writing themselves into my shoulder blades and spine and ribs, on the place where fire and stone had merged to become a part of my very skeleton.

I almost had it when the dragon came wide awake within me— angry, hungry, fierce, eager to rain fire and death upon its enemies. Sweat broke out all over my body as I fought a silent battle with the creature I had unknowingly invited inside my skin. It wanted out, to fly and hunt and rend. I felt a terrible desire to let it take me, to simply give up on human cares and hurts.

But if I did that, I would give up all my human joys, too—my friendship with Dave, my genuine affection for my school with all its quirks and characters, the deep bonds of love and pity that tied me to my mother . . . That last relationship—by far the most difficult—was also the one that gave me the strength I needed now.

If I let go of everything, my mother would have no one and nothing. My aunt's presence was temporary. When Noelle went back to the earth, my mother would have no anchor at all and she would be lost. I *couldn't* let that happen. No matter how angry she made me, I still loved her and she needed me.

Maybe that wasn't supposed to be the way the world worked, and thirteen was too young for that much weight to fall on my shoulders. But that didn't make it not true. That didn't relieve me of the responsibility to do what I could for her. I had to at least try to help her, and that knowledge gave me the strength to force the dragon back down into my bones, to bind it there, and put a deep sleep upon it using the powers I had been given—forcing it into a sort of hibernation.

I can't really explain how I did those things because it was an act of love melding stone and fire, and the words to describe it don't properly exist in either elemental tongue, much less in English. But I managed it and that connected me to the place where earth lived within my bones. I still couldn't touch the stone in my heart, but I didn't have to. When the powers moved *through* me, I felt the fire that tied me to my mother like a lodestone. That gave me the insight to find the bond between stone and father in my bones, if not my heart.

Turning slowly, I felt that bond pulling on my skeleton like the north pole on a compass. The link between the earthly Crown and its heavenly twin flexed, and a star that didn't exist appeared like a pointer in the sky. A star only I could see. Between the star and the tugging on my bones, I had it. There! My father was that way, and closer than I'd expected. Much closer. Within a few miles, if I was reading the signs properly. Fetching my bike out of the garage, I began to ride, barely aware of Josh close beside me on his bike.

I stopped at the foot of a tall hill in a small park in a neighborhood I'd never been to before. According to my watch, it was closer to three than two. Clouds hid the stars, making it very dark indeed, since there were no streetlights in the depths of the park. But I didn't *need* light. As soon as I got off my bike and my feet hit the ground, I just *knew* where everything was. Everything that touched or changed the ground anyway, all the dips and rises, every tree and each of its branches, a park bench I might have run into at another time.

Walking slowly with my bike beside me, I followed the line of the hill about a quarter of the way around until I came to an outcrop of stone like a flat wall. I slid the hand that shard of stone had melted into along the surface because I had a better feel for things of earth on that side. The wall was cold and hard—solid as a mountain. I was almost there, but not quite. I stepped forward into the stone. I should have broken my nose. Instead, I found myself pushing through what felt like a thick velvet curtain into an enormous cave. The darkness was as deep as that I had fought under the capitol, but empty and devoid of presence. I couldn't see, but again, I *knew* my surroundings. I stood within a great and hollow hill.

"Okay, this is all creepier than a drowned corpse." Josh's hand fell away from my shoulder, a contact I only noticed as it ended. "I don't suppose you thought to bring a light?"

Josh. Sigh. I wanted nothing more than to leave him in the dark, but I owed him. With a snap and a twist of my will, I summoned fire to dance along the fingers of my left hand, holding it high like a torch.

At the very center of the vast cavern, a broad natural-seeming staircase led into a hole perhaps thirty feet across, though it only went down three and a half steps. A smooth cap of stone blocked further progress. The pull on my bones drew me down into that well where I knelt and ran a finger along the floor. It felt like volcanic glass—slick and smooth as a frozen lake—with patterns that reminded me of a finely whorled marble as they gaudily reflected the red light of my burning hand.

"Where are we?" Josh had followed.

"I . . . I think this is where my father is trapped." I pressed both palms to the stone floor. "Yes. I can almost . . ." Letting the Crown guide me again, I bent and pressed my forehead against the slick surface.

CONTACT

A charge like cold lightning jumped from the stone to the Crown, flickering from point to point and filling my mind with . . .

—*deep, slow thoughts, like water trickling through cracks in an ancient vase—*

—*stone dreaming of self in an unsleeping mind—*

—*a fragmented presence—*

—*kinship—*

I shoved myself away from the floor, pushing so hard I fell over backward. The Crown tumbled from my brow with a metallic crash.

"I'm all right!" I hoped so, anyway. "I'm all right."

"Do I look like I care, Monroe?"

But I hardly heard. "I think I touched my father's thoughts. They were . . ." What was the phrase I wanted? "Not entirely human."

"That'd explain a lot," said Josh.

I ignored the dig. "It's like he isn't actually aware of himself as something distinct from the stone that surrounds him . . . as if he were thinking with a mind that's as much a thing of rock as it is of flesh."

I had a sudden insight. When I became the dragon, I thought as a dragon thinks. Maybe my dad had taken on the mental shape of the stone that contained him. "Yeah." I nodded to myself. "Yeah, that feels right."

"So, your dad's a rock that thinks? That's some pretty weird stuff, Monroe." For the first time Josh sounded almost interested, and I remembered that his family was . . . challenging. "Can you even talk with him when he's like that? Mind to mind, I mean? Because you're going to have some *serious* trouble convincing a boulder to become the Summer King."

I winced. "I don't know. I can feel he's there, but communicate . . . His thoughts are . . . well, let's just say stone doesn't much care about something as brief and fragile as flesh, even his son."

I felt a sharp, almost physical pain in my heart—a stab of loss that caught me by surprise. Here I was, closer to my father than I'd ever expected, and he didn't even know about it. How *was* I going to make a stone into the Summer King? I couldn't touch him or speak to him or . . . *anything*. Fear followed the pain. This wasn't going to work. How could it? Noelle had been right; there was no reaching my father.

I climbed out of the pit, breathing jaggedly and pacing as I tried to force down the loss and pain that filled my chest. *Don't think about it. Don't let it hurt. Don't. Don't. Don't.* I had lots of practice at not thinking about things that hurt, and soon enough the moment passed. When I was sure I had it together again, I retrieved the Crown.

I felt exhaustion fill me like water pouring into a vase then. "Holy crap, I'm beat." I looked at Josh, realizing only in the moment I did so that the flames on my fingers had faded almost to nothing. "I think we're done for tonight. Or, wait a second . . . bother. Sparx."

I really didn't have the energy, but I needed to leave a marker. "Ash and char, sun and star, wind and smoke, ash and oak." I touched one burning finger to the floor at the top of the stairs and drew the ideogram for a long-burning ember.

Now, if I could just make it home without crashing my bike . . .

The first challenge came at the exit. The wall of rock was every bit as solid on this side as it had been on the way in. But when the Crown fell off earlier, I'd lost that deep sense of connection with my father and the earth that had opened the way. When I tried to walk through the wall this time, I nearly did break my nose.

Josh laughed and let go of my shoulder. "That almost makes this whole trip worth it. If you could see the look on your face . . ."

"Gosh, thanks." I gingerly felt my nose and dabbed at a fresh cut on my cheek. "I'm so happy to be able to provide you with a show. I don't suppose you have any clever ideas on how to get through this thing? Because I'm not sure how I did it last time."

"You'd best figure it out quicklike. If we're stuck in here for good, I'm going to end up cracking your bones for the marrow."

As soon as he spoke, I realized the answer. With a sigh, I put the Crown back on and reached inward. It took three draining attempts to recapture some sense of connection to the earth that resided in my bones and open the way, and I pulled the Crown off again the instant we reached the outside world. As the heir, I could use its powers, but it cost me in a way I doubted it cost the rightful ruler.

In my exhaustion and with my earlier sense of the earth faded away, I ran into several trees and that park bench. Once we finally got back to the street, we climbed onto our bicycles and started the long ride back to my house. I thought for a moment that I saw a coyote slip out of the shadows under the trees and fall in behind us, but I was too tired to be certain.

When I got home at four I waved goodbye to Josh, then collapsed on my bed without taking my clothes off. I slept right on through till Sunday evening. As soon as I woke, I told an impatient Sparx how to find the hollow hill. I also told him I didn't think our plan would work, but I'd barely finished speaking when he vanished in a puff of smoke.

Despite all the things I needed to do, I headed for the attic after having a very late first meal. Dinfest? Breaker? Whatever. Sparx would be gone for a while and I needed to get my head straight. Pretty much since the day I first met the fire hare I'd been rushing from one emergency to the next with no end in sight. Now I was about to . . . what? Force my long-absent father—who happened to be a giant rock at the moment—into becoming the Summer King? How crazy was that?

It only took a moment to scamper up the shingles to my spot by the chimney. I'd come to love it up on the roof away from everyone, especially at night. It was incredibly soothing to simply sit and stare at the stars and pretend I was alone in the universe, and I found myself needing that more and more. For a little while at least, I didn't have to think about anything. Not the Crown. Not magic. Not my family. Not even me.

Time slipped quietly by until, "Kalvan!" My mother's voice, harsh and bitter, called up from the window below.

Her anger startled me. "Yeah, Mom? What's wrong?" I pivoted and used the chimney to pull myself upright—getting down and back in through the skylight safely was a bit of a process.

"I want to talk to you, now!"

"I . . ." Something in her tone made me pause as I grabbed for the roof-peak. "About what?"

"Your behavior. You've been sneaking out at night. I want to know why, and what you've been doing."

Instead of climbing down, I answered from where I was. "I

haven't gone out that much, and really I've just been going to the park. Sparx has been with me most of the time."

"I know there's more to it than that. Don't lie to me, Kalvan!"

"I'm not lying! I—"

"Last night when you were up there, I could smell the dark magic on you!"

I opened my mouth to try to explain about Mississippi's charm and Sparx acting the decoy, but closed it again without saying anything when I realized it didn't matter what I said. She was using her crazy voice. The angry version. I hadn't recognized it initially because she'd never directed it at me before. My heart went cold and heavy in my chest.

Growing up with my mom's mental illness had forced me to develop a sort of sixth sense for when she was . . . off. It was a survival skill, plain and simple. One that had grown stronger in the months since I drove Oscar away and his stabilizing influence on my mother failed. She was *way* off now, and she was off *at me* for the first time ever. I could hear it in her tone and her cadence, but most of all I could hear it in her certainty.

I don't know what she believed I'd been doing while I was out of the house, or even if the times I was gone had any correspondence with the times she *believed* I was gone. But really, it didn't matter. There was no reason the reality of the world had to have anything to do with the reality inside her head. What mattered was that there is no arguing with mental illness. Not my mom's anyway. Her brain is broken in a way that makes her believe things that aren't true— really believe them in her bones. I could argue the clock around and all it would do would be to make her more certain I was lying to her.

"Kalvan, you come down here right now and explain yourself!"

I didn't answer. There was no point. Instead, I settled myself back into the gap between the roof and the chimney.

"Kalvan!"

I looked up into the stars and tried to pretend I couldn't hear anything at all.

"You are going to be in so much trouble when you get down here!"

I clenched my fists until I thought the knuckles would pop right off, but I didn't answer, and I didn't look away from the stars.

"Kalvan, if you don't come in this minute, there will be severe consequences."

Don't-answer-don't-answer-don't-answer-don't-answer-don't-answer-don't-answer-don't-answer . . .

"I'll give you to the count of five. Then I'm closing this window and locking it."

I had to practically chew my tongue off to keep from responding.

"One, two, three—I'm serious, Kalvan—four, five."

Don't-answer-don't-answer-don't-answer-don't-answer-don't-answer-don't-answer-don't-answer . . .

"This is your own fault, Kalvan." The window closed, and I heard the lock shut with a sharp snap. My heart made the same sound as it broke.

I'd spent my whole life knowing my mother had moments like this, delusions that went every bit as deep as the depressions, but she'd never focused the anger they could bring on me before. I wanted to make it not have happened, but it had. I wanted to scream, but I didn't. I wanted to cry, but I couldn't.

"Kalvan . . ." It was Sparx's voice this time, and so quiet he might have expected me to shatter at the sound of my name.

I kept my eyes on the stars. "Go away."

"I—"

"Go away!"

Sparx vanished with a little popping noise.

Silence.

I needed that. Time passed and I realized I was cold despite the fire in my heart. I thought about going in to get out of the night air, but the window was locked. There were probably any number of things I could do about that, but none of them seemed worth the effort.

More time passed.

Hunger joined the cold. I tried not to care, but it didn't work. I would have to eat at some point, and it would be smart to get in out of the cold, but the window was locked.

The window was locked.

My mother had locked me out on the roof.

My mother.

My mother!

The fires that had been burning low in my heart suddenly flared wild and red and full of rage like nothing I'd ever felt. I moved without thinking, monkeying my way over and down to stare in through the locked window. The fires within grew hotter and angrier and my hand burst into a flame so intense I could barely look at it. I punched through the window, but it didn't shatter. It melted away from my burning hand and drops of molten glass dripped onto the counter below, leaving scorched holes in the laminate.

Twisting my arm, I grabbed hold of the lock, popping it open. The brass withstood the heat longer than the window had, but I felt the mechanism fuse in place an instant later. No one would ever lock me out like that again. With my other hand, I wrenched the window open. I slipped inside, dropping from the ledge to the counter to the floor.

I heard the door at the foot of the stairs open, and I almost turned to go back out the window. I couldn't bear the thought of dealing with my mom right now, but the voice that called my name belonged to my aunt instead of my mother.

"Kalvan? Are you all right? I heard some odd noises . . ." She trailed off as her head came into view and she saw the hole in the window and the smoke coming off the counter.

After a moment she spoke again, her tone gentle. "That's not good."

"She locked me out." The words fell out of my mouth seemingly in defiance of my will. "She locked me out, and then I punched a hole in the window."

Noelle nodded. "Your father broke a coffee table in half."

"I . . . what?" I couldn't make sense of what she was telling me.

"*Our* mother put her fist through a plaster wall—broke two knuckles."

"I don't understand."

"It's not your fault, Kalvan. Genny has that effect on people."

"But I broke the window . . ."

"It's. Not. Your. Fault." She sighed. "It's not her fault, either. She can't help herself."

"I broke the window."

"I know. I know. It's all right. Come here."

I flung myself into my aunt's arms in the same moment she opened them. She was cool and far more still than any living human could have been. It was exactly what I needed. Putting my head against her shoulder, I sobbed as I could never remember and she held me with all the patience of the dead.

Eventually, I was empty, and I stepped away from my aunt.

"It's not your fault," she said again. Then, "I'll go get some duct tape; that'll deal with the problem for now. Tomorrow, I'll see about getting it repaired."

Once she was gone, I went over to the window and felt the smoothly melted edge of the hole. This had to end. I had to find some help for my mother because I couldn't go on this way. If that meant conjuring my father out of his stone prison and stapling the Crown to his forehead against his will so he could do it, that's what I would do. And if it couldn't be done, well, then I would die trying and it would all be somebody else's problem.

"*sprths*al*erarha!"

With a flash of red light and a puff of heat, the hare appeared on the counter. "You summoned me?"

"We need to get to work."

20

The Door into Summer

THREE DAYS. That's all we had to take Oscar's notes and turn them into a spell I could use to drag my father out of the stone that entombed him and put the Crown of Summer on his head. Three days that also happened to be school days. Add in that if I stepped so much as an inch out of line, I could end up expelled with Child Protective Services knocking on my door and asking to see my mom five minutes later, and you had a recipe for one giant delight of a Monday.

Through it all, I had to keep Morgan convinced I was totally going to make her into the Summer Queen. Every time she gave me another package from Oscar provided a new opportunity for me to blow everything. I also spent a lot more time with Josh than I *ever* wanted to—which, to be honest, was anything more than thirty seconds—since he was providing me with spell advice and other support. I had to play stupid with Lisa the few times I saw her because I couldn't be sure whose side she was really on.

I kept trying to find a good way to talk with Dave about what was to come, but between his sisters keeping tabs on him and knowing Morgan could listen in on anything I said at school, it kept not happening. Not until the afternoon before the big day when I ducked into the bathroom—leaving Sparx behind with my bag. I was heading for the urinals, when . . . *POP*. A tiny circle of darkness appeared in the air beside my ear. On the other side was a note that said *"Stall." POP.*

So, I ducked into a stall instead. *POP.* This time, the circle that appeared at neck height was bigger than my head and a weird green light was shining out of it. It was parallel to the floor and opened downward. A moment later, Dave's alien hand poked itself out through the hole and made a beckoning gesture like he wanted me to come through the hole, which seemed like a *terrible* idea.

The hand vanished and reappeared with a note. *"Head. Hole. Hurry. Trust me."*

With a sigh and visions of my head going the way of Dave's original hand, I complied. Beyond was . . . weird. You know those nature documentaries where they're swimming through a kelp bed fifty feet down and everything is all greens and blues? Like that, only not underwater. A green sun hung over an endless grassy plain where things that looked like a cross between a *Triceratops* and a hippo happily munched on giant broccoli. Perhaps weirdest of all was Dave's head, poking out of a hole in space a few feet away and about five degrees off horizontal.

"Where are we?" I asked.

"No idea, but I think it might be my new hand's original place of origin." He poked a couple of alien fingers up underneath his chin. "At least, it's much easier to open gates into and out of this place than anywhere else I've tried, and the hand feels . . . at home here. But I can't hold two holes for long. So, talk fast. What's up?"

I did my best impression of an auctioneer as I told him what needed telling.

At the end he nodded. "How are you getting away from Morgan at the end of the school day tomorrow?"

"Working on it."

"In other words, you have no idea."

"Well, yeah."

"Let me cover it. Send Sparx to me. We'll sort out a distraction and he can clue you in on your part."

"Thanks, man. I owe you big-time."

"Don't worry about it, I'm keeping a running tally, and you can pay me back later. Ooh, hole's gonna collapse soon. Move." His head vanished and I followed his example.

The next day, I got up with the sun of my own free will. The ritual Sparx and I had figured out required me to create the entire spell between one dawn and the next. A challenge made considerably tougher by the fact I didn't dare skip school. As it was, I barely finished up my opening preparations—mostly a ritual shower that involved using some weird herbal soap Oscar had provided with his second round of instructions—before I had to hop on my bike.

I saw Morgan watching out a window as I parked at school—a great start to a day that passed like fingernails on a chalkboard. Around noon, I got called to the principal's office where they told me someone had stolen my bike—Josh and part of the plan, but they couldn't know any of that. Later, I had a run-in with Tanya about my paper. Not fun, but at least I could show her I'd made significant progress. Despite all the storm and stress, I eventually made it through to afternoon advisory.

Which was where things got chancy. Morgan and Oscar would be waiting out back to take me to my house so we could set things up for the ritual to transfer the Crown—a tricky bit of magic that had to be completed with tomorrow's dawn. Of course, none of that was going to happen.

Instead, after Dave made an Open Sesame distraction, he was going to collect Sparx and my bag with Mississippi's mud-jar charm and catch my bus. Morgan and Oscar would—hopefully—believe I was on board, too. When the bus got close enough to my place, Dave was going to attempt another bit of portal magic to get Sparx and the jar into my house. After that, he planned to catch a city bus home—arriving only a little bit late and ideally not getting in too much trouble with his mother.

If it all worked properly, Oscar and Morgan would be trapped on the wrong side of the wards around my house, certain I was double-crossing them, and they could spend their time and energy trying to break in. To aid in that deception, Sparx would continue to pretend he was me while making a lot of magic noise inside. But all of that was beyond my control and I wouldn't even know how any of it had gone until tomorrow—assuming I lived through my end of things.

With the clock showing one minute to the bell, I felt a hand touch my shoulder, though all I could see was the faintest shimmer like moonlight on water. It was go time. *Three. Two. One.* As the bell rang, I rose and passed my backpack to Dave in the same instant Josh extended his illusion to cover me.

We waited silently while the classroom emptied. Then, the fire alarms went off. That was our cue and we started moving. As we stepped out the classroom door, Josh yanked a couple hairs from my head.

"Ouch, what was that for?"

"You'll find out in good time. Come on. The bikes are parked on the far side of the capitol. We have a lot of ground to cover and very little time."

The original plan called for cutting across the lawns. But, after we went out the gym's fire door—the alarms were already ringing—Josh led me straight into the nearby court building.

"Where are we going?" I demanded.

"The bikes, but we're going by a different way. Trust me."

"Never." But I stayed close as he used his curtain of illusion to slip us past the metal detectors and other security.

"Your call, and I really don't care as long as you follow me."

"I don't have a lot of choice."

"True that. Ooh, perfect." He tugged me into an open courtroom after glancing at the schedule posted beside the door. "They'll be in session in fifteen minutes. Hang on." Josh pulled a big adhesive label out of the pocket of his denim jacket, sticking it to the bottom of a seat at the back.

"What's with the sticker?"

"Mazing, step one." He led me out into the hall.

"Huh? I don't understand."

"Draw a labyrinth. Charge it with words of power and a tie to the thing you want to hide—symbolically placing it at the heart of the design. In this case, some hair stuck to the adhesive backing. If someone, like, oh say, your uncle or the charming Miss Morgan

Shears, figures out you went missing along the way and tries to backtrack you magically, it'll look like you're in there." He pointed at the court. "The hair provides the sense of presence, and the labyrinth gives it complexity and substance that's hard to see through."

"So *that's* why you yanked my hair."

"Don't worry your pretty little head about that. It's plenty safe. If anyone tries to remove the sticker or use it for a sending in place, the spell will devour itself and your hair."

"I . . . oh." That possibility hadn't even occurred to me. "So, if that was step one, I gather there are more to follow?"

"Of course. You can break a labyrinth if you hit it hard enough. Or, more simply, if they come and look for themselves, it'll be obvious you're not here."

"What's the next step?"

"This." Josh sat on a bench and yanked me down beside him, producing a fresh sheet with four nametag-size labels on it from his courier bag. Each bore a dense pattern meticulously hand drawn in a dark reddish ink. "Let me see the bottoms of your shoes."

I crossed my legs so my left sneaker sole faced him. "More labyrinths?"

He shook his head as he placed the first sticker on my sole. "Mazes this time."

"There's a difference?"

"Duh. One is a single continuous path, the other can have dead ends and loops." He placed the second sticker and then quickly did his own. "If someone gets this far, they'll know I'm with you, but these will make following us a real headache. Now, come on. You've got a lot to do and not half enough time."

Josh led the way down a nearby stair into the tunnels linking the capitol with the surrounding government building. We covered maybe half a mile in a straight line and nearly twice that in actual distance over the next forty minutes. It was slow because Josh insisted we stop and spin three times around in place at a dozen or so spots along the way. Each time, he left behind a dense knot of thread. First red, then blue, green, gold, and back around to red. More mazing, presumably.

Then it was onto the bikes for the long ride to the hollow hill. We had three hours to sundown when we arrived, at best, and I was going to need every second. As we slid through the stone wall into the darkness beyond, I heard a sharp snap.

A cold green light blossomed in Josh's hand. "Chemlight, military grade. My dad keeps a big pile of them around for camping. I figured we needed some source of light that wasn't you this time around."

"Ah, is widdle Joshy afraid of the dark?"

"Do you want my help? Or would you prefer I break both your arms so I can watch you burn when the sun comes up and you haven't finished the spell? I'm here because Herself asked me, not because I care whether you live or die."

"Right. Sorry. Let's get started."

Josh dropped the chemlight and pulled another from his bag, snapping it into a cold brilliance as we approached the stairs into the well. "I'll be over there, Monroe. If you need anything, remember to beg nicely."

Josh settled on the lip of the well while I pulled string, a marker, and the sharpening steel from my mom's knife set out of my bag. The latter was fourteen inches long with a handle of polished oak. It was originally my grandmother's, but when I was little, my mother let me play with it. Some days I'd pretend it was a magic wand. Others, a sword. I'd chosen it for tonight because the spell called for a tool that meant something to me.

I used earth magic to force the point of the steel into the stone at the center of the well before tying one end of the string to its handle and the other to the marker. Stretching it tight let me draw a perfect circle twenty feet across with the steel at its center. Shortening my string, I drew a second circle inside the first.

Next, I pulled the steel from the stone. Moving to the outer circle, I sank the tip a quarter inch into the rock and started to trace the line of ink. I had to fight for every inch using earth magic that felt alien and cost me far more than my fire work ever had. Getting to the end of that first loop left me sweating and panting. A glance at my watch showed an hour and change gone already and I had another circle to carve before I could even *start* the ideograms and other detail work.

I felt time as an intense sort of pressure hammering at my nerves as I bent to start the second circle—like a clock ticking the minutes till dawn in double time. When I finished that one, I had a stitch in my side like I'd run a fast mile, and I wanted to barf. Since there was nothing in my stomach, I simply toppled over, lying on my back and trying to catch my breath.

Josh came and knelt beside me. "You look terrible."

"That's funny; I feel like sunshine and rainbows."

"You're not doing bad for a matchstick, but if you don't speed this up, you're going to die." He held up his cell phone with a clock face showing ten p.m. "Three hours eaten already and the sun's down out there."

"I don't suppose you want to help with the ideograms?" He knew what I needed, but I had zero leverage and I wasn't going to beg.

Josh sighed. "Want to, no, but when I spoke to Herself last, she did allow as I should give you a hand if it looked like you absolutely couldn't manage without me."

"Why didn't you say so sooner?"

"Because I didn't know if you could do it on your own. Now that you've proved you can't . . ." He sighed. "You've got earth and fire, so I'll take air and water. But after the elements, you're on your own again. Most of this is on you."

I groaned, but nodded and forced myself upright. "Ash and char, sun and star, wind and smoke, ash and oak . . ."

Behind me Josh started an incantation of his own, "Hawk and owl, cold winds howl, leaf and feather, hawk and heather . . ."

I blocked him out and focused on the fires within—spinning words into burning symbols and placing them between the two circles. Once I finished with fire, I shifted to the deeper tongue of earth and stone and went around the ring again. Then it was on to the Corona Borealis. As quickly as I could, I cut an uneven seven-pointed star into the floor at the center of the circle representing the seven stars of the constellation.

The next bit was terrifying because it was something I hadn't been able to practice, so I had no idea if it would actually work. Standing in the center of the star, I pressed the Crown against the scar on my forehead and asked it to help me. I couldn't command the Crown as the Summer King might, but Sparx and I hoped the affinity of the mark would be enough. Impossibly long seconds ticked past without any apparent response.

Please.

Nothing. I closed my eyes.

Please, I need this to help my mother.

Opened them. Nope.

Please!

I felt nothing, but Josh let out a startled exclamation. Crossing my fingers, I opened my eyes, and . . .

YES!

A filigree of light traced patterns and voids that covered every inch of space between the inner circle and the star. The Crown itself had given me the structures I needed. *On to the next test.*

I lifted the Crown from my head with a touch as delicate as if it were made from spun sugar and cobwebs. The pattern dimmed briefly, but then returned to a uniform brightness. *Almost there.* I gently set the Crown in the star and stepped back. The pattern flickered but held. Now, I just had to carve it all into the stone.

Just.

I began with a spiraling structure, then moved to another. On and on, with each line eating up more of the all-too-short night and my finite reserves of will and power. Josh helped—setting ideograms amid the silvery lace the Crown outlined—but not half so often as I'd have liked.

Hours passed like lightning in the dark. Then, suddenly, almost unexpectedly, I finished scribing a line into the stone and realized it was the very last. I had completed my preparations, and not an instant too soon. I couldn't see the sky, but through my connection to stone, I could feel the coming dawn as if the light were a weight pressing on the earth to the east. I had maybe half an hour to go.

"Monroe!"

"Huh?" I shook myself out of a long stillness I'd barely noticed. "Sorry. My mind was miles away, walking under the rising sun."

"You can go all mystical granola later. Right now you've work to do and little time to manage it."

"I know!" I took a moment to check my connection to Sparx. As far as I could tell, he was still playing decoy, so I moved back into the central star, placed the Crown on my head and started calling the elements.

"Issilthss!" When I spoke air's word, the corresponding ideograms came to light and life, hissing and sighing. Though Josh had placed them, he'd left them unsealed and now they belonged to me.

"Kkst*ta!" Fire and easy for me, activating the portions of the spell that depended on my home element.

"Bglbgleb!" Yeah, I was pretty sure I was still butchering water, because I didn't speak bubbledygook, and Josh looked deeply pained, but the symbols lit up.

"Drooododor!" I let earth's word speak itself from within my bones, though hearing something that sounded so like Oscar come out of my mouth gave me chills.

I was exhausted, but I couldn't waste an instant, and I moved on to the next step, which began with words of air. "Hawk and owl . . ." Etc.

Soon enough I came around to earth again. "Earth and stone, blood and bone . . ." Saying words I had first heard in my step-father's mouth drove another spike of uneasiness deep into my heart. But I had no choice.

I opened my mouth to begin the next round—tying in the Corona

Borealis—but I was preempted by a tremendous crash from the entrance off to my left. The whole stone wall had been slammed aside like some enormous door. Before I had the chance to do more than blink, a badly scarred delver led a pair of his fellows into the cavern, followed by Morgan and Oscar, who closed the gate again with a flick of his wrist.

"Oh crap!" Josh whipped his head around like a gopher searching for a bolt hole.

"Get inside the circle, you idiot!" I yelled.

Josh leaped across the twinned lines of the great circle.

I snapped out the next bit of the incantation. "Star and Crown, up and down, spoke and wheel, Crown and seal. The circle is closed."

With an electrical snap, the Crown found its place within the greater structure and a dome of many colored lights rose around us. I still had things to do but Oscar would have a devil of a time getting at us as I scrambled to finish.

"That won't save you, boy." Oscar stepped forward, gesturing imperiously.

In response, Morgan moved to stand behind him on the right while Cetius mirrored her on the left, and the other delvers fell in behind them. Though it wasn't obvious from where I stood, I could feel they had formed the five points of a star through the earth at my feet.

"Not a bad spell you've built, Kalvan, though it only answers for the Crown and won't save your mother. Your decoy ploy was positively inspired. I also have to compliment you on coming up with the idea of transferring the Crown to your father—though he's buried too deep. I hadn't realized you even knew where I'd trapped him."

"*You* trapped my father?!?" It felt like Oscar had punched me in the heart.

"Of course. He was far too powerful a rival to let run free. Look, I'm impressed with all you've done. Truly. But it's over. If you release the dome and let Morgan take her proper place as my Summer Queen, I'm still willing to fulfill the terms of the bargain I offered you. If not, I'll break your protections and do it myself."

"I thought you said you needed me."

"No, I said it was the simplest and surest way. The alternative is *quite* chancy. On the upside, it involves me cutting the heart from your living chest in the center of that pretty design you've built, and that would give me a great deal of satisfaction. It's your choice, but . . ." Oscar's face went suddenly pale. "Wait, who carved all those lines?"

I felt his will slip through the stone and touch the edges of my diagram. "That wasn't done with any fire magic." His eyes fell on Josh, and they held a cold anger I recognized from our worst fights.

Oscar raised his arms and a web of light formed between him and his companions, building quickly in intensity to something that seared the eye. An instant later, a brutal lance of pure magical force shot forth from the point of their formation. Where it touched, a patch of dome the size of my palm blazed up brighter than the sun and bent steeply inward while the whole structure flared and sparked.

"Kalvan, if you have a plan, now would be a *great* time." Josh's voice was husky, almost desperate. "Maybe if you—"

But another spike of power struck the wards, drowning out his voice as the dome shattered. The stone between the lines of the great circle spalled and cracked, destroying the ideograms there and freeing the magic within. It was like dumping a bucket of water into a toaster, and all that loose power arced inward. Lightning danced along the lines of my seven-pointed star and the magical impact drove me to my knees, but the protections held. Josh wasn't so lucky, taking the brunt of the discharge. He fell without a sound, his clothes and hair smoking faintly. I felt sick. I might hate Josh's guts, but I'd never wanted to see him seriously injured or dead.

But I had no time to focus on that as the web of light around Oscar faded and he spoke again. "That's one problem solved at least. The sun is almost upon us and I've left you the key part of the diagram. Will you perform the ritual and pass the Crown to Morgan? Turn me down and I will kill you without remorse or hesitation."

I opened my mouth, but no words came. Too much had happened too fast and I was, quite simply, overwhelmed. I thought briefly of shifting into dragon shape, but I didn't know what that would do to my connection with the Crown's magic and the spells I needed to save myself and my mother.

"Your time's running out, boy."

I looked at Oscar and shook my head. "Six years."

"What?" He blinked.

"Six years you were my stepfather and you never once figured out how to motivate me. All you've ever done is yell and threaten. I wanted to like you at the beginning, but I never could. I used to think that was as much on me as you. I was wrong. You are simply a horrible human being and a worse dad."

"Is this going somewhere?"

"Yes. A lake. As in, why don't you take a long walk off a short dock."

Oscar shrugged. "I would have preferred to do this the easy

way, but I think we can manage to remove you and still preserve the important parts of that spell you're standing on."

Oscar's right hand contracted into a tight fist and a boulder the size of a car ripped itself from the floor and flung itself at me. It should have killed me, but in the instant before it smashed me to a pulp, a surge of earth power pulsed up from the ground beneath me, moving through my body. In response, my left hand whipped up and out, like a man catching a baseball. I felt a sharp stinging slap on my outstretched palm and the great boulder burst into powder-fine dust.

Oscar looked genuinely startled. "Interesting. It wasn't the other boy who carved those lines for you, was it? And, the buried father yet lives, acting now through the son who inherited his element. It won't save you, of course, though it closes the ways of earth for me."

It wasn't until he spoke that I realized I'd felt something like love come with the power from below. Reaching down through my bones into the stone, I could feel my father had awakened to the conflict and that he would do what he could for me. I doubted if he could save me, but at least I wouldn't die alone.

"Morgan, it's time you proved your worth." Oscar made an *after you* gesture. "What's left of the diagram will serve, but only if it is left unharmed."

In that instant of distraction, I sent a column of fire roaring toward them. With a lazy gesture and a sharp gust of wind, Morgan snuffed the flames as easily as I might have blown out a candle.

Morgan smiled. "Not bad, Kalvan. It won't save you, but not bad. Let's see how you handle this."

Morgan moved a couple of fingers—the tiniest of gestures—and knives of wind slashed across the space between us. If I hadn't expected an attack, air hardened to the density of steel would have cut me into bloody ribbons. Instead, the killing wind met a wall of heartfire, shredding it into a thousand ribbons of flame that flickered wildly and then went out, taking the wind blades with them.

I tried a rolling wave of flames next, but Morgan casually batted my best aside.

She upped the ante a heartbeat later. This time, the winds that answered her gesture met my fires and doused them without slowing. But, at the very last second, death failed to take me. The cutting winds simply vanished without touching me, though I had no idea why.

"What?!?" Morgan shouted, and I was no less surprised. "Impossible!"

21

All Fall Down

A SOUND LIKE great blades shattering on a wall of rock came from a distant part of the cavern—Morgan's attack diverted to another target somehow.

"Impossible!" she repeated.

"I do not think that word means what you think it means." Dave laughed behind her. "Though it certainly wasn't easy."

I looked past Morgan and spied Dave at the entrance to the cavern where the stone wall had been pushed aside once again. A huge coyote stood beside him on three legs, the other held close to her chest. "Sorry we're late, but that door was a tough open even for me."

Oscar turned and made a pushing motion that sent a great wave of liquid rock rolling across the floor to crush the pair. But they were gone by the time it arrived—stepping through a bright circle in the air to appear beside me.

I'd never been happier to see anyone. "I love you, man. How did you know where to—"

Dave cut me off. "Lisa, but we can talk about it later. We've got like five minutes to win this fight. Speaking of which." He made a sweeping gesture with his alien hand, opening one gate in front of us and another a few feet away. A great sledgehammer of wind passed through, turning back on Morgan in the process. She flicked it aside with a finger, though it knocked Cetius to the floor as it passed.

"Right," said Oscar. "We'll have to do this the hard way even if it risks the diagram. Cetius, get up!"

Through my feet and my connection to the stone beneath us, I felt the points of the star formed by Oscar and his companions grow suddenly active. My first thought was there was no way we could survive a blast like the one that had taken down the dome. But that was swept aside a moment later as stone brought me the message of more arrivals. Three of them. Sparx, my aunt, and . . .

"Mom, no! It's too dangerous! Get out of here!"

A sort of sick horror filled me as my mother dashed toward us. Sparx could take care of himself, and Noelle was already dead, but my mom had no real power of her own. No way to protect herself from the oncoming doom. Even as that thought passed through my mind, Oscar struck, releasing another devastating lance of pure magical force—and my mother was between us.

There was nothing I could do except watch. Noelle, who was trailing behind my mother, on the other hand . . . With the slightest nod in my direction, she turned and stepped into the beam. I expected it to tear right through her and go on to devour my mother and the rest of us an instant later, but the dead are made of tougher stuff than the living.

When the power struck Noelle's chest, light fountained outward from the point of contact, outlining her with an intense corona, like the halo around the moon at the height of an eclipse. It seemed for a moment that she might even survive, but then her edges blurred and burned away, and she erupted into a great column of fire that scorched both floor and ceiling—momentarily blinding me.

Trying desperately to keep track of Oscar and his followers, I shifted my attention entirely to the earth beneath us. The sense of presence that was my father trapped in his stone prison had grown enormously, acting like light in a dark room. Through him, I could feel the whole shape of the sealed gateway between worlds—its ins and outs and every piece of its functioning, right down to the way it might be opened again if I only had enough power.

There was so much weight of magic and information there I had to fight hard to "see" past it. First to where my aunt's second death was slowly burning itself out, and then onward to put "eyes" on Oscar. I was surprised to find that his formation had suffered a momentary fragmentation.

As my eyesight returned, I saw why. Noelle had managed to reflect much of the blast back at those who had sent it. The hair of Morgan's bangs and eyebrows was actively smoldering, and Oscar's crown scar looked as red and livid as if he had only just received it. Deepest hate stared out at me through his eyes as he gestured for Morgan and the others to re-form the star.

"That was your last reprieve, boy." Through my feet, I felt the power of the star begin to build again—slower this time, but much stronger. "Now we do it the hard way. Morgan, kill everyone but Kalvan."

The girl spun her upturned fingers in a half twist. A wind rose in answer and began to circle the well where we stood, moving faster and faster as Oscar fed it power from the star.

Oscar smiled. "This will be a genuine pleasure."

Before I could reply, my mother arrived with Sparx. Throwing her arms around me, she hugged me wordlessly. What I wanted to do was melt into her embrace and let her make everything better, but my whole life told me how that would end.

"Sparx?" I asked over her shoulder. The building whirlwind snatched the words from my lips and tugged at the air in my lungs.

"I can't stop that. Nothing can."

"Dave?"

"I've been trying everything I can think of," he gasped, "none of it gets through."

"Lisa?"

The coyote shook her head and let out a mournful howl, but the wind sucked it away an instant later. I could hardly breathe myself and I couldn't see any way out.

Wait, *see*. That word . . . I still didn't understand my earth powers, and that might be the reason for my failure to even think of using them actively thus far. I had been blind to the possibilities of my father's heritage. Ironically, my aunt's death and the temporary loss of vision it had brought was the thing that forced me to look beyond sight, if only for a time, and truly *see*.

I closed my eyes and reached down through my feet into the ground below, seeking desperately . . .

There!

The gate matrix. I had touched it earlier, but pushed that awareness aside in my desperation to find Oscar. I couldn't open the gate
with the power I currently had. Not fully anyway, but I might be
able to crack it far enough to . . . yes!

I pushed on the matrix of the gate with everything I had, and it
gave. Not much. Barely at all, really. But enough. For one brief second I opened my end of the gateway between two worlds. The floor
beneath us faded away for perhaps thirty feet. Gravity took over
and we fell. Or, began to. My strength was expended before we
dropped more than a few yards, and the gate closed around us—
sealing us in stone in the very second Morgan released the full
force of her whirlwind.

It struck the magically hardened rock of the gate and rebounded
harmlessly. I had saved us all from death at the cost of trapping us
deep in stone . . . and more than stone. I felt the difference when
Sparx tried to slip through the rock of the gate and failed.

How could I know all that? Because I was my father's son and a
child of the earth as much as I was my mother's and a child of fire.
The gate stone was no ordinary marble or quartz. It was as close to
the pure heart of earth as it was possible to get. I understood now
why my father had diffused his consciousness into that stone. Not
out of fear or desperation, but out of wonder. It would be the simplest
thing imaginable to join in the long slow thought of that ur-rock of
which all other rock was but an imperfect reflection.

But I was also a child of ever-moving fire brightly burning and
I had trapped others with me. Others who could not so easily join
with the rock. I reached out, finding my mother, Sparx, Dave,
Lisa . . . oh. I realized with a start Josh was with us, too, and alive.
His slowly beating heart sent echoes through the matrix of stone

and magic that held and healed him. For *that* was a gift of the urrock as well. Those it contained, it protected and cared for.

I could feel it working. Quickly on the burns that had nearly killed Josh—close to the stone and the surface as they were. More slowly on inner hurts like Lisa's broken foreleg. Slower still on that which went the deepest, like Dave's asthma—which his power had eased but not ended. Where Josh's skin would recover in a matter of minutes or hours, it might take days to fully restore Lisa's leg, and months to reshape Dave's breathing. Sadly, my mother's problems were beyond such simple healing.

I don't know exactly how I knew that, only that I did. Perhaps, despite myself, some part of me was already thinking with the great stone mind that surrounded me. I understood then in a way I never had before that I couldn't *fix* my mother. Her mental illness was a part of what made her the person she was and it could only be addressed to the extent she wished it. Even that had limits I had no part in setting. I might, if my magic grew in the right direction, help her, but only so far as she would allow.

But none of that would free any of us from the trap I had used to save our lives, and now I forced my mind away from the beautiful temptation of thinking the slow and gentle thoughts of stone—how had I ever hated this element? I had put us here, and I had the responsibility to free us, but I had no idea how.

Then, suddenly, unexpectedly, irresistibly, my attention was wrenched upward. Through the stone I *saw* Oscar limping down the stairs to the sealed gate, his scalp raw and blackened even where the Crown had not burned him all those weeks ago. His eyes were threaded with red lightning from broken blood vessels. Neither Morgan or Cetius followed as he crossed to the center of the stone well and knelt on the freshly smoothed rock. I could feel him shaking with rage as he ran a hand over the surface.

"So close," he whispered. "So close, and now it's gone." He bent and spoke directly into the rock. "Curse and blight you, Kalvan. You could have walked away with a cure for your mother, but you chose ruin instead. Yours as well as mine."

Oscar stood then, though the effort clearly cost him. Without so much as a glance at his companions, he limped across the stone floor of the cavern to the exit where the first rays of the rising sun peeked through.

The dawn had come.

DAWN

I felt a sudden pressure on my brow as the Corona Borealis answered the dawn. How do you describe the feeling of becoming one with a season? Sunshine. Green leaves. Warm rain. Flowers bursting. Frantic life racing to reproduce. But that was only the beginning. Summer is the season of heat and light and rot and sudden death on hunter's wings. Summer is all that and so much more. Most of all?

SUMMER IS

And I *was* summer. But only for an instant. There is too much summer for one mind to hold. Too much for a thousand minds even. The rush of feelings and images and sounds and scents and every sense stuffed to the brim faded away, though it left many gifts. Not least of which was the sense that I was more alive than I had ever been, more than *anyone* had ever been. I was brimful of life and of the power that came with it. Too full. If not for the healing power of the stone encasing me I would have burst then—come apart in a thousand flaming fragments.

Even with that support, I knew I could not hope to contain this power for long. I needed to . . . wait. With the power of Summer came a deeper connection to the Crown and the knowledge it had been built to contain. Could I . . .

I reached for the structure of the gate. I had more than enough power to hold it open for as long as I needed now. Only . . . I couldn't get at it from this side. With senses turned up a thousandfold by my ascension to Summer's Throne, I could see things I hadn't noticed earlier. When Oscar sprang the trap that sealed my father here, he had made certain no one within the gate could move forward into our world. But he had reckoned without the power of the Crown. If I wanted to, I could open the gate. Of course, I would die in the next instant, but at least I could free the others.

A last resort that. What else could I do? Didn't doors open both ways? With a flick of my will, I turned my attention in the other direction, searching for the place where my father lay trapped. I still didn't want to open the gate and die, but if it turned out that was the only option, I wanted to send my father through as well. Somebody would have to take care of my mom. Besides, I was beginning to get the inklings of another way, though I'd need help and a lot of luck.

So, could I . . . No.

The way was closed in that direction and I couldn't hope to open it by myself. But, then, maybe I didn't have to. Not all the way, at any rate.

Perhaps . . . yes.

With a wrenching effort of will, I forced part of the gate aside, pushing enough stone out of phase with reality to let me crawl to Dave's side. I could feel the power burning brighter within me as I did so. Though the ur-rock still surrounded me, I was no longer in full-body contact with it and I could feel myself starting to cook from within. I would have to do this quickly. Dave was lying on his back, still and quiet.

—*hibernating*—whispered the voice of the ur-rock.

—*bide*—

—*there, he wakes*—

Dave blinked his eyes and looked at me. "Dude, has anyone told you you're glowing?"

"Huh, am I?"

"Yeah, you're shining all green and gold like, whoa. Especially the Crown. You look like something out of a commercial for unicorn hair spray. By the way, where are we?"

"Trapped in the gate between our world and my father's. Long story and I'll tell you all of it if we get out of here in one piece. But holding even a part of this thing open without lighting myself on fire is taking everything I've got and then some. I need help."

"All right. What do you need me to do?"

"I . . . um, I'm not sure, really. The Crown and I had a quick convo and now we need to go down because my dad's that way and if we go up I turn into a human fireworks display. That involves opening a path through this." I waved my hands at the ur-rock. "I figured opening is your thing now, so . . ." I trailed off at that point because I didn't know what came next.

"All right. I can work with that . . . I think. But you have to promise not to laugh." I nodded and crossed my heart, and Dave turned his gaze toward his alien hand and began to speak to it. "You kind of showed up on your own, and you've usually steered me right when I ask, so, hey, let's do this."

Seemingly of its own accord, the hand reached up and touched the central gem of the Corona Borealis. I felt a sort of jolt that arced from head to heart to the soles of my feet and back again. Then, as if a door had opened in my mind, I saw what to do.

"Dave, touch your palm to the stone beneath us."

Once his alien hand was in place, I knelt and covered it with both of my own, focusing my power through his just . . . so. Around us, a large circle of rock thinned and vanished, revealing the others. Most appeared to be in the same weird unconscious state Dave had been in when I'd first found him. All but Sparx, who gave me a look that told me I was in for quite the lecture. But when he opened his mouth, I shook my head.

"You can yell at me all you want later—I certainly deserve it. But right now I'm still working on getting us out of this mess. Hopefully, alive."

"Fair enough. What's nex—argh!"

Even as he spoke, I made a magical twist. The floor below us stopped . . . well, *floor*ing, as stone shifted halfway into another sort of matter entirely, becoming something midway between solid and gas. That eased the stress the Crown was putting on my body as we began to sink, a bubble of clear space, moving a bit slower than a stone falling through water.

Down.

Down.

Down.

Until, rather suddenly and unexpectedly, we hit a hard bottom and stopped. At which point I had a surprising realization. "That's . . . odd."

Dave looked at me. "I don't like the sound of that. Why'd we stop?"

"We just crossed the line between being mostly in our world and being mostly in my father's."

"And?" he demanded.

"I'm not the Summer King on this side of the line. The Crown's power doesn't reach here. On the upside, I'm no longer a candidate for sudden conversion into messy special effects. On the downside, I'm running out of tricks . . ."

"Kalvan, son . . ." My father's words preceded him out of the stone around our clear bubble of space. "You've freed me from my long imprisonment. But what's this?" He touched the Crown on my forehead. "You're far too young to bear this burden."

"I am, but I've just had an idea." I'd dreamed of meeting my father for years, and I wanted to say more, to do more, but it would have to wait. If I took the time now, we might all be trapped forever.

"What?"

"The structure I built to transfer the Crown is gone, and the moment to use it passed, but we're kind of still attached to it through the memory of the ur-rock. I'm thinking we might be able to bend the rules here beyond the edge of the world if you're willing to accept the Crown. Dave, do you think you could take the Crown from my head with your magic hand and put it on my dad's?"

"Maybe . . . this hand is about halfway between a familiar and a part of me." Dave touched his temple with the hand and his eyes went far away for several seconds. Finally, he nodded. "I might be able to at that. Only, it won't be quite that simple. Both of you, kneel."

I looked at my father, and he nodded. "Do it."

We both knelt. Dave rotated his alien hand slowly through space while pulling it down and toward him.

POP . . . POP

A pair of circles opened in the space above our heads. As Dave reached his human hand into the one above my dad's head, it came out through the one above mine and caught hold of the Crown. A moment later, he set it on my father's head. I felt my connection to the Crown begin to fade, taking what little energy I had left with it. *Maybe this* would *work . . .*

My father extended a hand to my best friend. "I'm Nix. Dave, is it?"

"Yes indeed." They shook.

"The thing you were doing with my son to move through the rock. Do you think you could do it with me? The power of the Crown may not reach here, but I have this." He touched his ear and the sapphire there suddenly shone out as bright as any star.

"Yes." Dave took my father's hand again. "It was mostly the hand and Kalvan before, but I think I learned what's needed."

Sweat broke out along my father's brow and we began to rise. I had about a million questions for this man, but I knew *exactly* how much what he was doing took out of you, and I didn't dare interrupt. In fact, with the Crown gone and now that I wasn't so focused on keeping us moving, the world was getting mighty dim around the edges . . .

A supreme effort of will allowed me to ease myself down onto my back instead of simply falling over.

"Kalvan?" Sparx sounded alarmed.

"'m all right. Everyone all righ'?"

"Yes." He nodded.

"Even Josh?"

"He'll live."

"'s good, cuz 'm gonna take a quick nap."

Lights out.

22

If It Wasn't for Those Meddling Kids

I **WOKE TO** a song of stone, realizing as I did so that the wordless music had threaded itself through my dreams, easing sorrow and soothing pain. It was tempting to go back to sleep—as I vaguely remembered doing at least twice before. But this time my curiosity outweighed my exhaustion and I forced my eyes open.

At first, all I could see was the ceiling some eight feet above me. It was a curved sheet of some densely patterned rock unlike anything I'd seen before. Imagine lapis lazuli threaded with natural veins of silver like Celtic knotwork and you will have some sense of it.

"At last, the sleeper wakes." Lisa's voice, and I could almost *hear* her smiling—an expression she confirmed a moment later by leaning over my . . . what? Bed?

No, that didn't feel right. Something heavier than covers pressed on my body. I glanced downward, unsure what I would find and . . .

"Am I really buried to the neck in sand, like some idiot at the beach?" I seemed to be in a deep cup in the rock floor—a cup filled mostly with a fine and powdery white sand, with only my head and neck exposed while Lisa sat cross-legged on the floor beside me.

She nodded. "More or less. They are healing earths; the Crown very nearly destroyed you."

"All right. Weird, but all right." I took a breath, bracing myself for a major effort, and tried to sit up. The sand flowed around me as easily as water, but . . . "That's . . . odd. I—oh."

The attempt revealed several things that made me reluctant to finish getting out of my strange bed. For starters, I didn't have a shirt or any kind of pajama top on, and I couldn't tell if I had bottoms, either—not something I wanted to find out with Lisa as my audience. Also, it nearly knocked me out. Apparently I still had some healing left to do. Reluctantly, I settled back into the sand.

"Okay, then. How long have I been asleep? And where are we? And where's Sparx? I would have expected him to be waiting. And what are you doing here? Not that I object, but . . ."

She waved her hands for me to stop. "So many questions. Start with Sparx. He's off somewhere with Dave, but I imagine he'll be along momentarily now that you're awake. As to how long you've been out? Just shy of three days. What else? Oh, yes. We are in the caverns under your basement."

I looked at the beautiful stonework again. "Are you sure? Because last time I checked, they didn't look anything like that."

"Your father has been making some changes. Which also explains why I'm here."

"It does?"

"Sure. Given your injuries, someone with appropriate magic

had to keep an eye on you at all times. I volunteered to take up the slack as needed, since I'm at loose ends now and still deeply in your debt."

"For what?"

"Freeing me from Morgan, among other things."

"I think I must have missed a step."

"When Morgan forced me to tell her about you going to the hollow hill, it gave me an opportunity to sever our connection." She moved her left arm, and for the first time I noticed it was in a sling. "Painful, but worth it."

"You're only getting me more confused."

"Years ago, Morgan rescued me from a trap. By the laws of my people, that bound me to her service until either I paid my debt by saving her life in turn or she broke the compact. She was very angry when she realized that you had slipped away and left a decoy in your place, so angry she lost her cool when she realized I'd been concealing things from her. She kicked me and I caught the blow with the same leg that had been in the trap."

"I'm still confused. Why were you in a tra . . . oh. You're a coyote who becomes a girl, and not the other way around. That's why Dave calling you a werecoyote irritated you so much."

"*Half* of why it irritated me. If I'm a were-anything, it's a were-girl, but that doesn't begin to cover it. I was and am a force of nature."

"When you warned me about bodies shaping minds . . ."

"I was looking at it from the other end, yes. You humans are all kinds of bizarre, and I've picked up some awful habits living as one of you."

I decided to leave that alone in favor of another question. "So how did you come to arrive with Dave there at the end?"

"I knew you'd need help to face Morgan and Oscar together, so I went to fetch Dave. We'd have gotten there sooner, but I only had three legs to run on."

"Why didn't you use the phone?"

Lisa blinked several times and then shrugged. "Sometimes I think like a girl. Sometimes I think like a coyote."

I remembered being a dragon and nodded, but that brought back other memories. "What about Oscar and Morgan? Oh, and Josh?"

"Last first. Josh is all right. Still a jerk, but all right. Your dad wanted to put him in a healing pit, too, to minimize the scars, but he told your dad to get stuffed and left. We don't know what's become of Oscar—he was pretty badly hurt but he slithered off into some hole and pulled it in after him. Your dad's looked but hasn't been able to find him, even with the help of the delvers. Morgan is . . . well, Morgan, and back in school acting like nothing ever happened."

Before I could respond, a sudden *POP* sounded and Sparx dropped through a circle cut out of the space beside my "bed."

"The sleeper wakes at last."

"I do. How's Dave?"

"More or less under house arrest, but he thinks his mother will relent soon."

"I wish there was something I could do for him. He saved my life, he and . . . Noelle." Thinking about my aunt hurt.

Sparx shook his head. "Her time was past, Kalvan. Long past. She would have gone back into the grave soon after the change of the Crown no matter what. From what I saw of her—and that was a good bit more than you did—I don't think she would want you to carry her second death on your shoulders."

My mother spoke from near the doorway then—I'd missed seeing her come in. "She would not."

"Mom?" I spoke cautiously, uncertain what her mental state might be after this second loss of her sister.

"Trust me, Kalvan. She loved you." My mother sounded better than she had in a long time.

Lisa got up and made a shooing motion at Sparx. "I think now would be a good time for us to find someplace else to be for a bit."

Sparx nodded. "Good plan."

Once they were gone, I turned back to my mom. "How are you?"

"Mostly sane." She grinned to take any sting from her choice of words. "Thanks to you. I have problems that are always going to be with me at some level—my brain wiring is kind of a mess—but for the moment I feel more like me than I have in years. I've been drowning in my own head, and you found me a lifeline by bringing Nix back."

My heart started to beat a little easier, releasing a deep tension that had become such a part of me I had all but forgotten it was there. "That's wonderful, Mom. Are you two . . ." I didn't even know how to ask the question.

But my mother understood me and shook her head. "We're not, or not yet at least, and possibly never again. We've been too long apart to get back together so quickly. That's one of the reasons I need you on your feet as soon as you can manage it. While I'm delighted that Nix has been able to help me find my way, I don't want to have to lean on him for long."

"I'm not sure I understand where you're going, Mom."

"You're an earth power, too, and if I have to have someone helping me keep my hold on the world, I'd prefer it was my son. If you're willing, of course."

I swallowed hard. That was a lot of responsibility, but I was finally ready to face up to it. "If I can help, Mom, you know I will. I love you."

"I love you, too, and thank you. Now, if you'll hold on a second, there's someone else who wants to talk to you almost as much as I did." She went to the door and returned a moment later with my father. "Kalvan, this is Nix; you lost him too young to remember much of him. Nix, your son. I'm sorry you didn't get to watch him grow up. It's been an adventure. Especially the last few years."

"Kalvan?" Nix smiled a shy sort of smile, and I felt some part of my broken heart begin to mend.

"Dad . . ." I made another attempt at sitting up, but it didn't go any better than the first had.

"Rest, son. You came so close to . . ." Tears started to slide down his cheeks and he stopped speaking for a moment as he knelt to put his hands on my shoulders. "For more than ten years I've hoped for this day. I . . . don't know where to begin."

My mother caught my eye. "And now it's my turn to give you a little privacy."

"You don't have to go, Mom."

But she just smiled. "I've had days to talk with Nix while you slept. You've never had the chance at all. Don't worry, I won't be far."

For several long seconds, neither my father nor I spoke as we looked each other up and down. Here was the dark skin and facial structure I had inherited, the face I'd never seen on anyone else ever. I'd been waiting for this moment all my life, yet, now that it was here I didn't know what to do or say.

"Dad, it's been so many years, I don't even know how to start."

"That's all right, Kalvan. After talking to your friends and familiar about what you've done over the past few months—for your mother, for the domain of the Corona Borealis, for me—I know exactly how to begin."

"How?"

"Like this: Son, I am so, so proud of you."

Author's Note

The Free School of Saint Paul as depicted in these books is not the Saint Paul Open School. Though my time at the latter certainly informs my creation of the former, all of the characters and situations in these volumes are fictitious and creations of my imagination rather than reconstructions from memory. That said, my eleven and a half years at the Open School are fundamental to my life and to my work as an artist, and I would be a very different person without them. I owe so much to the school, its teachers, founders, and my fellow students. Thank you all. The me that I am today wouldn't be possible without you.

It is also worth noting that the downtown Saint Paul of this book differs in some significant ways from Saint Paul as it is now. It's been thirty-five years since I used to sneak off to play hooky downtown, and the version of the city I describe in this book is a mixture of Saint Paul as it was then, as it is today, and pure fancy that serves the purpose of my story.

Finally, on the subject of mental illness and its treatment within the book, there are things I can't say without violating the privacy of people I love, but I will note that I occasionally take anxiety medications and also that I grew up in a house with people who had significant neurochemical issues, including paranoid schizophrenia and major depression. To this day, I have people I love who have serious mental health issues. I come at the subject very much from the inside.

Acknowledgments

Extra special thanks are owed to Laura McCullough, Jack Byrne, Holly West, and Jean Feiwel.

Many thanks also to my Web guru, Ben. My family: Carol, Paul and Jane, Lockwood and Darlene, Judy, Kat, Sean, and all the rest. My extended support structure: Matt, Mandy, Sandy, Kim, Jonny, Lynne, Michael, Steph, Tom, Ann . . . and so many more. I also want to thank the departed members of the feline horde who have been with me through every book I've ever written. Moonshadow, Spot, Leith, Meglet, Jordan, Isabelle, and Ashbless, the company you provided was hugely important to me and my writing, you are all very much missed.

Feiwel folks who have been instrumental in making my books here the best they can be: Ilana Worrell, Kim Waymer, Liz Dresner, Christine Barcellona, Ashley Woodfolk, Heather Job. Thank you all so much.